Miriam was a small, young Quaker girl with a demure appearance and a gentle manner. But she had enough spirit to leave the village where her grandparents had brought her up, in search of independence and a new life. She came to Tancred . . . and her expectations crashed about her. The household was sinister, brooding, rotting . . . its inhabitants seemed to be under the spell of the past . . . She determined to discover the secrets of Tancred, but she faced a conspiracy of silence, subterfuge and half-truths . . .

Also by Diane Pearson

THE SUMMER OF THE BARSHINSKEYS
THE MARIGOLD FIELD
SARAH WHITMAN
CSARDAS

and published by Corgi Books

Diane Pearson

The Bride of Tancred

CORGI BOOKS

THE BRIDE OF TANCRED

A CORGI BOOK 0 552 10249 0

Originally published in Great Britain by
Robert Hale Ltd. under the title *The Loom of Tancred*

PRINTING HISTORY
Robert Hale edition published 1967
Corgi edition published 1968
Corgi edition reissued 1976
Corgi edition reprinted 1977 (twice)
Corgi edition reprinted 1979
Corgi edition reprinted 1980
Corgi edition reprinted 1982
Corgi edition reprinted 1983
Corgi edition reprinted 1985
Corgi edition reprinted 1986
Corgi edition reprinted 1987

This book is set in 9/10 Times

Corgi Books are published by Transworld Publishers Ltd.,
61–63 Uxbridge Road, Ealing, London W5 5SA,
in Australia by Transworld Publishers (Aust.) Pty. Ltd.,
15–23 Helles Avenue, Moorebank, NSW 2170, and in New
Zealand by Transworld Publishers (N.Z.) Ltd., Cnr. Moselle
and Waipareira Avenues, Henderson, Auckland.

Printed and bound in Great Britain by
Hazell Watson & Viney Limited,
Member of the BPCC Group,
Aylesbury, Bucks

*For My Father
and for My Mother –
the Best Raconteur I Know.*

1

When I was eighteen I learned of my illegitimate birth and many things, until that time not properly understood, became clear to me.

There is, in all truth, nothing very unusual about bastardy. In every small society, every village and hamlet, there is at least one of those defensive—and sometimes belligerent—folk who pass their lives in an apology for the waywardness of their parents. But in a small Quaker village such as ours, the accident of a fatherless birth occurred less often than in most places. This is not to say that we were not as subject to sin and temptation as other folk, but in our farming community there was, perhaps, a tighter code of morality stretching its white fingers rigidly out from the Meeting House in the center of the village and into every cottage and farmhouse in the vicinity. And indeed most families were too concerned with wresting a living from the soil to have time to sin in any grand manner. The young people were set to work as soon as they could be trusted with plough and ox. There was little leisure left in which to indulge in the pleasures of wickedness.

I was, therefore, something of an anomaly in a society where every grandparent, every fifth cousin twice removed could be accurately named in the network of family relationships, where all were sure of their antecedents and to whom they were related. I had been clothed and fed fairly, for the people in the village were kind, and charity and forgiveness were part of our teachings. I was included in the small events that made up the social life of our village: the suppers and marriage meetings, the picnics at the end of harvest; but always I was aware that my presence was suffered as a Christian duty, that I was, in some way, different from the other children of my own age.

As a very small child I remember the first time I became conscious of my isolation in the closely-knit Quaker community. It was on an April Sunday, a day of bright clearness and I was, I suppose, no more than four years old. I could dress myself, for we learn to be useful at a very early age, I could fasten my own apron and collar and get myself ready for going to Meeting. But the stiff bands of the starched white cap were difficult for a small girl to manage and when my grandfather saw me struggling, growing red-faced and sticky-fingered with the effort, he put down his Bible and called me over to where he sat.

'Here, Miriam, I will fasten thy cap.'

My hair was knotted and tangled, twisted all around the bands of the cap and after fumbling for a while my grandfather sent me to fetch my brush. He was a quiet, gentle man, and in his own reserved manner, he was, I think fond of me. When I came back he pulled me up on his lap and began to unravel the knots in my hair.

We are taught not to heed our personal vanities and it is to my shame that I confess I am proud of my hair, the only beauty I am ever likely to possess. It was, and is, extremely thick, golden-brown in color and quick to spring forward when released from the tight braids. I have often regretted that the custom of our women insists that the head should be covered, for certainly with my hair hidden away from my face I am an extremely plain and insignificant person. My grandfather, humming very softly to himself, began to brush my hair in curls around his fingers. I think he had really forgotten what he was doing; his mind was occupied with other things and he had become absent-mindedly interested in the movement of his fingers. At last he set the cap on my head and tied the tapes neatly beneath my chin, pulling my hair out at the back so that it sprang forward around the white, starched wings.

'There,' he said softly. 'Now thou art ready for the Meeting.'

I slid from his lap and went over to the stove to climb on the box by the mantle, the box that enabled me to reach up and get my Bible. And at that moment my Grandmother came into the room.

When I think about her now I realize that she was, at that time, probably a very handsome woman. She had dark hair and a strong energetic face. She moved quickly, in a sharp decisive way, always sure of herself, always brisk and commanding. It was in some measure necessary that she should be that kind of woman. She had a farmhouse full of menfolk, uncles and cousins and suchlike, as well as a dairy to run. But to me, a child only too-well aware of my own short-comings, she was a frightening, bewildering woman.

She came into the kitchen wearing her Sunday cape of good black serge and her eyes darted briskly from Grandfather, staring dreamily out of the window, still holding the brush, and across to me reaching up for my Bible with my cap perched at an angle and my hair bouncing jauntily out at the back. In two strides she was across to where I stood. I felt the cap wrenched from my head and my neck was seized suddenly from behind, clasped firmly between her two hard hands.

'Is it so soon thee encourages vanity in the girl?' she hissed at Grandfather. 'What is it, when a man of God sends his own granddaughter to the house of the Lord with her hair about her shoulders?'

She sat in her black, wheel-spoked chair and gripped me tightly between her knees. Then she began to braid the hair back from my forehead, pulling it so hard that small peaks of skin were drawn up along my scalp. Grandfather watched her and then said gently, 'She is only a child, Sarah. There is no need to be so harsh.'

7

She gave my hair an especially sharp tug, a tug that made water stand out in my eyes and hurt the top of my nose.

'Evil is already in her,' she snapped. 'We must guard against the devil and the corruption he breeds.'

I did not really understand what I had done, or indeed what Grandfather had done. I knew my Grandmother did not like me and that, of all the family who lived at the farm, I was the one who drew her most quickly to anger. I thought I must have done something very bad, very wicked, to be always provoking her so.

Again, there was the time when I stole a cake, and the humiliation of that occasion still has the power to move me to embarrassment. I had been washing down the dairy and I came into the kitchen to find a batch of cakes cooling. Childlike, without thinking properly of what I did, I took one and ate it, and was immediately terrorized by the enormity of what I had done. I felt the lump of guilty dough resting heavily in the middle of my chest, and as the afternoon progressed, the lump grew bigger and bigger.

My Grandmother waited until the grace had been asked over the food that night and then she looked tightly round the table and said, 'There is a thief amongst us. I wish to know who took food from my kitchen, for he who steals is doomed to everlasting damnation.'

It was almost a relief to climb down from my stool and stand by the table. The ultimate had happened. I had been caught and found guilty and my punishment could certainly be no worse than the misery of wondering whether I would be found out in my transgression.

Even at that time I was small for my age and I remember, with an inconsequential clarity of detail, that when I stood, my eyes were just level with the top of the table and my Grandmother's face was seen through a forest of plates and dishes.

'Yes, Miriam,' she said serenely. 'Of course, it would be thee.'

Strangely enough she did not seem angry with me, but almost pleased. She smiled slowly at Grandfather, a smile that offered proof of something vaguely triumphant.

'Leave the room,' she said softly. 'Pray to the Lord for forgiveness and I will tell thee thy punishment later.'

She did not strike me; the way of our people deplored violence and children were never chastised in this way. I was made to take my food in the big scullery for two weeks, sitting alone on my high stool with a tin plate held on my lap. Even while I admitted that I *was* a thief, some stubborn spark of defiance made me question the justice of my punishment. My cousin Stephen was always raiding the larder for food and once, when he was tearing a wing of chicken from a cold roast bird, Grandmother caught him and laughed at his 'boyish spirits.'

As I grew older, I learned not to answer back and to try and keep unobtrusively out of my Grandmother's way. I learned, too, not to make any attempt at forming friendships within the Meeting; for although the other children knew no more than I about the details of my background, they were quick to sense, in the cruel way of all children, that I was an apology—a freak of some kind—allowed to exist only by the grudging permission of adults in the village. It is true there were other children who had no parents, who were raised by kinfolk, grandparents and uncles; but these children could point possessively to a well-tended gravestone, claiming that piece of ground as particularly their own. It was an entry of admission into the respectable hierarchy of the village and they did not, as I did, receive letters from a mother who was never seen and could not be remembered.

I asked Grandfather why she never came to see me. My father was dead, I was told, and so my mother had to earn a living for herself. Then why, I persisted, did she not work in the village where she could come and visit with me? I accepted his answer with the unquestionable faith of a small child who believes implicitly in the omnipotence of grown-ups. There was special work to be done with the Friends in Cumberland—teaching work—and my mother was needed there. Was my mother a teacher then?

When he spoke of my mother, Grandfather's customary reserve would vanish and his face would grow animated and alive as he spoke of his only daughter: of what a pretty child she had been, how quick with her needle and pen and how she could even play the harmonium, a rare vanity amongst our people. I would watch his face soften with warm affection and I wanted, oh so desperately I wanted, to be exactly like her, to have the power to turn my Grandfather from a quiet, reserved man into a person alive with pride. I could do nothing about being pretty, for it was apparent that I resembled my father in appearance. But if industry could force comparison with my mother's other gifts, then I should be the best needlewoman and scholar in the village.

My Grandfather, for a man who was after all only a farmer, had an exceptionally fine collection of books; and partly because I was lonely and partly because I wished to emulate my mother, I immersed myself in the wild, extravagant world of Mr. Dean Swift, Jane Austen and the exciting Bronte sisters. The world, once entered, could never be left again. If I was lonely, I did not know it, for the characters in my Grandfather's books were more real, more satisfying by far, than any friends I ever wanted to have.

I wished to become, like my mother, a teacher. Quakers, so we are told, have advanced ideas about the schooling of their womenfolk. Certainly our women seem to have more learning than others of this age, and with the example of our reformer, Elizabeth Fry, before us, it seems that a thinking woman can sometimes succeed where a man either cannot, or will not. But when the time came for me to finish with schooling, Grandmother would not hear of any such scheme. Again references were made to my inherent wickedness, to the ever-present evil lurking in my soul. I must not, should not, be encouraged to ideas above my station. Humility and a life of service was my greatest hope for redemption and so, stifling an inward rebellion, I was apprenticed to the village seamstress, a pleasant little woman named Miss Llewellyn.

And then, when I was seventeen, the tenor of my life was smashed, for I fell in love with Joseph Whittaker.

Courting started early in our village; early and without too much waste of time. It had to be fitted in between the autumn ploughing and the spring sowing, and every Easter and Whitsuntide there was a new crop of betrothals, the products of the somewhat more leisurely winter months. Without being told, I knew that it was not my place to join in the annual wheeling and pairing that commenced every year with the harvest supper. Games were called at the end of the big, oak-floored room and there was giggling and fidgeting with caps as the boys chose their partners for forfeits and apple-bobbing. Naturally I found myself helping Mrs. Jenkins, an arthritic, in and out of her chair, fetching plates of lardy cakes and buns to where the matrons sat in a gossiping circle and, if I was lucky, being allowed to empty another bag of apples into the tub. Whatever great wickedness had kept me precluded from childhood friendships continued to act as a barrier to intimacy in my adult life. My great sin, whatever its nature, was enhanced by my uninspiring appearance and I really did not blame the young men for looking elsewhere. To be truthful, it did not really bother me. Compared to the heroes in my books, the village boys were a rough, unromantic group of young men. It did not bother me, that is, until Joseph Whittaker arrived in the village.

He came in the summer. His father, mother and three sisters moved into the farmhouse at the bottom of the hill. He was twenty, with thick, curling hair and dark eyes—the most beautiful young man I had ever seen. The black garb worn by our men is not a flattering one. It tends to contrast garishly with work-red skin and hands and make the pale look sallow. But Joseph Whittaker had a deep, olive skin and in his black suit he was a poet, a knight, a hero straight from the pages of Sir Walter Scott—and I was not the only one to think thus.

On the first Sunday that he and his family appeared at Meeting there was a wild fluttering around the Meeting House. I watched the girls darting swiftly, one to the other, on the pretext of borrowing a handkerchief or a Bible. They were anxious to see him and, more important, to be seen by him. When the Meeting was over, Grandfather welcomed the Whittakers to our village and invited us to offer our hospitality. I watched the families come up, one at a time, and speak to them. Prudence Collier, she with the large violet eyes, sighed up at him and lingered a little and I was forced to admit that no man could help being overwhelmed at first onslaught by Prudence's blue and golden looks.

I rose from my chair to leave the Meeting and, as I was near the door, I heard Grandfather's admonitory tone calling after me.

'Miriam? Thee has forgotten thy courtesy to the newcomers. Come and give thy greeting.'

I turned and mumbled some kind of apology. I shook hands with Mr. and Mrs. Whittaker and their three daughters. And then I came to Joseph and suddenly found I could not look up at him. I choked out a garbled and awkward welcome and then turned and hurried quickly out of the Meeting House, back to the safety of books and anonymity.

I did not speak to him again in the weeks that

followed, but I watched him. And I watched Prudence Collier and Elizabeth Jenkins and all the others who tried to tempt him to be their partner. I found that Mr. D'Arcy and Heathcliffe and all my dream heroes were no longer so satisfactory. The dark-lashed face of Joseph Whittaker came more and more between me and the pages of my books.

And then one day, as I stood to collect my purse and Bible, I heard his voice close behind me.

'Miss Miriam.'

I turned and he was waiting, his face slightly blotched with a nervous blush; I was so flustered I dropped my purse.

'Miss Miriam,' he said again, then stooped and picked up the purse from the floor. 'Miss Miriam, I should like to walk thee home from the Meeting.'

It was unfortunate that he spoke at a time when everyone else in the room had suddenly stopped speaking. The silence echoed ominously through the room and was broken at last by a plopping gasp, a noise I defined as coming from Prudence Collier who stood with her lower lip hung open. I felt both confused and embarrassed, but for Joseph more than myself. Apparently no one had told him that I was a wicked, ill-dispositioned person who was not to be included in the normal village rituals—a person who was tolerated but no more than that, and one who certainly was not chosen to court with.

My eyes, hunting frantically round the room, fell suddenly on Grandfather. He was watching me in a strange, sad kind of way, but then he nodded and smiled very distantly in Joseph's direction. He, Joseph, coughed and spoke again.

'Miss Miriam?'

I realized suddenly what had happened. All the excitement and delight of being chosen by Joseph Whittaker, flooded suddenly up in my throat. Small, and as Grandmother had told me many times, ugly both in looks and bearing, I had been selected by the glorious, eminently desirable Joseph Whittaker. I smiled widely, and perhaps a little unkindly at Prudence Collier. Then I turned to Joseph and handed him my Bible and purse to carry.

Of that walk home I can remember nothing. Nothing save the sea of astonished faces at the Meeting House. I could not look at the boy by my side and I am sure I did not speak, but I remember being afraid that he would hear the noisy thudding of my heart. We paced carefully along the path, a well-measured three feet between us, both anxious in case a hand or an arm should accidentally brush and turn our formality to a licentious abandonment of the flesh.

Our arrival at the farmhouse was marked by an awkward clearing of the throat on Joseph's part and a recurrence of flooding color over my face. We stood for some seconds looking down at the rutted soil of the path beneath our feet; there was another cough from Joseph, a cough that was a preliminary to speech.

'I should like . . . Would thy grandfather mind if I sat with thee in the Meeting tonight?'

I took enough courage to look at his face. Small beads of nervous moisture were gathered over his forehead and I suddenly felt a whole lot better.

'Perhaps if thee were to ask him . . .'

He swallowed hard, then handed me my Bible and purse.

'I will come this evening,' he gulped. 'In good time for the Meeting.' He turned abruptly, so abruptly that he tripped on the uneven ground, recovered, and hurried away down the hill to his own house. At the bottom of the hill he turned and waved before vanishing into the trees, leaving me with a big shout of happiness bubbling up into my throat. We do not dance—dancing is an abomination—so I ran, riotously, wildly, hilariously up the path, feeling that if necessary I could run all the way to the next village and still have enough

14

energy to shout aloud and jump over the Meeting House roof.

When I went into the kitchen. Grandmother was waiting for me.

She was still wearing her cape. Her hands, clasped icily before her, moved swiftly as I stepped through the door. I felt my arm caught suddenly in a vice-like grip and I was turned painfully to look into her rigid face.

'Sinner!' she hissed. 'Vile and corrupt sinner! Is there no end to the evilness in thee. Must I continually be reminded of the shame of my house?'

She could always arouse a sense of panic in me—a knowledge of guilt and shame without knowing what I had done to be guilty or ashamed of. My uncles were seated round the table eyeing me with somber, severe faces. The shame in me grew deeper for having witnesses to my disgrace. Suddenly she shook me violently by the shoulder and my guilt was replaced by panic, the fear of one who has grown up in a world unused to violence.

'Jezebel!' she spat. 'Is it always left to me to bring order and decency to such a wanton creature?'

She shook me again and the indignity of being humiliated before my uncles moved me to stubborn defiance.

'I have done nothing wrong,' I burst out. 'Grandfather said he might walk with me.'

'Nothing wrong? Nothing wrong? When you have walked through the village flaunting thy wickedness for all to see?'

I could feel hot tears welling up angrily at the back of my eyes. A furious resentment drove me on to further protest.

'Grandfather said I might,' I shouted. 'He said I might. And Joseph Whittaker is coming tonight to ask if he can sit with me in the Meeting.'

Her mouth twisted angrily and she shook me again, hard and painfully.

'There will be no coming to speak with thy Grandfather. Nor sitting together in the house of the Lord.' She let go of my shoulder with another rough shake and began to re-tie the tapes of her cape.

'Get to thy room this instant. Before I forget my Christian charity. Josiah!' She turned to my uncle Jos who stood immediately and came round to join her by the door.

'Jos, thee will come with me. We go on the Lord's work.'

'Where?' I asked thickly, still trying in some measure to keep a semblance of dignity about me. 'Where is thee going with Uncle Jos?'

She was halfway out of the door, her head erect and strong, and I could sense the leashed power in her as she waited before striding down the path.

'Where?' she repeated proudly. 'I go to right the iniquity done in this house.'

She hurried out of the house, her cloak flying out behind with the speed of her movement. I was not quite sure what she intended doing, what the dreadful purpose of her journey was. But I did know, with all the certainty of my cowering spirit, that in some way she was going to turn Joseph Whittaker against me. I saw the glory of the bright morning disappearing down the path with my Grandmother's formidable black. Tears, angry and defiant, surged hopelessly down my face and, seeing my cousin Stephen grinning nastily at me, the last attempt at pride vanished from my soul. I ran down the path and caught hold of her cloak.

'Please don't go to the Whittakers! Please don't go!'

She snatched her cloak away from my hand. The sudden, unkind gesture, trivial and futile as it was, broke the misery in my heart into a fury of hatred against her. The teaching of humility, of gentleness and modesty, flared into a momentary outburst of rebellion.

'Thee is cruel! Cruel and spiteful. Thee shall not speak to Joseph! Thee shall not . . .' I could not finish.

16

Anger and tears together choked my words, blinded my eyes and I did not know how to stop.

Through a watery haze I saw Grandfather enter the gate. Grandmother pointed to me, her eyes shining with triumphant pride and, even in the wild misery of that moment, a small detached part of me appreciated that she was enjoying the high drama of the scene.

'See!' she spat at Grandfather. 'See what evil we have spawned in this house. Even her own mother, wicked though she was, never spoke to me in such a way.' Grandfather tried to stop her as she strode past him on the path but she pushed him out of the way.

'There is work to be done,' she said and she and Uncle Jos were away, following the same direction that Joseph Whittaker had trodden only a short time before.

Grandfather watched me for a moment as I stood, completely without shame, sobbing in the middle of the garden path. Some small fragment of compassion, or perhaps it was embarrassment, made him touch me gently on the arm and try to draw me back into the house.

'Hush, Miriam,' he said quietly. 'Thy grief is angry now, but perhaps it is best that this episode is ended, before it begins.'

'It is not ended!' I was angry with him, angry and hurt. Why did he always let Grandmother chastise me and use me for the scourging of her spirit? Why did he let her dictate the pattern of my life when one small word from him would have sufficed to rebuke or correct me. I wanted nothing more than a single note of praise, a commendation from my Grandfather, but never, however hard I tried, did I receive anything but reserve and silence.

'It is not ended. He will come tonight. Thee will see. He will come and we shall sit together . . .' Again I could not finish. The fight had gone from me and, without protest, I let Grandfather draw me back into his

17

house. I looked once at his face and saw that his eyes were full of tears.

Joseph Whittaker did not come that night. He did not even come to the Meeting and I wished with a desperate fervor that I, too, could have remained at home.

I do not cry prettily, as some do, and I sat that evening between Grandmother and my Uncle Jos, aware that there were curious glances toward my swollen eyes and blotchy cheeks. My pride kept me there, sitting upright and looking straight ahead, and pride kept me from crying again. That night, lying alone and drained of all emotion, I promised myself that never again would I let Grandmother see me weep. She enjoyed it too much.

The following Sunday Joseph smiled unhappily across to where I sat. Then he crossed to Prudence Collier and later, after the Meeting, they left the House together.

I was no lonelier than I had been before, in fact less so, for the little desire I had ever had for converse or friendship now vanished completely. Talking was unnecessary, pleasantries completely without meaning or use. Sometimes, about the house or dairy, a word was needed or a sentence necessary to define a task; but mainly it was better to be still, to wait for peace to enter the heart and in time I knew tranquillity again. I knew that I had grown uglier, pale and even thinner than before, but this did not matter. Things outside the spirit did not matter and I found that when Prudence and Joseph were spoken together in the Meeting House and stood up to be blessed, it did not even hurt.

I wonder now what would have happened to me if I had stayed in the village, becoming more withdrawn and more detached from the things and people about me and I suppose in time turning into one of those strange women who live alone and are laughed at by the village children. Certainly if I had not overheard one day a conversation between Grandmother and my cousin Stephen, I do not think I would have left the village.

Stephen was a fat, mean-spirited youth. For two years he had been trying to find a girl to court with, but his natural disagreeableness soon repulsed any girl of sensibility. I was shelling peas outside the kitchen door when I heard his voice through the open window, loudly lamenting his misfortunes with the village girls.

'It is her fault. If *she* were not here people would soon forget.'

I sat very still because I knew the *she* was myself.

'If she would only leave, go away, they would soon forget there was a bastard in the family. At least her mother has the good sense to stay away so that we are not all constantly reminded of our shame.'

'Hush, Stephen.' I heard my Grandmother say, but the rebuke was for the usage of the unpleasant word and meant nothing. Stephen was my Grandmother's favorite grandchild.

The basin of peas rested quietly in my lap and everything became strangely clear and simple to me. I had not known I was illegitimate but now that I did I was neither surprised nor concerned. Knowledge could not alter my life, and in any case I was contented enough. I wished for no suitors, no friends. I put the affair from my mind, tucked it away with other things that I did not wish to remember, and I finished shelling the peas.

But during the following days, the words of Stephen teased at me and, in particular, I thought about my mother; about why she never came to visit and why, in spite of Grandfather's stories, she worked so far away. I knew he loved her, indeed he loved only her, and when letters came they were addressed always to him. I admitted at last that I wanted to learn more of my background, to hear the story that had prompted my cousin Stephen to complain: the story that everyone in the village knew—everyone except myself.

19

The opportunity came one day when I was working with Miss Llewellyn.

She was a nervous, garrulous little woman whose tongue sometimes said things her heart did not mean. But she could be kind, and once when I suffered an earache, she let me lie on her sofa and fetched a piece of warm flannel for me to hold. She was not one of our Fellowship; she had worked in all sorts of different places and had come to live in the village when her sister was ill. But still she was a kindly creature and the stories she told—of various houses she had worked in—were better than books.

The day came when we were to stitch a gown for Prudence Collier who, although pretty, had no great skill as a needlewoman. It was a dark-blue lawn to wear for her marriage to Joseph Whittaker, and Miss Llewellyn was very uncomfortable as she handed over the bodice for me to stitch. We worked in silence for some time, with Miss Llewellyn ticking and tutting every few minutes, stealing secret glances at me full of concern and worry. At last, unable to keep her tongue still any longer, she burst into passionate speech.

'It's quite disgraceful! Shameful! To sit here sewing that creature's gown when it should be your own.'

I smiled at her. Like everyone else in the village, poor Miss Llewellyn seemed to think that I was still fretting over Joseph.

'It is of no concern, Miss Llewellyn,' I said. I bit off a strand of blue cotton and tied a knot in the remaining thread. 'I have no wish to wed with Joseph Whittaker.'

'No,' she snapped. 'And you'll wed with none other if you stay in this village.' She stopped suddenly and clapped her hands quickly over her mouth as though regretting her words. I finished the shoulder seams of Prudence's gown and began to bind round the neck. Miss Llewellyn fretted in silence for a while longer, then put her work down and came to sit beside me.

'Miriam, why don't you leave the village? Take a post

20

in a house. You're a clever girl with your needle and you read and write better than most. I know a house down in Sussex would be pleased to take you.' She paused, then added jerkily: 'If you stay here you will always be living in your mother's disgrace.'

The chance was there, the opportunity to find out what had happened to my mother. Miss Llewellyn did not belong to the tight community of silence that held my past strictly from me. I felt my face growing hot, but I forced myself to say the words.

'I should like to know my mother's disgrace, Miss Llewellyn. For up till now, no one has seen fit to tell me.'

She stammered and looked distressed, trying to cover up her indiscretion with nonsense and chatter. At last I put the blue dress down on the table and turned to her.

'Tell me, Miss Llewellyn. Someone must tell me. Surely it is not right that I should be the only one who does not know?'

She faltered a little at first and tried to make excuses. But at last, in the face of my determination, she gave in and told me what I wished to know.

It was a drab, pitiful little tale. The same sourness of spirit that my Grandmother now turned on me had been vented on my mother since her birth. Some strange kind of jealousy had made my Grandmother resent her own daughter, and at sixteen my mother had run away from the farm and taken a post in a private house. Grandmother was angry and when she found that Grandfather had helped my mother to find the position and had abetted her in her escape, my Grandmother's wrath turned in full fury upon him.

Recoiling not only from Grandmother, but also the Fellowship of Friends, my mother had married outside the Meeting, a man twelve years older than herself, and a man—she discovered too late—who already had a wife. What had possessed him to be so cruel as to go

21

through a form of marriage with my mother, I cannot guess; but it had left her forever embittered against everyone. She was forbidden to come home and she had no wish to. My Grandmother had been spiteful enough when she was at home before and now, unmarried and with a child, she knew her life would be unbearable. She tried to find work where she could keep me with her, but it was a futile effort that had ended in an east London lodging house fighting a recurrence of a lung fever she had contracted as a child. She was forced, against the wishes of her pride, to ask my Grandfather for help.

He had made the journey to London, a terrifying one for a man who was a simple farmer and a Quaker. Seeing the condition of both my mother and myself, he had insisted that I return with him and live on the farm. He had dispatched my mother to Friends in the north of England who knew her story of misfortune but did not have my Grandmother's malice of spirit. With a quiet determination that he was apparently sometimes capable of, he had defied my Grandmother and brought me home and I, although a constant reminder of my mother's disgrace, had at least been fed and cared for. My presence, however, was something my Grandmother could never forgive, anymore than she could forgive Grandfather's rebellion.

We finished Prudence Collier's gown that day and I went home. But when I stepped through the door of the farmhouse that evening I knew I could never feel the same about any of the family again, not even Grandfather who had done what he thought was right for me. I looked around the table at the big circle of men eating and talking of crops and cattle. Then I looked at Grandmother seated at the foot of the table—proud, straight-backed, iron-willed—and I thought of my mother alone in Cumberland, ashamed and forbidden to come home.

I came to no hasty decision. Many things contributed to my final departure from the village. Miss Llewellyn, once she had told me the truth, repeatedly pressed me to accept the offer of employment in Sussex. In her foolish but kindly way she tried to tell me that if I stayed in the village the years would all be the same, lonely and barren.

On the evening of the day that Prudence Collier stood up with Joseph Whittaker to be married, I spoke to Grandfather about going away to work and was relieved to find that he was not surprised.

I realize now that he had always known I would leave the village, and in his own way had prepared me for a life where it was unlikely I would marry. It was unthinkable that I should wed outside the Fellowship— my mother had proved the disaster of this kind of union—and certainly no young man within the Fellowship, knowing my history, would desire me for a wife. Seeing this, my grandfather had equipped me as best he could for a life where I could stand on my own in an unfriendly world.

He wrote that night to the house in Sussex and to the Friends in that part of the county. Eventually, after some correspondence had been exchanged, he agreed that I could go away. My new position offered six guineas a year and for that I was to act as needlewoman, companion and general factotum, both to the mistress of the house and to her twelve year old granddaughter. If I had waited, perhaps I could have found a better post; certainly the stipend was a meager one considering my duties. But my decision once made, my immediate longing was to leave the village, to leave my Grandmother and everything that reminded me of my background.

If I had thought that Grandmother would protest my leaving, I was mistaken. With my departure she was once more the only woman in a household of men. She predicted acidly that I would be unable to keep my position for more than a few weeks, but she limited her unpleasantness to sharp comments and messages of warning. I waited in vain for the command to stay at home. It did not come.

I made my farewells, realizing bleakly how few there were to make. I packed my small handgrip, kissed my grandparents respectfully on the cheek, and left the place that had been my home for eighteen years.

Thus it was, in the winter of that year, I came to Tancred, that great dark house crouching on the bleak side of the Downs and casting its forbidding presence over all who dwelt there.

2

The South Downs of England are immeasurably old. I do not know when they were shaped, what ice-age or volcanic upheaval served at their creation; but in their shadows—their oppressive boulder-like immensity—lies some kind of primordial instinct. A racial memory. Huge and round-summited, they loom ominously over Sussex and Hampshire; the only living thing on the hills is the wind, racing from the Steppes of central Asia, across the plains of Germany and France, to scream itself to death on the slopes of southern England. On the tops of the hills are great stones, brought there no one knows how or why; strange altars to even stranger gods, old with the ritual of blood long before the Romans came.

And here, on the seaward side of the hills, the house of Tancred had been built: a great monolith of gray stone perched on a chalk crack and stripped clean by the wind.

My journey from the village had been a miserable one. I had quite enjoyed the first part, for it was only the second time I had traveled on a train; and the excitement of the unknown, the sense of adventure that possesses me even now whenever I set out on a journey, made the morning a bright one, a day of hope and promise. Foolishly, with all the gay optimism of youth, I considered that with the village and Grandmother behind me, life would be rich and colorful, filled with new friends and daring adventures. I sat tightly in the corner of the railway carriage watching the smoke from the engine drift past the window and holding my carpetbag firmly on my lap in case someone should come to wrench it from me. The problem of not speaking to strangers did not present itself, for no one climbed in to share my carriage and it was with a superb air of confident independence that I alighted from the train into the noise and confusion of Brighton station.

There was no one to meet me. I sat for three hours on a bench waiting for a conveyance to come, growing steadily more depressed as the hours passed.

Payment for a carriage was out of the question. My rail fare had been lent me by Grandfather and the few shillings that were left I needed to keep by me. At last, in the afternoon, I found a vintner's wagon that was going to Loxham, a village three miles from Tancred and I decided I had better accept the driver's offer to ride along. We agreed that I should pay a sixpence for the twelve mile journey and he threw my red and black bag up onto the cart, then lifted me up beside him.

For the first few miles we did not speak, indeed I could not, for I was struck dumb by the bewildering spectacle of the Brighton streets. The houses were packed so tightly together that I did not see how the people could breathe; but breathe they did and yet had enough energy to bustle and chatter through the crowded lanes. There was so much wealth, so many fine carriages and splendid dresses that I felt I was traveling through one of the Bible's legendary cities, Tyre or Damascus or maybe the city of Jerusalem when the ships laden with cedar and bronze used to bring wealth from the ancient world. Then I began to notice other things, women behaving in a lewd, unfamiliar way, standing outside innyards with gentlemen who seemed to have taken too much wine. A carter was flogging a horse and the beast was jumping up and down and screaming with fear. I began to feel a little sick and decided that the town was more like Sodom and Gomorrah than Tyre and Sidon. I looked in vain for a Quaker cap or black suit. There were Quakers in Brighton—I had been told to seek them out at the first opportunity—but they were hidden, drowned in the sea of color and noise.

We left the town and the road began to pass through fields and villages that appeared to be more like those in my own part of the country, although the hills were bigger and bleaker and there were not so many trees. The vintner's wagon pulled higher into the Downs and the wind grew sharper so that I pulled my cloak up about my ears. The driver reached back and rummaged under a box; then he drew out a plaid blanket which he gave me to wrap around my legs.

'It gets cold here, Missy. Ye'll need a thicker cloak if ye're planning on spending the winter in these parts.'

He looked at me curiously, obviously wanting to know why I had begged a lift on his cart in the middle of January. He had a heavy, thick-set face, but his shirt was clean and buttoned up at the neck. I smiled and thanked him for the blanket and said that indeed it was cold, very cold.

'And why would you be wanting to go to the Tancred Hills. There's nothing there, 'cepting for the old house.'

'I'm going to work at the house.'

He dropped the reins in his lap and turned to look at me, his eyes were startled, ringed with some kind of unpleasant query. He said nothing, just continued to stare at me, and the horse, although unreined, plodded dutifully along the road. At that moment we came through a gap in the hills facing directly onto the sea. The wind swept through with hurtling force, screaming along the road so that the horse stopped and all the breath was knocked from my body. I could hear nothing above the raging wind but I saw the driver swallow suddenly and then his mouth moved and formed the word 'Tancred.' For two miles we could neither speak nor hear, indeed I was hard put to keep my seat on the wagon and the poor horse had his head well down into the wind as he trudged round the hill road. We moved at last behind a sheltering promontory of land, and tucked away at the back of the Down was the village of Loxham.

The driver stopped the cart and turned toward me. 'I unload here. Then I make back to Brighton, and if ye mind me, young woman, ye'll ride back with me. I don't know your business nor why you've come to these hills, but you look to be a quaint little thing and I do know that the black house up on that hill is no place for a young girl to live.' He climbed down from the cart, tied up the reins and lifted me down.

'Now you go and sit in the inn till I've unloaded. Then I'll fetch ye back to Brighton.'

'I thank thee, but I am going to Tancred. I have a position there.'

I was cross. It was very fine for this vintner's man to say where and where not I should work. He, no doubt, had a loving wife and a family to welcome him when he returned home, not a sour Grandmother and a village full of knowing smiles and complacent eyes. He looked sharply at me, then asked, 'How old are ye?'

'Eighteen, Sir,' I did not think it necessary to add that I was eighteen by only a couple of months.

'Well I'll tell ye, young Missy. If ye'd been sixteen I'd have bundled ye up and taken ye back to Brighton, whether ye liked or not. Maybe I should do it anyway.'

'I'm obliged to thee for the ride,' I answered coldly. 'So now I'll give thee thy sixpence and be on my way. No doubt thee has thine own affairs to manage, as I have mine.' I took the sixpence from my purse and held it out to him. To my surprise he shook his head.

'Keep the sixpence. You'll need every small comfort you can get at that place.'

'Sixpence was the price we agreed upon. I wish to be under no debt.'

He shook his head angrily and reached up to hand me my bag. 'May God forgive me for bringing anyone to

Tancred at all. Let no one say that Reuben Tyler took money for such a task.'

He handed me my bag, and as it was plain he would not take the sixpence, I put it back into my purse. 'Will thee point out the path to me, the way through the Down?'

I did not like having to ask him. I was still annoyed with his high-handedness, but it was obvious I would have to walk the last three miles and there was only about an hour of daylight left.

He answered abruptly. I suppose I had been a little rude, and he was determined to wash his hands of me as my mind was made up. 'Down through the village to the next opening in the hills. Then a track off to the right which will take you round the side of the Down and up to the brow of the hill. Once ye're on the sea side, ye'll see the great stone tomb ye've set your heart on living in.'

He turned his back on me and began to unbridle his horse. I was not sure whether to speak to him again, to thank him for his concern and maybe ask the reason for it, but so busy was he with the horse it appeared he had dismissed me from his notice. I picked up my carpetbag and started to walk down the road. Then I heard a shout and looked back to see him running after me, waving the plaid blanket.

'Here. Take this. Ye'll need it up there for there's no flesh on ye to keep the wind out. And remember, if ye're needing to leave that place quickly ask for Reuben Tyler of Wat's Lane. Anyone will tell you where it is. Remember now, Reuben Tyler of Wat's Lane.'

His eyes searched my face with concern and I felt suddenly ashamed of my rudeness. He was a good man and I held my hand out to him.

'Bless thee, Reuben Tyler. Thee is a true man of God.' I clasped his hand for a moment—a big, rough hand— and then I turned and continued down the road. When I

29

looked back he was standing in the middle of the track gazing after me.

The village of Loxham was empty as I hurried through its main street, indeed its only street. There was not even a dog wandering by and its curious stillness depressed me, even made me shiver a little. Once I thought I saw a curtain move in a window, but when I turned to trace the movement there was nothing.

I found the path off to the right and began to walk up along the chalky track leading round the Down. It took me a long time to get through the hills and I began to grow worried that it would be dark while I was still looking for the house. I could hear the wind, that terrible wind that will live with me and scream through my head for the rest of my life. I was still protected by the lee of the hill, but as I approached the sea the gale grew louder, screeching and whining like a living thing. Then, for the first time since leaving home, I was frightened—a fear that did not leave me during all the months I stayed at Tancred. The driver's remarks began to murmur quietly in my mind, and although he had not said definitely what it was that made the house a bad place to live in, it was this very omission, this unspoken dread, that made me nervous. The hills were so big, so lonely, and it was very quickly turning to night. I whispered a quick prayer to the Lord, apologizing for being afraid of something so foolish as darkness and wind and then, suddenly, I was out facing the sea, high, high up over the Channel, and the gale shrieked and buffeted me back against the steep grassy slope behind. I turned. There above me, squatting like a gray animal on a ledge cut from the hill, was the house of Tancred.

It was a tremendously long building, stretching in a raw, ugly gash across the side of the Down. It had, so far as I could see, four storys, and above it one could see the bleak, grassy slopes rising to the summit. Obviously the house had been built so wide and so high because the narrowness of the ledge, cut in the chalk, could mean that there would be space for no more than two rooms in depth anywhere in the building. In later years I have traveled to many parts of England but never, never in the whole of my life have I seen a house so gray, so austere and cold.

I was shivering, and not entirely because of the cold wind. I told myself that the house only looked severe because there were no trees or shrubs about it and no lights in the windows. I assured myself that inside it would be warm and welcoming. Had not Miss Llewellyn spent several hours telling me what a fine place it was!

The climb up the hill was easier than I expected, for now the gale was behind me and at times almost lifted me into the air. The skirt of my dress was pressed flat against my legs; the starched wings of my cap were repeatedly being whipped forward, slapping me painfully about the cheeks. At last I stood on the narrow, shingled courtyard that stretched along the front of the house, and trying foolishly to smooth my dress I mounted the stone steps and pulled hard at the bellrope by the door.

There was no answering chime from inside. I took hold of the rope in both hands and tugged as hard as I could.

The rope came down so suddenly, curling itself in a snakelike coil about me, that I screamed—and immediately hushed myself for having done so. The scream was whipped away into the night wind and a fresh assault of the rushing air caught me briefly off balance and threw me sharply against the iron handle of the door. When I felt the hard edge of metal bang savagely into my shoulder, I gave up trying to pretend that everything was normal and just as it should be. I considered the nightmarish possibility that I had come to the wrong place, a house of the same name and same address, but still the wrong place. I sat down on the steps and wrapped the plaid blanket around my shoulders. The shivering had spread to the whole of my body. I was cold, tired and miserably lost on the side of this grim hill.

I thought of the farmhouse kitchen at home, light and noisy, full of big men clumping about in boots and making a fearful din with their plates and knives. There would be a huge pan of soup simmering away on the stove that always grew red with heat this time in the evening. There would be lights from three lamps, for Grandmother would have no false economy on the saving of lights, and it had been one of my more unpleasant tasks to clean and trim them every day. Grandmother came unbidden into my mind and I imagined her, chiding and triumphant because I could not even gain an entry into my place of new employment. I could hear her words of gloomy prognostication in my mind, and suddenly I stood up and folded the blanket into a neat square. I went back to the big wooden door and banged on it with my fists.

There was no answer. I began to feel angry. For six guineas a year I was at least entitled to be let into the house, even if I was not considered of sufficient importance to be fetched from the station.

There was obviously no point in standing on the steps banging the door. At the knowledge that no one was going to answer, I started to walk the length of the house in order to see if I could get in at the back. It was not quite dark and I held my hand against the stonework as I moved. No moss or lichen grew between the beveled stones. The wind did not allow any living thing to usurp its territory. It was a house stripped clean of vegetation.

As I had thought, the building was a shallow one. I tramped wearily along its length and found, when I reached the end, that it took me only a moment to arrive at the back. At last, with a surge of relief, I saw a thin knifeblade of light in a window, set down below the surface of the ground.

There were steps down to the basement window, steps that I raced down, anxious to get inside as soon as possible to the welcoming light gleaming through. I could hear laughter and the movement of a chair. The sound should have cheered me but it took on instead a strange, sinister quality in keeping with the rest of the night. I heard a woman's shrill voice, then the thick answering growl of a man. I tapped on the window but the laughter continued and I heard the woman shriek and a cup smash on a stone floor.

I could bear it no longer. The hateful wind and strange noises of the night made me lose what last thread of control I had and I beat frantically on the glass, not caring whether or not I broke it, crying: 'Let me in! Let me in!'

The voices stopped at once, and I was filled with the horrid notion that perhaps the light and the people inside would disappear into the night, leaving me alone on the hill with only this terrible house for company. Then, at last, I heard the rattle of a door chain and the sounds of bolts being drawn back. A door by the side of the window opened slightly and the frightened, somewhat suspicious face of a young woman peered through the crack of light.

'Yes?'

'Please! Let me come in!'

'What for? What do 'ee want, wandering alone on the hills when it's dark?'

I pushed forward quickly into the light in case she changed her mind and closed the door again. 'I am Miriam Wakeford. I have come to work for Mrs. Tancred and I have walked all the way from Loxham. I want to come in! Please, let me come in!'

I forgot my manners so far as to press my hand against the door, and the girl hesitated, just for a second. I suppose she was just as unnerved by the unexpected encounter as I was. She eyed me warily then moved her hand back to unfasten the chain on the door.

'Aye. Well, I suppose ye'd better come in.'

The welcoming strip of light grew wider, and the minute it was big enough I thrust through into the warmth and light of the room. My eyes were filled with water from the sudden change of light and heat and again I began to shiver.

'You're cold,' said the girl disinterestedly. 'Here, ye'd better drink some o' this.' She thrust a tin mug into my hand and I could feel the heat from it bearing through to my frozen fingers. My teeth chattered noisily against the blue rim and I took a deep swallow. Some kind of scalding spirit seared its way down my chest, nearly choking me with raw heat. I coughed and spluttered and again heard the deep throaty laughter of the man's voice. The liquid began to warm me; slowly my eyes cleared and I searched in my purse for a handkerchief to wipe my face.

'Ye feeling better?' asked the girl.

It was difficult to tell how old she was. Perhaps she was in her twenties, but she seemed in her manner to be older, far older than I. She had a round face, pleasant enough, but her hair was stringy and greasy, and she wore no covering at all on her head. Her dress was torn under the arm and on each side of the skirt were two big, black grease marks where she had wiped her hands. It appeared that I was in the kitchen of the house. There was a poor fire burning in a range and on the floor lay a heap of dirty saucepans and cutlery. The floor was made of the same gray stone that the rest of the house was built of, although it was so covered in droppings of food and dirt that the color was not apparent. Something unpleasantly nauseous was cooking in a stained pot on the fire, and as my stomach turned queasily at the smell I realized I had not eaten since breakfast that morning.

From the far side of the room there came again that coarse, thick laugh, and I heard a male voice say, 'Right. Now let's have a look at her.'

34

The woman moved aside and the man walked forward. I looked once, then could look no more. Never, in all my years growing up amongst a family of boys, had I seen a sight so shocking, so shameful.

He was a big man, inclined to fatness. He had the greasy, shiny complexion that some fat people seem to have. Thick red hair grew low on the sides of his cheeks and over the back of his collar. He was generally rather repulsive in his countenance, but what made the color rise in my face and kept my eyes fastened to the floor was the sight of his naked chest and belly covered in matted red hair. Not only did he wear no shirt under his open coat, but his breeches were undone at the top.

He came right up to me and put his hand on my neck. It was fat and moist and made a damp place on my flesh when he took it away. 'Mmm. A quiet little pigeon this one.' I tried to stand without shuddering at the nearness of his body. He was so close that his great stomach was nearly touching me.

'See. It even has its own two white wings to fly away on.'

He knocked the peaks of my cap, then forced my face up so that I could do no less than stare into his eyes. 'You won't be able to fly far from Tancred, little pigeon. The house will come after you and eat you up.' His big stomach quivered with a fresh bellow of laughter. He bent his face close to mine. His teeth were decayed at the front and a wave of foul breath blew suddenly into my face. I caught another glimpse of his fat nakedness and closed my eyes against the shame.

'Haa,' he said with the air of one who has discovered a new toy. 'Look, Mary. We've got an old-fashioned one here. Watch, see how she blushes when a man stands near her.' He brought his other hand up and placed it again on my neck. 'I'll take a wager with you, Mary. I'll wager there's a Bible tucked away somewhere in that shabby old bag.'

The girl looked uneasy and pushed him roughly out of the way. With relief I felt his hands leave my face and neck.

'Leave her alone, Math,' she said uncomfortably. 'She's here to look after the old lady and the girl. Not for you to sport with.'

His interest darted quickly to her. He caught hold of her hair and twisted her to face him. I felt sorry for the girl but glad that, for the moment, his attention was diverted from me.

'Are you jealous then? Jealous of a skinny little black crow like this one? Watch her. Look. See her flushing up again. How long, Mary, how long since you blushed because you were standing near a man?'

He laughed again and she tried to join him, but the noise she made was merely an unhappy echo of his. I sensed something unpleasant, something wrong in the air about me. The very atmosphere was charged with unhappiness and ... something more, something unwholesome that could not be attributed to the loathsome brew bubbling on the stove. The girl, Mary, was worried, and she looked nervously from me to him.

'You go now, Math,' she said. 'Go and see to the master's fire and I'll take the girl to her room.'

He rubbed a fleshy hand over his fat stomach and grinned at me. 'Goodbye, little crow. Mind I don't catch you one dark windy night.'

His laugh echoed along the passage as he left the kitchen. When he was gone Mary looked warily toward me. 'You don't mind Math. He don't mean no harm. It's just his way. Don't let him frighten ye.'

'No. He doesn't frighten me,' I said stoutly, and I think it was the truth. He made me ashamed but I don't think I was frightened of him.

'You come now,' said Mary. 'Come and see where you are to sleep.'

She led me out of the kitchen and up a small flight of stone stairs to a long, narrow passage that dis-

appeared into the distant gloom. The lamp she was
carrying cast a dim, smoky reflection on the walls
which were panelled in dark wood. At one time they
must have looked quite splendid, but now the wood was
pocked with wormholes and in several places great
sections had fallen away to reveal the stone underneath. Heavy doors led off from right and left and
at frequent intervals the passage was crossed by a
smaller one.

We came to another flight of stone steps and
ascended. I began to wonder if I would ever be able to
find my way back to the kitchen, for certainly that was
the only place where there was any life in the house. At
last, after another upward flight of steps, the girl
stopped and opened one of the depressing, mahogany
doors.

'Here ye are,' she said, and I stepped into the darkened room leaving her to follow with the lamp.

It was a big room and because I could not hear the
wind so clearly I knew it must face into the hill. The
floor was covered in some kind of undefinable brown
carpeting and over the windows were hangings in the
same drab shade. Three chests, two wardrobes, a
ewer and basin on a very fine white marble stand and
an enormous four-poster bed were the furnishings of
the room. Using the light from the lamp she carried,
Mary lit a lamp that was standing on one of the chests

'Is that all ye got?' she asked, pointing to my small
carpetbag, and when I nodded she looked annoyed.

'I spent a lot o' time turning out these cupboards and
things. The mistress was set on everything being right
for you. Math and me got that ewer set in special. This
is the finest room in the house, exceptin' for Mrs.
Tancred's o' course.'

I stared dismally about me, pondering on the general
aspect of what was considered the second best room in
the house. It was the largest room I had ever slept in,
but it was also the shabbiest and the coldest. There

was soot lying in the fire grate where obviously no fire had been lit for many years. There was a damp, musty smell in the air, and I wondered uneasily how long it had been since the room had been cleaned. I began to unpack my bag. Two spare black gowns, one of good dimity for afternoons and wearing to Meeting, half-a-dozen spare caps, aprons and collars. Four chemises, two nightgowns and a pair of shoes. I arranged them carefully, along with my stockings and handkerchiefs, in a drawer in one of the great chests standing in the corner. They lay drably on the bare wood looking lost and meager. Mary, her arms folded across her body, leaned against a wardrobe watching me.

'Could I have some hot water for washing?' I asked diffidently.

She looked rather sullen and unfolded her arms. Beneath the sullenness I sensed embarrassment and an unwillingness to make excuses for the general condition of things. She wiped her hands down the sides of her gown, over the two greasy bands already there.

'There ain't none until later. When the dinner is over, I heats some water for Mrs. Tancred and the master. Miss Esmee washes in the kitchen by the fire. If you want to come down and wash in the kitchen you can.'

'No.' I said hastily. 'That's all right. I'll use the cold water in the jug.'

The thought of standing in the kitchen unclothed where Math could come in at any moment and see me was abhorrent. I shook my head again and hurried over to the washstand to slop some water into the basin, in case she should insist that I should go back and wash in the kitchen.

'I'll come back for ye in ten minutes.' She seemed relieved that I was not going to make any fuss about the hot water; she even managed a half-smile, then left the room and closed the door behind her.

It was bitterly cold when I took my dress off. I stood

38

in front of the ewer feeling the skin on my shoulders pinching up into the damp air. The water in the jug was even colder, and when I had finished washing I wrapped the good Mr. Tyler's plaid blanket around me and tried to stop shivering. I was hungry, hungry and cold, and I was also terribly homesick. I longed for the big, warm farmhouse, for Grandfather sitting silently in one corner reading his Bible. I even felt a momentary nostalgia for Grandmother. At least she made a bustle and noise so that one did not wonder if everyone else in the world had died. I tried to pray, for prayer is a great comfort in times of distress but all I could think about was Uncle Jos bringing in logs from the woodshed and me hurrying off to bed clutching a hot brick wrapped in a piece of old flannel.

Irritably, I told myself how foolish I had been to listen to Miss Llewellyn and her stories about the splendors of Tancred. She was a romantic little woman given to exaggeration and the painting of vivid descriptions. And I had allowed myself to be swept along with her dreams of fine houses and promising positions of employment. This was a cold, miserable place. Where were the thick beautiful carpets and velvet drapes she spoke of? And the throng of servants, one to every room and then some to spare. And the lamps. She had always impressed upon me that there were no lamps to compare with the famous Tancred lamps, each one made of silver and at least a hundred of them riveted along the lengths of the passages.

Mary came back into the room without knocking, and I was still huddled on the bed trying to get warm. She darted a quick, searching look at me. 'Ye're crying.'

'I am not.'

She said nothing but picked up my dress and passed it to me. 'Hurry now. The mistress wants to see you.'

She watched while I put on my dress and cap. I turned my back before I removed the blanket for I do not like strangers staring at me while I dress. When I was ready she went to the door, then turned and coughed. 'The room's all right like, ain't it. I mean you're satisfied with the bed and all, aren't ye?'

I realized suddenly that she had probably spent a lot of time getting the room ready, that in spite of the surly manner and lounging ways, she was eager to have my approval, anxious for a word of appreciation for the room.

'It is a very fine room.'

'And everything's clean for ye?' She watched my face carefully.

'Very fine,' I said again. Her face lightened and she opened the door out onto the passage. I was glad she could not have seen me earlier, turning back the bedcover to make sure the sheets were clean. I suppose it was an uncharitable thing to do but since entering the room I had been beset by the fear that the bed linen was dirty. My anxiety had been dispelled. It was very thin and worn but it was at least clean.

She led me once more along the passage and down the steps to the ground floor. Then back along another dreary passage until she stopped before a door identical with mine. She tapped deferentially before turning a handle and guiding me in.

This was a splendid room, not gaudy, but with a somber dignity that matched the old woman sitting in a wheelchair by the fireplace. I noticed that in spite of the richness of the room there was still no fire burning. The walls were covered in a dark red paper, heavily embossed with gold. There were some rather grand portraits hanging over the marble fireplace. The floor was well-carpeted, again in a somber red, and the furniture and ornaments were all quite splendid. Everything was immaculately clean and well-polished and there, on a walnut chest, stood one of the elegant silver lamps that Miss Llewellyn had spoken of. But amidst the well-regulated order of the room, one strange, incongruous item stood out from everything else, jarring bizarrely against the rest of the room. I had no time to observe it properly. I was hardly in the room before I was called over to Mrs. Tancred.

She was old, black-haired and black-eyed with long, incredibly thin-fingered hands. 'Here, Miss Wakeford. Over here into the light where I can see you.'

She had a gaunt, high-boned face and although she was crippled, she sat straight and tall in the chair. A shawl covered her legs, gray like her dress. I hope she did not expect me to curtsy, for we bow to no one except the Lord. I held my hand out to her and if she was surprised at my apparent familiarity, she gave no sign. She clasped my hand briefly in hers, then turned me into the light.

'Yes, well I knew you would dress like that, though it does seem a pity for such a young girl to be constantly wearing black. Still, you will find we will not interfere with your customs in this house. You are free to worship as you wish.' She inclined her head graciously, and gave me a long appraising stare.

My eyes were drawn to the strange object in the corner of the room. I knew what it was. I had seen one before back in the village, in the teacher's house. It was a tapestry loom, a big, ugly wooden thing with strings hanging down from a top bar. It was not just the strangeness of such a thing that made it leap out from everything else in the room. It was the colors that were on the half-woven tapestry. The weaving of a tapestry is, I have been told, a restful and soothing occupation. But this tapestry was peculiar, frightening and garish. It did not belong in the graceful room with the proud, tidy old woman in the wheelchair.

It had no picture. It was formed entirely of splashes of vivid color thrown angrily over the loom in big jagged weals. The colors, harmless in themselves, were horrible in proximity to one another. Purple hung lividly against orange, crimson bled into a crude

41

yellow. Bright colors need soft ones to set them in their
beauty. There were no soft colors on the loom, only
black against the wild collection of savage colors fighting against each other . . .

'You are smaller than I expected.'

I looked away from the loom, back to Mrs. Tancred.
She was watching me, ignoring my scrutiny of the tapestry. I stood up a bit straighter and clasped my hands
together in front of me. 'I am very strong, Marm.'

'Perhaps so, perhaps so. I hope you have good eyes.'

I would need good eyes if the sparcity of the lamps
were any indication.

'Did Miss Llewellyn tell you what your duties would
be?'

'I am to help with thee and thy grandchild, and to act
as seamstress.'

The imperious old woman looked a little uncomfortable. She moved the wheels of her chair slightly so that
her face was turned away from me. I was to discover
that she could manipulate her chair with a cunning
dexterity. She used it as other people used their bodies,
to convey a range of behavior and emotion. My eyes
glanced back to the tapestry. Surely this old woman
had not sat before it and spun those weird designs. I
brought my attention back quickly before she had time
to notice where I was looking.

'You will find that Mary can attend to most of my
modest needs. She is a trifle rough perhaps, but she is
used to my ways. Esmee, however, does not respond to
Mary's words. The child's mother is dead you understand, and my son has left the disciplining of the child
to me. You are well-schooled I believe?'

'I have been told so, Marm.'

'Perhaps you could restrain the child a little. Even
try to induce some small learning in her.' She hesitated, then added, 'You may find her a little . . . strange
for her age. She is twelve and has been left for too long
without proper tuition.'

I wondered just what she was trying to tell me. I had no time to consider the matter. She began to speak again.

'Since my accident, I have directed the house from this chair, but I find myself unable to manage as well as the house needs. I shall want you to help me conduct the affairs of Tancred. Mary is a willing worker, but she has no idea of order.'

'How many girls are there, Marm?'

This time there was no mistaking Mrs. Tancred's discomfort. Her thin, loose-skinned neck stiffened and the lizard-like black eyes regarded me with dislike. 'At the moment we have only Mary. And Matthew, my son's man. One or two things have become a little disorganized, but there is nothing that diligence and industry cannot repair.'

It seemed I was to earn my six guineas a year. Mrs. Tancred wanted a housekeeper, a governess, a seamstress and, as there was only Mary to do the work, a housemaid as well. As though fearing my thoughts she asked me quickly, 'Are you pleased with your room? I instructed Mary that you should have the best in the house and she has spent many hours preparing it.'

'It is very pleasing, Marm.'

I could not tell her that it was cold, dark, and miles from anywhere. Having seen some of the rest of the house I could well believe that it was the best room. She was relieved at my answer and hastened to add, 'I am so upset that you had to journey here on your own. We had thought you would arrive tomorrow when Matthew would drive to Brighton in the trap.'

My journey had not been a pleasant one, but in retrospect I decided that a fifteen mile ride with the repulsive valet downstairs could have been far worse.

'I managed, Marm.'

'Of course it was too dark for you to see the house, but tomorrow you shall see how splendid it is—the only one of its kind on the Downs. We have had five kings

43

who have visited at Tancred. There is no other house to equal it in the whole of Sussex.'

I thought she was making some kind of clever jest. A joke about the house to cover up the shame she must feel about its general condition. I looked at her face and saw only pride there, pride and a fierce sense of possession, and I perceived, almost with pity, that she really believed the house was a place of beauty and splendor.

'Did Miss Llewellyn tell you anything of Tancred?'

'A little, Marm. She told me she came here with you when you wed with Richard Tancred, and that she stayed with you for ten years.'

She leaned forward in the wheelchair, her hands clasped together, and on her face was a rapt excitement. 'He was my cousin and all my life I had wanted to be mistress of Tancred. You should have seen the balls and dinners we gave then. Every week there was a party or a concert. The path up the hill had to be widened especially to accommodate the carriages. Every window, even in the servants' rooms, were lit with lamps. We had our own musicians who lived here all the time, and an Italian gardener who cut the garden out of the cliff at the back of the house. The whole county came to Tancred. Here,' she rapped impatiently on the arm of her chair. 'Push me out into the passage and I will show you what Tancred means.'

She took the silver lamp from the chest and held it carefully on her lap. Her eyes were so wild, so excited, that they did not seem like those of an old woman. She tapped once more on the arm of her chair and I obediently wheeled it through the door and out into the passage.

'Down here, down here,' she said sharply and we rustled along the eerie dark passage for what seemed an interminable length of time until we were stopped by a huge iron door. I unlatched it—for that was obviously what I was supposed to do—and wheeled Mrs. Tancred inside.

44

We were in an enormous gallery. Above me I could see the shadow of a balcony running the entire length of the room, and a series of portraits stretched into the endless distance.

'See!' She pointed the lamp to a small, dark painting. The colors were so somber and the gallery so dark that I could make nothing of the picture.

'That is the first of us, Mandel Tancred, who fought with the Black Prince and received these lands for his gallantry. Here,' she swayed forward ecstatically, 'here is his bride, a princess from Scandinavia whom he got in exchange for a shipload of sheep-pelts.'

I wanted to laugh, but I think my laughter was not only because of a bride bought with sheep's wool. There was something uncanny about the old woman, she was too bright and glittering. She frightened me a little.

'Push me forward, Miss Wakeford.' I did so.

'Here is the next, Edward, and there his son, the second Mandel. John Tancred, after whom I named my son, rode with his men to welcome Henry Tudor when he landed to fight with Richard Crookback, and *his* grandson became rich robbing the Spaniards under the old Queen.'

She spoke as though the old Queen (and I perceived she must mean Queen Elizabeth) had been dead only a short time. She was swaying imperceptibly back and forth and although she was speaking to me I had the strange feeling that Mrs. Tancred was, in reality, communicating with these long-dead men and women.

The procession along the gallery continued. This one beheaded, that one morganatically married; Mandel III, insane after imprisonment by the Inquisition. The old masters of Tancred were paraded before me with their brides until my head whirled and my arms ached from pushing the heavy wheelchair. Then we came to the end of the gallery, to another heavy iron door like the one we had come through. But the door at this end was slightly ajar and, thankful to break the macabre pageant of ancient Tancred, I asked:

'Where does this door lead to, Mrs. Tancred?'

Unformed words bubbled away on her lips. I watched her turn back into an old woman in a wheelchair—a woman who lived alone in a red and gilt room with a weird tapestry loom for comfort. She stared uneasily at the open door and I again caught that shifting, sideways look that she had given me when she spoke of her granddaughter.

'They are my son's rooms.'

'All of that half of the house!' I had worked out that the gallery was right in the center of the long stone building, and until now I had only been on the western side.

'Beyond is the part we no longer use. It is locked and there is nothing of interest there.' Her voice was completely devoid of expression, flat and cold, saying nothing. I tried to see her face but she kept it stonily turned away from me, and her shawl partially draped the lamp.

'Over to the other side, Miss Wakeford. You have not seen all of the Tancreds yet.'

The long walk back started, the portraits changing slowly as dress and the fashion of artists altered with the centuries. Hugh Tancred, decapitated by the round-heads. Osbright Tancred, restored by Charles II. Another Hugh, this one the first of the great merchant sailors, for during the last two hundred and fifty years the Tancreds had accumulated their wealth from bartering across the seas.

Then, half-way down the gallery, we came to the last painting, and for the first time my attention was riveted on the man it portrayed. For I have never seen a face both so beautiful and so evil.

'Who is this, Mrs. Tancred?'

She was gazing at the last portrait but one and droning softly, 'William, killed at the Battle of Waterloo, married to Fiona, daughter of . . .'

'Who is this, Mrs. Tancred?' I repeated in a clear, ringing voice, trying to dispel the ghosts of the great gallery.

Slowly her head turned toward the last portrait and I saw that her face was ravaged and twisted with an old hate that still gnawed at her. 'My late husband, Richard Tancred. Painted before our marriage.'

We stared silently at the portrait. It showed a young man leaning against a marble column, with a background of cloudy sky. The setting was a typical one for painters of the mid-century, but there was nothing modern or fashionable about the face of the man himself. Long narrow dark eyes slanted out of a young-old face. The mouth was sensuous, beautifully-shaped, corrupt. He was not smiling, but the whole portrait seemed to grin malevolently at me. The light flickered unevenly over the walls and I thought I saw the man move his head, inviting me into the picture. It was a face coming forth from the pages of *Revelations*, a likeness painted in the pit.

The wind had started to blow again and as we were now on the seaward side of the house I could feel it blowing sharply through the cracks in the walls. I looked at Mrs. Tancred. She was crouching forward, her hands clasping the arms of her chair, and her lips were moving soundlessly as she stared into the picture.

'Shall we go back, Mrs. Tancred?' The wind caught my words and blew them away up the gallery.

'Mrs. Tancred?'

She was murmuring something that I could not hear, so I bent my head. All I could catch was 'Richard Tancred, Richard Tancred, Richard Tancred,' repeated over and over again.

'Mrs. Tancred! Please come away! Please!' I shook her by the shoulder, shouting at her, trying to break whatever terrible communion she was engaged in with the man in the portrait. At last she seemed to hear. She lifted her head and stared at me as though wondering who I was. Then she raised the lamp a few inches and said wearily, 'It is time for dinner. Take me back.'

Thankfully I pushed her from the gallery and closed the iron door carefully behind us.

Dinner that night was one of the worst meals I have ever eaten. There was some thin, oily soup that had a faint flavor of fish, then a gray slice of meat followed by cheese that had apparently had the mould cut from it. At home they would be sitting down to game pie and roast potatoes. And there would be baked apples to follow, with large bowls of newly turned cream set on the table. If anyone still had appetite after that, Grandfather would pass round a crumbling Worcestershire cheese. Nevertheless, I was so hungry that I ate each insufficient portion of food as it was placed in front of me, in spite of the obnoxious smell and the hair that was embedded in the cheese.

We sat, Mrs. Tancred and I, one on each side of a square mahogany table. Two other places were set but no one came to join us, and after a brief glance at Mary, Mrs. Tancred ignored the other places.

I had not been sure whether I was to eat with the family or not. My place in this house seemed a strange one, neither housekeeper nor maidservant, governess nor nurse. When I had wheeled Mrs. Tancred into her place at the table I had waited to see what I should do. She looked at me and smiled, and I caught a glimpse of the gracious woman she had once been.

'You will eat with us, Miss Wakeford. There, opposite me.'

Mary served the soup and I waited for the Grace but none was said, so I quickly shut my eyes and said the words in my head. I need not have bothered to be so reticent. When I opened my eyes Mrs. Tancred was so busy gulping her soup that she did not even look at me.

We are not a rich family but Grandfather's people have farmed their own land for many years, and during that time we have collected a few good pieces about the house. Grandmother has a pair of Georgian candlesticks and a cabinet of Spode, so that I know a fine thing when I see one. When I looked down at the small piece of meat placed before me I was surprised to see it was resting on a Wedgwood plate. I looked at Mrs. Tancred's dish. It was porcelain, and as I gazed about the table I saw that all the china, all the cutlery and glass were old and exquisite; but all of it was odd —no two pieces matched and much was cracked or chipped. At the end of the meal when Mary, still wearing the torn dress, came to remove the plates, Mrs. Tancred said quietly, 'Where is Esmee?'

Mary shrugged and picked up the remains of the cheese in her fingers. No doubt I would be expected to eat it at some later meal. 'Somewhere about. She'll come when she's ready.'

She clattered a few more plates together and left the room. Mrs. Tancred gave me that odd, uneasy look that I was coming to associate with her.

'My granddaughter will be here soon.'

She looked again at the two places laid at table and added, 'My son does not usually eat with us. He prefers to stay in his own rooms.'

I had been at Tancred only a short time but already I ceased to wonder at the strangeness of a family where grandmother, son and granddaughter never met. In this unhappy house it seemed the normal thing to do.

Then the door opened quietly, very quietly, and a child slipped into the room. She stared at me curiously but did not speak. She went straight over to Mrs. Tancred.

'Bonsoir, Grand-mère.'

'English, Esmee. English!'

She was a queer little girl, thin and black-eyed like her grandmother, wearing a dress that was too long under a soiled apron.

49

'Grand-mère does not like me to speak French,' she said conversationally to me. Mrs. Tancred was angry, and in some odd, uncanny way, she was afraid of the little girl.

'Esmee, this is Miss Wakeford who has come to school you and teach you the duties of a daughter of Tancred.'

The child did not answer, just watched with her curious, glittering black eyes.

'Has thee eaten?' I asked her, for no one else seemed to care.

'Hmm. I ate with Matthew.'

She began to move with a ritual precision about the table in a peculiar little dance. Mrs. Tancred hastily pushed her wheelchair away from the table.

'Miss Wakeford, perhaps you would care to see Esmee ready for the night. Her room is along by yours and soon there will be water for washing.'

'I shall wash with Mary, in the kitchen.'

'Thee will not,' I said firmly, for I had no intention of sharing my first introduction with Esmee in the presence of that man who appeared to walk in and out of the kitchen as he pleased.

When, late in her room, I began to undress her for bed, I was appalled to see that she wore no stockings or bodice underneath her frock. And, moreover, her body was none too clean. I made her stand in the bowl while I scrubbed her down, and all the time she was singing a strange sharp-noted little song in a language that I thought must be French.

'Esmee, why does thy Grandmother not like thee to speak French?'

She looked at me furtively and stopped singing long enough to answer, 'Maman was French. She taught me the song.'

It started again—the monotonous chant—the same phrase repeated again and again, and it began to worry me. When she was clean I braided her hair.

50

'Tomorrow I shall wash thy hair. And see to thy stockings and bodice.'

'Why do you talk like that?'

'Because I am a Quaker.'

She tilted her head on one side and asked, 'What is a Quaker?' but before I could answer, she had started singing again.

'Now say thy prayers and go to bed.'

The song stopped abruptly, and once again I received that curious birdlike look.

'Why should I pray?'

'To speak to the Lord, and thank Him.'

'What shall I say?' she asked curiously.

I was at a loss. Quaker children know their prayers almost from birth. What could I tell this child to say, she who apparently knew nothing of God and who swayed to and fro while singing. Then from some dim recess of my mind an old childish rhyme came to my head. I cannot think where I heard it—certainly not in the village, but I made her kneel on the bed and fold her hands.

'Matthew, Mark, Luke, John,
Guard the bed that I lie on.
Strong and brave and clothed in light,
Keep the evil from the night.'

She began to repeat the words, sly and bright-eyed, and then, as she finished saying the verse, she became frightened.

'Will it work?'

'Will what work?'

'Will they keep me safe? Away from Grandfather and the noise?'

I felt the hair on the back of my neck rise, and something cold moved down my spine.

'What noise, child? Thy Grandfather is dead. He can make no noise. Come now. Climb into bed.'

I pulled back the sheets, then screamed when I saw what lay there.

51

Something black and shiny moved into a crease of the sheet, and on the far side another of the same kind moved quickly out of the light. I was held rigid in a cold revulsion that crept up my body. I managed at last to turn my face toward the door and scream, 'Mary, Mary!'

It was an age before she came, running up the stairs, her face white with fear and agitation.

'Look! Look at this.' I dragged her into the room and pulled the covers back again. The revolting black things in the bed scurried again for the hidden crevasses of the sheet. To my surprise she took no notice. She sat trembling on the edge of the bed, holding her hands tightly together. I, too, would have liked to sit down, if only to ease the trembling in my legs. But I dared not sit on that horrible bed. And I felt afraid to turn my back on the sheets and walk away—as though, once I could not see the things, they would run riot all over the room. Mary slowly released her hands and color seeped back into her face.

'Is that all? I thought . . .'

'Is that all! Is it not enough? Bring some fresh linen and let us make the bed. What we can do with the overlay I do not know, but at least let us have clean linen.'

'There is none,' she said sullenly.

'No linen?' This was nonsense. Everyone has clean linen somewhere about the house.

'There was only one pair of sheets. All the rest are ripped and worn. The mistress said you was to have the clean linen.' She paused and then added spitefully, 'She's afraid that if you ain't treated properly, you'll leave.'

We stood, three women, sharing only the mutual bond of our sex. There was no other link between us, no shared communication to use as contact. Then Esmee smiled secretly.

'But you won't leave. You see you can't, not now.'

52

Of course I could leave whenever I chose. I could pick up my bag and go straight from the house this very instant. I thought of trying to find my way out of the house, and then wandering down the hill in the heavy night. I swallowed hard and looked at Esmee. She was perched up by her pillow, seemingly not bothered by the condition of her bed.

I did not want to do it, for there was something about the child that worried me; but I could not, in all faith, let her climb into that dreadful bed.

'Esmee, tonight thee will sleep with me. Tomorrow we shall see about the linen.'

Together we went to my room and later I lay down beside her. My mind was so tormented that I was afraid to rest in case I should be haunted by the events of the day. But hardly had my head touched the pillow when I fell asleep and, strangely enough, that night I dreamed of Joseph Whittaker.

3

I awoke to a thin, gray light filtering through the worn parts of the curtain. Esmee was gone and I reached over and put my hand on the place where she had been lying. It was still warm and had a very faint scent, a strange almost non-existent odor of cheap soap covering a mossy, wood-like smell. I had taken care not to touch her in the night. I like children and no doubt, when I had grown accustomed to Esmee, I should like her too; but the unearthly aspects of the previous evening had served to make me hold back from her—to withdraw into a wary constraint.

I threw back the bedcovers and let myself slide down from the high bed onto the floor. The clear light of morning and a good night's sleep should have restored everything to normal and made the house and the people ordinary and common-place and my task a mundane, if poorly paid one. But I awoke with just as much depression as had been with me when I slept. Even in daylight, the house was still strange, not merely in the way of an unfamiliar house, but strange and sinister. Mrs. Tancred was a gracious lady. Perhaps she was too concerned with the pride of her house, but she was no different from many old ladies who are consumed with the past. And yet she did not quite fall into the accepted pattern of a great lady. She was odd—and there was the loom . . .

I went to the window and drew back the curtains. A cloud of dust bellowed out into the room, then settled again as the curtains were still. The Down rose steeply before me, and running up the hill was the small figure of Esmee Tancred. She was throwing her arms wildly up and down in the faint light of the early morning, and over her nightdress she was wearing the plaid blanket tied loosely and trailing on the ground. I opened the window and shouted at her to come back. Either she did not hear or she took no notice. She ran like an animal, darting swiftly from side to side in the wild unpredictable way of a field creature. I watched her carefully; and then I sensed a curious pattern in the rhythm of her movements. I tried to define why the pattern was familiar, why I knew what speed her next few steps would take and when she would pause for a moment on the hill. It came suddenly when I realized I was silently measuring a tune; the strange song that she had sung last evening was going through my head, brought there by the design of her running. Eventually she came to the top of the Down and disappeared, and hurriedly I turned back to the bed to dress, remembering that it was my task to control the child, not stand in the window and watch her.

Mary was in the kitchen, lying on a small pallet set by the stove and with a shudder, I saw that she also slept in the torn dress with the grease marks. She was sitting up on the pallet, yawning and running her fingers through her tangled hair.

'Mary, Esmee, is away, chasing over the hills in her night-shift.'

She stretched her arms up in the air, then pulled the cover back up over her shoulders.

'Aye. Don't worry yeself. Sometimes she's gone for two or three days at a time. She'll come back when she's ready.'

I wrestled with the chain and locks on the back door and at last managed to bang the swollen wood away from the frame. It was cold outside, though the wind had dropped a little and I started to run, trying to catch up with this contrary-tempered daughter of Tancred. She was certainly, as Mrs. Tancred had said, undisciplined, and as controlling the child had been set upon me, then control her I would. While I was in charge there would be no two or three days spent running over the hills. It was no wonder the child was strange, left without schooling, taught no prayers or even how to wear a bodice. It was time she was brought to some kind of order.

The hill was steep and very soon I was forced to slow my pace. When I reached the top of the Down, there was a pain in my side from trying to run too fast and I felt more than a little cross with Esmee Tancred.

The tops of the Downs are deceptive. Looking up to the grassy humps from the valleys below, one supposes that the other side falls smoothly away like an upturned basin. But the summits are a strange world of their own, rising and falling in small hummocks, little hills standing on big ones. A hundred yards in front of me stood a circle of Druid's Stones, some tall, some almost buried in the grass, but all intimating an unstated pattern of command so that unbidden one's eyes were drawn to the primitive archway standing at the eastern end of the circle. Looking over the hills, here and there, I could see odd stones arranged in a nebulous design that was no design at all, each stone waiting, ancient and gray.

They must have been weird people, the old Britons who had dragged the great monoliths up the Down without horses or wagons and set them in the chalk. The wind hissed lovingly around their sinister shapes, remembering what no one else could ever remember. I heard a high, soft laugh from somewhere on my left and I hurried down, then up and over a small tussock but Esmee was not there. The laugh came again but this time it was from the Druid's circle, and then it moved to a single stone and left that and wandered about the hill.

I was angry, angry that a child could confuse me so and make me unsure of where to look. Then the wind caught hold of that strange little French tune, the child's thin humming echoed about the hills and purposefully I moved quickly to the circle, determined to catch Esmee before she disappeared again. The song began to back away from me so I ran up to the circle and in and out of each stone in turn until I came to the arch. She was not there either but still further back, and again I ran, faster, away from the stones, up to another summit standing against the sky.

I do not know to this very day what made me stop in time. Some quick instinct acted on my balance and held me back, right on the crumbling edge of a great gash in the chalk. Four hundred feet below me boulders of chalk and stone lay in a confusion of rubble dotted here and there by stunted bushes of thorn. I could see the village of Loxham quite clearly, sitting snugly in the valley at the foot of the chalk cliff. For one wild, indecorous moment I thought I was going to be sick. The speed of my own foolish running and the thrust of the wind behind had all but toppled me over the edge. Even while I stood, holding my hand against my throat and swallowing hard, I felt the ground crumbling beneath my left shoe. The singing had stopped.

Very carefully, anxious that no sudden movement should start a downward tumbling of soil, I drew back from the edge and started back, back down the grassy mound to the circle of stones, into the wind and the view of the cold, steel-gray sea, high on the line of sky.

And then, on the far side of the stones, standing and looking out to sea, I saw the figure of a man. He was turned away from me, only his right side was visible, but the unexpectedness of his appearance, as though he had risen silently up out of the stones, made me halt my steps and keep quite still. For one insane, ridiculous moment my heart jolted nervously with the thought that it was Joseph Whittaker come to fetch me from home. There was a certain superficial resemblance, the coloring was the same, dark hair and olive skin, but

57

there the likeness ended for this was a big man—too big, I suppose, to be considered a fine romantic figure. It was John Tancred. I knew with complete and utter certainty that this was the master of the dark stone house below us, the man who was Esmee's father and Mrs. Tancred's son. There was something of both in him, something in the way he stood that was unmistakeably reminiscent of the old woman and the strange child. And—though I tried to push the thought away—there was also a vague likeness to the portrait of the man in the gallery.

He was old—at least in his middle thirties—very big, wide-shouldered and thick-hipped, with probably a tendency as he grew older to increase in weight. His hair, although thick and curling, was far too long, and it gave him a careless, untidy look, an appearance intensified by the fact that he wore no more than his breeches and a loose-sleeved shirt. I was cold even in a serge dress but he did not seem to be bothered at all by the wind. He just stood there, looking out over the water, apparently impervious to any vagaries of the weather. His face, although heavy, was beautiful— smooth and well-shaped.

He turned his head to look at me and I felt my body stiffen with shock. I managed not to gasp, sensing that if I did I would regret it later on. But it was not at all easy to control myself when I saw the other side of his face. It was disfigured, ugly and horrible, with a welter of angry scars. His eyes was unharmed, but the cruel distortion of his cheek twisted the corner of his mouth into an unhappy parody of a smile. I forced myself not to look away, for I believe that folk who are maimed or crippled in any way find an aversion to their afflictions being ignored; it is, in its way, more hurtful than having people stare. Faced up to honestly, the horror of the wounded cheek faded a little and I began to sense the misery of the man behind the face. We stared at one another: I not knowing quite what to say, and he glaring at me as though he wanted me to scream and run away.

'Do you like my face?' His voice was harsh, rough and curiously deep in texture.

'It is worse than some—and better than many.'

His eyes wandered disinterestedly over my black dress and white cap and collar. 'What are you doing here?'

'I am Miriam Wakeford. I have come to care for thy daughter and to manage thy house.'

'Miriam Wakeford.' He repeated the name dreamily. Then his eyes went queerly opaque, shutting off whatever thoughts were in his head. 'And how old are you, Miriam Wakeford?'

'Eighteen, sir.'

Another hard stare from the blank eyes, then he turned his head suddenly and looked back to the sea. 'Have you a home, Miriam Wakeford?'

'I live with my grandparents, sir. On a farm.'

'And why did you leave your farm?'

They were odd questions to ask of someone who was a servant in the house. I began to feel he didn't want me there.

'I wanted to come out to work, sir.'

'And you chose to come here?'

'Yes, sir.'

His face twisted back suddenly to face me. This time I knew what to expect and the sight of the marked cheek did not jolt me quite so hard.

'You were foolish to come here, Miriam Wakeford. You should have stayed on your farm, wherever it is.' He spoke softly, so softly that it was difficult to hear what he said. 'Go back to your farm and your good grandparents. Pack your bags and leave us. There is nothing you can do here.'

He moved quickly away from me and began striding down the hill, his shirt blowing loosely against his thick chest. I was bitterly cold, and moreover, I was growing tired of these Tancreds who insisted on wandering about the hills without warm clothing. I was also hurt. It would not have been asking too much for him to have offered his hand, to thank me for the miserable task I was dowered with—that of caring for his unruly daughter. I began to follow him down the hill, not so quickly, for my legs were not nearly so tall as his, and he vanished into the house while I was still some way up on the hill.

From this angle the house looked odd, a line of stone with the sea right below it. The garden that Mrs. Tancred had mentioned last night had been painstakingly cut out of the chalk on the hillward side of the house. Perhaps at one time it had been agreeable but now nothing had survived the wind except ivy and ewe. Broken parts of old statues lay on the ground partially covered with grass and soil. I could see the eastern wing of the house, the part that was used by John Tancred and the portion that was locked. Right away at the very end, the building had already turned into a ruin. The roof was broken and the windows were all out, with neither glass nor boards to replace the damage.

A door was banging, open and shut, open and shut. In spite of this, and in spite of the wind, there was an unpleasant stillness about that eastern end of the house. I found, as I walked down the hill, that I was moving gradually over towards it drawn not entirely by curiosity.

Tancred was always a still house. I never once saw a bird fly over, although there plenty on the cliffs nearby. But this eastern wing was so agelessly quiet that I was almost afraid to place my feet on the shingle drive.

The door, swinging to and fro, appeared to lead into a small passage and I waited a moment before deciding whether or not to go in.

There was a small animal-like flurry past me, the

noise of a darting creature. Esmee, panting and wild-eyed, flung herself in front of me and stood with her arms stretched over the door, barring the way to me.

'Keep away, keep away,' she snarled. 'This is my place.'

The plaid blanket had slipped from her shoulders and I could see that her bare feet were blue with cold. She looked small and somehow pathetic, and I knew a moment's ridiculous embarrassment for having been afraid of her earlier that morning up on the hill.

'I shall not go in if thee does not wish it,' I answered gently, turning away to go back to the kitchen.

She watched me worriedly, still defending the door with her thin, poor little body. 'No one can go in here except me.'

'I have no wish to.'

I thought she must have a child's secret place in there, the sort of game that all children play to themselves. I remembered making a secret garden in the hollow trunk of a walnut tree, planting violets and nettles there. They had flourished, too, until my cousin Stephen followed me one day and trampled on the flowers.

When she saw I was walking away she cautiously left the doorway and followed me, the gap between us growing less very gradually. She gazed up at me and in a tone of sweet calmness said, '*Maman* is in there.'

For one horrible second I thought she meant it. The evil miasma of Tancred had already seeped into my soul and I could almost believe that the dead woman was locked up in that gruesome, derelict part of the house. Then I recalled the games and the imagination of childhood and smiled to myself.

'No, Esmee. Thy mother is in heaven.'

She looked curiously at me and shook her head.

'No. She is in there. Look.'

She took my hand and pulled me to a halt, then propelled me around to face in the direction from which

61

we had just come. The empty window spaces stared back, blank sockets. 'There, in there. *Maman* is there. Can't you see her? In the wind?' She swayed slightly from side to side, watching the door swinging on its hinges. 'To and fro, to and fro,' she chanted.

This time I had truly had quite enough. A chase over the hills nearly to the edge of a cliff, an encounter with the surly Mr. Tancred and now this precocious child (dragging *my* blanket in the dirt) filling her head and mine with superstitious nonsense. I grasped her firmly by the hand, pulled the blanket tightly about her neck and began to march her back to the kitchen.

'There will be no more of this,' I said coolly. 'From now on thee will dress each morning when thee rises and thee will tell me where thee is going. Now, no more hanging about in the cold. We are going back to breakfast.'

She shrugged her tiny shoulders.

'No point in going back yet. There won't be anything to eat for hours.'

'Oh yes there will,' I said determinedly, and I meant it.

Five hours later I had the kitchen floor scraped of dirt and gleaming with the deluge of seven pails of water. A pan of bread was rising over the stove and Mary, some-what sulkily, was dicing up cubes of leathery cold meat into a saucepan.

I had made some breakfast, a reasonably nourishing thick porridge which had at least been hot, even though there was no sugar or cream to eat with it.

We had stripped all the beds of linen, including Mary's nauseous pallet by the stove, and I had done what I could to repair enough sheeting for that night. I felt I did not want Esmee sleeping with me again. I reproached myself for my selfishness—my lack of charity—but unwittingly I found myself recoiling from the child. The linen of the house was in an appalling condition. What was not filthy was ripped and worn. No attempt had been made to turn or repair the sheeting, and as the linen wore out it was thrown dirty into a dresser drawer. Esmee's overlay I pulled out into the yard and burned and what came out of that burning mattress made me shudder. Some have a great fear of spiders or maybe lizards and garden creatures, but my own particular horror has always been of lice and unwholesome things that breed in dirt. I found an overlay—very damp but at least clean—in one of the countless rooms stretching along the length of the house and Mary and I dragged it down and set it by the fire to air.

I would have liked to suggest that Mary remove her gown and wash it while we had so much cleaning and soaping going on, but a suspicion—later proved correct—that the young woman had only the one dress, made me hold my speech, and I was glad that I did so. She was a good-natured girl. Many would have resented a stranger coming into the house and setting the place on its ears, and although at first she was a little sulky, a little inclined to take offense at every new action of mine, she grew more cheerful as the day proceeded and she found I was quite prepared to do my share of the scrubbing and unpleasant chores.

The pantry was a depressing place considering the size of the house. No preserves or chutneys had been laid up, no fruit dried or syrupped from the summer, and there was not much in the way of flour or meat either. I asked Mary who did the buying for the house.

'Mrs. Tancred gives me some money each month to go down to the village and purchase food.'

Esmee turned eagerly from the other side of the room. I think she had hoped to go running over the Down again, but I had washed her hair and made her sit by the stove. Then, deciding that it was time she learned how to help, I set her slicing onions for the broth.

'When Mary comes back, we have pheasant and cream and Matthew has wine . . .' She stopped as Mary glared at her and shook her head.

I felt angry. Mismanagement of money always makes me cross, especially when there is only a little in a house. I, no doubt like everyone else in this place, was both cold and hungry, apparently because no one had bothered to organize the housekeeping. I could see no joy in spending what little money there was on rich things and then living like paupers for the rest of the month. And I was especially cross at the thought of the fat valet having enough for wine while we lived on thin soup and moulding cheese.

'But that's not fair!' I said indignantly, and watched a flush creep slowly up Mary's neck. I forced myself to speak quietly, remembering that she was older than I and had been here for a long time.

'It doesn't seem right that we should live well for a few days and then starve for the rest of the month.'

'I do the best I can,' she said sullenly. 'If you think you can manage better, you're welcome to try.'

I was quite sure I could do better. For one thing I should see that Math Johnson did not supplement his wages out of the housekeeping.

'Well, Mary, if thee does not mind I think I should like to try. I have done the marketing at home for a big household. I feel I can buy for six without too much worry.'

She sniffed and shrugged her shoulders with an expression of indifference. 'Please yeself,' she said sulkily. 'If you think you can feed six on what she gives me I'm sure I don't care.'

That made me a little apprehensive, and later I became worried in case I had antagonized the girl. I could not afford an enemy in this weird household. But the thought of living on bad meat and sugarless porridge for the rest of the month made me stick to my decision. Maybe we would not be able to have meat and milk every day, but I was sure we could eat better than we had last night.

When the time came to eat that evening I was tired. I had worked all day, and looking back over that strange time at Tancred, I admit to myself that my industry was not only a desire to set the house to rights. Whenever I was unoccupied, I found that I was filled with an uneasy dread, searching for something in those endless rooms and passages or listening for Esmee humming her peculiar little foreign tune. I tried, when working, to make some cheerful noise about the place —the homely clattering of cooking utensils or the bumping of furniture as it was cleaned—but the house was so huge and the everlasting wind so violent that noises quickly echoed away into the gloom.

I wheeled Mrs. Tancred into supper that night, and in spite of my weariness I felt a small piece of pride when I looked at the table. There was a clean cover and fresh table napkins which had been part of my wash during the day; and Esmee, her hair clean and braided, sat waiting in one of the other places. I think Mrs. Tancred was a little surprised to see the child there, especially tidy and neat with clean fingernails.

'Bonsoir, Grand-mère.'

Again, as she had done the night before, the old woman stiffened at the words. Esmee watched her grandmother slyly from beneath lowered lids, waiting for something to happen. I wanted no repetition of the weird events of the previous night, no bizarre carnivals around the portrait gallery looking at the likenesses of the dead. Neither did I want the uneasy communication between grandmother and grandchild that I sensed whenever they came together. I put Mrs. Tancred's chair to the table and said brightly, 'From now on, Marm, Esmee will be eating with us. She is old enough to learn good manners and how to conduct herself at the table.'

The old woman nodded, looking strangely subdued. Again she gave me that soft, brilliant smile and the encounter with John Tancred came to my mind. I watched how the smile transformed Mrs. Tancred's face and I wondered if the silent man in the east wing ever smiled and, if he did, whether it relieved or intensified the grimness of his face. In view of Mrs. Tancred's affability to me this evening, I was tempted to ask about her son, but I thought better of it. The most inconsequential subjects took on a forbidding aspect with this family.

Mary brought the food in. Again there was no attempt to ask a blessing, so just as I had done the night before I shut my eyes and said the Grace as quickly as I could. When I looked up, Esmee was watching me, smiling.

'Why do you shut your eyes?' she asked loudly. Mrs. Tancred was startled. She turned to look at me and I felt my cheeks flooding hotly as I stared hard at my plate.

'I was giving thanks for the food.'

Esmee sniggered. Even Mrs. Tancred had a quiet, amused kind of smile on her face, and from the far side of the room I heard Mary giggle. Esmee had decided to be evil-dispositioned that evening.

'Do all Quakers wear ugly clothes and say prayers in front of everyone?'

I waited for the old lady to reprimand her. I could hardly say anything when her grandmother was there. There was silence around the table.

'And the way you speak. Do you all speak like that— like old men and women?'

I would not have thought that a child's words could have hurt me so much or made me feel so old-fashioned and dowdy.

In the village, amongst my own people, I had always been the smallest and plainest of persons and now, here with these ungodly folk, I was conscious not only of my unprepossessing appearance but also of the fact that I was an oddity. I tried to keep my back stiff and straight but I felt exactly the same as on the day Grandmother had called me a thief at the table—ashamed and wanting to cry. Mrs. Tancred had stopped smiling and she said sharply to Esmee, 'You are impertinent. Apologize to Miss Wakeford at once.'

'Sorry.' She sang the word. In a shrill high voice, and almost at once, she relapsed into her everlasting song. I thought Mrs. Tancred would rebuke her for singing at the table. She looked at the child almost with dislike, and then turned wearily to her plate.

I had made a good, thick country soup with plenty of vegetables and what little meat there was left. As there was nothing to follow, one of my new loaves was sliced on the table with a tiny dish of butter. Mrs. Tancred looked questioningly at her cutlery, only a spoon and a knife, signifying that there were no more courses to come. Then she raised a querying eyebrow at me.

'Is this how one eats in a farmhouse?'

It was a spiteful thing to say, for I had spent a lot of time making the best meal I could with what little provision was in the pantry. I could have answered that if we had sat down to a meal like this at home, my Grandmother would have blushed with shame. No doubt Mrs. Tancred preferred to carry on with the facade of imitating a formal dinner, the onion water for soup, the meat lost, one piece each on a delicate plate. However, having made her protest, I observed that both she and Esmee ate rapaciously, taking slice after slice of the new bread and asking Mary if there was more broth.

I had made up my mind to speak to the old lady that night. There were several things I wanted to make clear, including the fact that I should do the kitchen buying. When we had finished eating, Mary took Esmee away to the kitchen and I was left alone with Mrs. Tancred.

'I am sorry if thee does not approve my cooking, Marm. I did what I could with the food in the house.'

She had the grace to flush a little. 'It was appetizing.' she conceded stiffly.

'I could, no doubt, provide something a little finer had I the planning of the buying. With thy permission, Marm, I should like to hold the monthly purse.'

I waited for the rebuke. To my surprise she seemed pleased and smiled most affably. 'Perhaps that would be best.'

'Then, Marm, there is the matter of Esmee's clothes. She has no stockings, nor bodices, nor neat dresses.'

The smile faded at once, giving place to a look of strained distress. 'She has managed up to now.'

'It does not seem fitting, Marm, that she should go chasing over the hills in her drawers and coverall.'

She was acutely embarrassed and murmured something that was quite inaudible. When I asked her to repeat it she said, 'I will speak to my son about the matter.'

I could hardly see the scarred, silent man I had met that morning on the Down concerning himself over his daughter's undergarments. Mrs. Tancred tapped her fingers uneasily on the arm of her chair. She obviously wanted to speak no more of the matter.

'It does not necessarily mean new garments, Marm. If thee has some length of old stuffs I could soon make dresses and pinafores.'

I must have struck the right note, for her face cleared suddenly and she stopped her tapping on the arm of the chair. 'Of course. I had forgotten. Come, Miss Wakeford, take me to my room. I think I have something suitable for Esmee.'

I pushed the chair back along the passages, back to the opulent red bedroom, the splendid chamber that was so out of keeping with the rest of the house. I looked at the loom, it did not appear to have changed at all. The colors still jarred angrily over the wooden frame.

'Behind the wardrobe, Miss Wakeford, you will find a trunk. Pull it forward here, into the center of the room.'

It was a big, old tin box and very heavy. I pulled and dragged at it and at last got it in front of Mrs. Tancred. When I opened the lid a smell of old, musty clothes blew up into the air, a combination of dampness and lavender.

'These are all the things I had as a young woman. So many dresses I had, so many. We can cut them to fit Esmee, can we not?'

'There is still the matter of the stockings.'

She dismissed this as of no importance and leaned forward to pluck a garment out of the chest. 'This blue velvet. This should do for something.' She held it up before her and stroked the fabric with her thin, white fingers.

'It was the dress I wore when I traveled to Paris after my wedding. There should be a cape to match. And I had a blue cambric hat trimmed with osprey.'

She looked almost happy, smoothing out the creases and fastening the buttons on the old dress. I had to admit that the fabrics were beautiful, all of excellent quality; and the gowns were well made. They were crumpled and fusty but she was right, they could be cut into quite splendid robes. I began to feel excited. A seamstress in a Quaker village does not work on anything very splendid. The dresses are always black or dark blue, the material wool, linen or occasionally a dimity. These old robes of Mrs. Tancred's were exquisite, in colors like flowers. The woollen capes were of a superb quality—soft and very warm in beautiful shades of green and blue.

She pulled a gleaming satin out, and the color was so gloriously crimson that I gasped with pleasure. 'My ball dress,' she said proudly, 'for the first time I received as mistress of Tancred. I had a lace dress too, cream, and I wore it with pearls.' She wrinkled her brow as she tried to remember something. 'Where would that dress be? In the other chest. Bring it over the wooden one.'

We opened the other box, and like children we held all the beautiful colors up in the air; silk and velvet was strewed all about us on the floor. Satins, muslins, bombazines, taffetas, heap after heap thrown on bed and washstand. Crimson, emerald, white faded to an old ivory, amber and green. I was drunk with color and texture. We had both forgotten our reserves and for once there seemed no guarded barrier of hidden fear and secrecy. We were drawn together for just this brief time in a mutual regret, for neither of us could ever wear such lovely things, she because she was old and crippled and I because I was a Quaker.

She must have seen the longing in my face, for she rummaged deeper into the first box we had opened and finally handed me a dress of black silk. It had a wealth of yardage in the skirt and had obviously been worn over a hoop at the time when that fashion was at its height. The silk was quite splendid and it was a heavy one, corded here and there with a knotted thread.

'Here, child. I know your teaching forbids you to wear anything but black. This is a good silk, an Indian silk brought back on one of the Tancred merchant ships. Take it and cut it down to fit you.'

I had never been so tempted before. I wanted that silk so much I could have cried, not that I would have looked any different in it, but I would have felt so fine and maybe a little less insignificant. I held it in my hands and thought just how I would make it over, with a buttoned bodice and a neat waist. I had to refuse it quickly, for otherwise I would not refuse it at all. I stroked the fabric once, feeling its invisible softness under my hand. Then I thrust it swiftly back into the trunk.

'I thank thee, Marm, but a silk dress is a vanity.'

I think she was as disappointed as I, for the excitement

faded from her face and she looked slowly about the room at the dresses and capes and petticoats lying everywhere.

'What a mess we have made,' she said dully. 'Well, take what you need and put the rest away.'

I picked out some woollen garments, and some of lawn and flannel that I could cut down into drawers and bodices for Esmee. As I turned to go I thought of Mary. She could not possibly go on living and sleeping in the one dress. It made my stomach recoil to think of it, but then it was all very well for me to set myself up so grandly about Mary's dirty frock. I had three dresses and six aprons and I could afford to clean my things whenever I fancied.

'Could I have a dress for Mary, Marm?'

She waved her hand irritably in the air in a gesture of assent. She had lost all interest in the clothes and she just wanted them out of the way. I hastily selected a blue woollen dress and put the rest back in the boxes. I left her sitting with her hands folded in her lap, staring darkly into the distance.

When I reached my room, Mary was waiting inside for me. 'You'd best go and see Esmee,' she said tiredly. 'She won't get into bed until she's seen you.'

The child was sitting huddled tightly into a corner of her bed. The pupils of her eyes were dilated and there was something inhuman in the way she cowered in the shadows. I wished I could like her, for I liked most children. She stared at me queerly as I came in.

'I've forgotten the magic words.'

'What magic words, Esmee?'

'The spell to keep Grandfather away.'

I was shocked to find that the prayer I had taught her had become no more than an incantation for something unpleasant. I tried to reason with her. I did not want her to be concerned with this fear she had for her dead Grandfather.

'Thy Grandfather is dead, Esmee. He can never come

71

back here, not in any way, for God will not let him.'

'God will be afraid of him. Everyone is afraid of Grandfather. *Maman* was, and *Grand-mère*, and my father, too.'

She crouched forward, like a cat ready to spring, her thin, wild face tense and unchildlike. The suspicion I had tried to push away from my mind ever since meeting her last night stirred again, and this time it would not go. I had tried to put the child's behavior down to her unusual background—the lack of discipline and the fact that she had no other children to play with. But I was becoming increasingly conscious of the fact that Esmee Tancred was not a normal child.

'God is afraid of no one, Esmee.'

She smiled at me, a smile without joy or humor. Her teeth were small and sharp, her tongue darted back and forth over her upper lip. 'He will be afraid of Grandfather.'

The old woman downstairs had gone into a trance when she looked at her husband's portrait. The child lived in terror that he would come back to haunt her. The man on the hillside had told me to go away. I wanted to know why.

'Why is everyone afraid of Grandfather, Esmee?'

'Because of the noise.' The wind echoed her words and shrieked suddenly through the cracks round the window and we both jumped.

'Was that the noise, Esmee?'

'No. You listen. You'll hear the noise. It goes on—and on—and on . . .' Her words drifted into a chant and the chant became the song, as I knew it would. I felt bewitched by her. I could not speak because of the dryness in my throat. Her song became softer; she leant right up close to me, her face thrust into mine.

'You're afraid, Miss Wakeford. Aren't you?'

I turned away to run out of the room but she screamed at me, 'The words, Miss Wakeford, the words!'

I could battle no longer. It was wrong, but how could I let a child go to sleep in terror when an old rhyme would keep her fears at rest. I repeated the prayer and she said the lines after me and then curled quickly into her bed. As I blew out the lamp and left the room she said, 'Goodnight, Miss Wakeford, and don't you forget to say the words.'

In my room I undressed and went to draw back the curtains. There was a bright moon lighting the hill in the front of my window, and small feathery clouds scudded quickly inland.

Half way up the hill a figure waited on a horse, a dark figure on a lightish colored animal. The rider was dressed in breeches and a white shirt. He wore no coat, and even at this distance I knew who he was. He was looking down at the house, toward the east wing and beyond to the locked ruin at the end. Then he turned and spurred the horse and the two of them disappeared over the top of the Down.

I turned away from the window and went to kneel by my bed. I prayed: all the usual prayers, for Grandfather and Grandmother, for all the uncles and cousins and people in the village. I prayed to have my sins forgiven and for help in overcoming my innate wickedness. I asked my private prayer, the one for my mother and then I stood up and climbed into bed.

I suppose it could do no harm, I told myself. There was no reason why I should not use the childish prayer that seemed to bring Esmee so much comfort. I perceived, suddenly, to what depths of foolishness the house was bringing me, and I turned over and tried to compose my mind for sleep.

4

In the weeks that followed, I tried hard to draw close to that strange, isolated family living on the windswept Down. I endeavored to fit myself into the routine of the household, to assist where it was needed, but without being thrusting or forward. I was willing, if anyone so desired, to offer my sympathy and friendship. Indeed, in those early days I was so anxious to succeed at this, my first position of employment, that I would have gone to any trouble, taken any abuse if only I had felt my company was needed.

It was an effort that was wasted. I was wanted merely as a drudge, someone who could set the house to rights and from whom nothing more was needed. I did not have to worry about a routine, for there was none other than that I made myself. I was told what things were wanted and it was left to me to see that somehow, anyhow, the results were achieved. It would not have mattered if I had gone through the passages drunken and a slattern, provided the meals were served, the beds were ready for sleeping and Mrs. Tancred's room was kept in a spotless condition.

On a few occasions Mrs. Tancred would send for me in the afternoon and demand that I read to her. The first time she sent for me I was conscious of a feeling of pride and a desire to offer the very best company I could for the old lady. Armed with a selection of my favorite works, I hurried in to see her. She was waiting, staring out of the window with her hands idle in her lap, and she did not look up when I came in. I paused a moment, then coughed. Still she made no movement.

'Marm?'

She turned her head slowly and looked at me, vaguely and without interest.

'Thee sent for me, Marm. To come and read.'

She raised her black eyebrows reminiscently and moved her chair slowly forward into the room.

'So I did, Miss Wakeford. So I did.'

'I have some books, Marm. Some of my own, unless you prefer something more learned . . .'

She did not give me time to finish. She moved her fingers briefly in the air and said, 'Anything will do, anything.'

I was not sure which one to select, but finally I picked up Thomas Hardy's *Under the Greenwood Tree*, thinking it would be suitable for an afternoon's enjoyable reading. I had read no more than two or three pages and was just beginning to enjoy it—Mr. Hardy being one of my favorite authors—when she interrupted me, looking angry and upset.

'You are reading a novel, Miss Wakeford?'

'Why yes, Marm. I did not think . . .' It had not occurred to me that she might be strict and not approve the reading of novels. Surely in a house where no Grace was said and no prayers taught, she did not insist that only learned works were read.

'It is a romantic novel I believe. If my memory serves me right, Mr. Hardy usually indulges in foolish nonsense of that kind?'

'I suppose it could be called romantic, Marm,' I faltered.

'Then read no more. What else have you?'

I looked down at my small collection of books. *Wuthering Heights, Sense and Sensibility, Shirley.* 'I suppose, Marm, they might all be considered as romantic.'

She tutted irritably and told me to put my books

75

away. Then she bade me fetch a history book from one of her chests, an account of Cromwellian policy in France and Germany, I believe it was. And very dull reading it made, too. However, it was Mrs. Tancred's fortune to choose her own reading and at least she wanted me, had deliberately picked me to share her afternoon. I began to read, trying to make the lists of charters and agreements as exciting and colorful as I possibly could. The book went on and on, and with it went the power of my voice. The afternoon drew in to early evening and still she did not tell me to shop. I began to fret, it was time for me to see to the dinner, to fetch Esmee in from the hills and get her washed. I came to the end of a chapter and looked at Mrs. Tancred. She had pushed her chair back to the window and was once again staring out, though by this time she could not possibly have seen anything. I waited. She said nothing, just continued to watch the night moving slowly past her window.

With a jolt of hurt pride I realized that she was not listening, and indeed had not been listening for some time. I had been speaking into the empty air; a dog barking or a chicken scratching would have made a noise just as meaningful to her. I stood up and waited, then walked across to the door. She did not even know when I left the room, and neither do I think she remembered I had been there.

I was called in again on some afternoons, though why she bothered I could never ascertain. I would read—always a dry book of politics or history—for as long as it was convenient to the business of the house. Then I would rise and leave her, staring into some forgotten dream.

Strangely enough, I found that after a little time had elapsed the one person who had cause to resent me, became my friend—a distant and somewhat wary friend, but at least a person I could talk with. I think, if I had been in Mary's place, I would have resented the coming of a younger girl who entered the house and took over the planning and marketing, instructed what meals were to be cooked and how, and generally interfered in the management of the house.

She had been prepared to dislike me, and then she found that I did not ask her to do anything I would not do myself. I would scrub and empty slops, peel onions, rake out the stove and sit in the corner seaming at the sheets and garments for Esmee.

Of necessity we drew together, and then we found that each was a balm for the loneliness of the other. Two young women in a silent, unhappy house are bound to form a union of some kind; they depend on each other for kindness and a piece of comfort when they are out of sorts. It did not take us long to discover that friendship—even such a one as ours, with all its limitations of reserve and secrecy—was something that neither of us had had before.

I won her finally when I made over the blue dress of Mrs. Tancred's. I let her think I was fixing it for the old lady and then, on the day it was finished, I handed it across the table to her.

'There, Mary. That is for thee.'

She gazed down on the woollen fabric with a puzzled line over her eyes. 'This belongs to the mistress.'

'It did. She said I could have it to make over for thee.'

Her face slowly smoothed itself of the frown and I watched her biting her lower lip between her teeth. 'You been working on it a long time.'

'Yes. But thee will find it fits. I have a fair hand at seaming and stitching and the stuff is good, very good.'

I suddenly felt terribly ashamed, for I thought she was going to cry. Her face was suffused with color and her eyes, fixed lovingly on the blue wool, seemed unnaturally bright. I always feel uncomfortable when people thank me for something I have done. I said quickly, 'Come now, try it on and let's see how it looks.'

She stood up quickly and unfastened the wretched

gown she had worn since I had arrived at the house. Giggling slightly, she pulled the blue wool over her head and waited for me to tie the tapes at the back.

'Thee looks very fine,' I said, and she twisted around so that the material of the skirt billowed out into the room. She did look well and I realized, not for the first time, that when she was not looking sulky or unhappy she had a very handsome face. She was tall, much taller than I, with a splendid figure; she filled the dress out and gave it a style it would never have had on me. I had a notion to see just how grand she could look.

'Let me wash and braid thy hair,' I said. 'Then, with gloves and a cape, thee will look just like a lady.'

It was a cruel, unfortunate thing that at that moment Matthew Johnson came into the kitchen, heard my comment, and saw Mary, flushed and smiling in a new blue dress.

I did not like him, and not just because he was fat and uncouth. The men of my village are, it is true, only farmers and countrymen. But they have an inborn courtesy and a sense of the fitness of things. Math Johnson had no courtesy and even less consideration for others.

He and I had settled into an uneasy truce. When we encountered one another I made a point of being especially polite and even-tempered so that he would have no cause to pick a quarrel with me. I sensed that it was his wish to make me angry, to provoke me into some kind of rebellion so that he could mock at my teachings. Sometimes, when I came across the yard, he would lean against the door watching me. Once or twice he had deliberately come out of the stable to stand in my path, dodging from side to side when I tried to step around him. He laughed a lot, nastily in a big thick roar that came deep from his stomach. Now, as he came into the kitchen and saw the two of us standing together in pleasure over the new gown, the laugh came again, and I turned to see his great belly shaking as he leaned against the jamb of the door.

'A lady! Oh my God! Mary a lady!' He laughed so hard that it turned into a bout of coughing and he turned to spit into the yard.

'Ho, Mary lass! Watch out, or the little black crow will have you praying and going to meeting next. A lady! Our Mary a lady!' His great laugh bellowed out again and I watched the pleasure in Mary's face turn into pinched misery—saw her change from a pleasing young woman back into a drab. He had spoilt the morning. A small knot of anguish in my breast swelled slowly into something more than pain; it grew and filled the whole of my heart and then burst into seething anger.

'Thee is a lout, Math Johnson! A clumsy, spiteful lout! If thee did more of thy fair proportion of the tasks instead of leaving us to swill the yard and fetch the wood, she would have more time to be a lady!'

He had spent a lot of time trying to make me lose my temper and now that he had succeeded, he looked surprised. Then a slow grin spread across his greasy jowls and I was furious that my words had had so little effect on him. I sought angrily for something that would pierce his thick hide. 'And if thee did more work, thee would not be such a fat lump either, Math Johnson.'

It was rude and childish and I did not care. Nothing makes me more angry than spitefulness, and this horrible man had taken away what little pleasure there was in Mary's depressing existence. My allusion to his fatness got through, and for a second he was annoyed; then he grinned and came over to where I stood.

'Well! At last we've made Miss Prissy forget her lovely manners. See now, take off the stiff collar and there's a sly little cat there, just like all the rest.'

He put his hand on my neck. He was forever touching me whenever we met, patting my face with his thick fingers or trying to squeeze me about the waist.

'Take thy hand from my neck, Math Johnson.'

'What will you do if I don't? Fight me?' He burst into

his huge laugh again and then put his other hand round my waist and pulled me up to him.

I have no excuse at all for what I did next. I had lived for eighteen years in a community where violence was deplored, where the harming of another being was never considered, not for one instant. The teaching was so inherent in me that I could not even wring the neck of a chicken, and now this fat, loathsome man set years of carefully instilled tolerance to nothing, for I reached up and slapped him hard across the mouth.

From the other side of the kitchen I heard a tiny gasp and then the sound of Mary crying, but I was too appalled by what I had done to go and comfort her. A red mark was beginning to stand out on Matthew's face, and when I saw the way his eyes narrowed at me I wished even more that I had not done it.

'You little bitch,' he snarled. He got hold of the bodice of my dress and lifted me into the air by the material. My feet hung emptily above the floor. Then he shook me so hard I thought I heard my teeth rattle. Mary screamed and ran across the room to catch hold of his arm.

'Leave her, Math, leave her for pity's sake. She meant no harm.'

She was sobbing noisily, pulling and wrenching at his sleeve, but he was so angry he did not hear her. She shouted again, 'Math!' so loudly that at last he put me down on the floor, still clutching my dress.

'You ever do that to me again, girl, and I'll kill you. You hear? I'll whip you so hard you'll wish you'd never left your namby village with its gutless men.'

My knees were shaking so hard I could scarcely stand but I was not going to let Math Johnson talk down to me. 'And I'll tell thee Matthew Johnson. If thee ever so much as touches me again I shall have thee dismissed.'

It was a foolish threat and he knew it, for with a sudden change of temper he threw back his head and gave another great shout of mirthless laughter. 'Dismiss me? They daren't. No one can dismiss Math Johnson. I know too much.'

'Math!' There was no mistaking the guarded warning in Mary's cry. Their eyes met briefly, then darted apart.

'You go now, Math. She didn't mean nothing. You didn't, did you?' she said, turning quickly to me.

She was so distressed, so very anxious about something, that I could do no less than mutter a resentful apology for hitting him. I thought he was going to say something to her but he changed his mind, and going to the stove he lifted off the bucket of corn mash that had been heating there. At the door he once again stopped at though he wanted to speak, but Mary hurried over to him.

'Go, Math. Take the mash to the stable before it gets cold.'

His small, red eyes looked across the room speculatively at me; then he opened the door and went out. I could hear him laughing all the way to the stable. Mary turned anxiously back to me.

'You shouldn't have said that to Math, and you shouldn't have hit him. I don't mind him laughing at me, but you shouldn't have hit him.'

I was hurt by her defense of the hateful man. I had made her the dress and I thought we were friends. Should it come to an upset, however, she stood by him rather than me. My annoyance was short-lived. I looked at her face and saw how all the excitement of the morning had gone, turned into a dull apathy, and there was more than apathy in the way she had spoken to him. I thought, indeed I was sure, that she was afraid of something. Uselessly, fighting against the general malaise of the morning, I tried to salvage something of her gaiety and interest in the new dress.

'He is a stupid, ignorant fellow,' I said and then, when I saw her face grow frightened again, hastened to add: 'But still, I will not fall out with him again.'

She plucked miserably at the stuff of her dress.

'For all that he is a man, and what do men know of frocks or ladies? I know a good thing when I see one and I know thee looks very fine.'

She smiled thinly.

'Now we shall heat water for thy hair and I will lend thee one of my ribbons. It is black of course, but good velvet just the same.'

I tried, but it was useless. Her happiness had gone, carried out of the kitchen with a bucket of corn mash and a mean-minded man. We pretended, both of us, that we had forgotten the incident, but it was there, hanging morosely in the air between us.

Later, when Mary sat with her head bent forward to the fire, I wondered why she was so quick to defend him. What tenuous link held her in some strange kind of loyalty to him? I recalled how on the night of my arrival they had been laughing together, and it struck me—ludicrous though it at first appeared—that perhaps she had a liking for the fellow. To me he was an odious, unpleasant man who stank of horses and sweat, but not everyone sees things and people in the same way. A toad is a diamond in a duck's eye and perhaps, to Mary, Math Johnson was a fine, upstanding man.

'Mary, are thee and Math courting?'

Her eyes were huge with astonishment as she lifted her face from the fire. 'Courting? Me?'

'Well, I thought perhaps thee might be.'

She smiled, a queer, unhappy sort of smile. 'Who'd want to court with me?'

'There's plenty. If thee doesn't fancy Math, there's sure to be some suitors in Loxham.'

'There's none there would want me, neither.' Her face was red—from crouching over the fire, I suppose.

'Surely they sought thee out before, when thee was younger?'

'No.'

'But they must have,' I persisted. 'There's not many girls up in these hills, and farming folk aren't keen on tramping into towns looking for wives.'

She stood up so quickly that she upset the stool. A sneer spread bitterly across her wide-boned face. 'There's no one would come near me. Not in Loxham, nor in Brighton. Nor, come to that, in the whole of the county.'

'But that's foolish talk!' I said heatedly. 'Thee would make a fine wife, comely and a good worker.'

She stared hard across the room, two bright spots of color flaring on her cheeks. 'And who'd want a girl that the old man had finished with—a girl who was rotten, bad and nasty like the old man himself was. There's nothing could come away from him that wasn't hateful. No one, I say, no one in the whole of Sussex would want me now. He finished me, just like he did everyone else in this house.'

There was a tap dripping in the corner of the room, a well-spaced interval of plopping that seemed more important than it actually was in the silent room. I concentrated on its regular, even beat because there was something quite wholesome about the noise and I did not want, not just yet, to understand the meaning of Mary's words.

'I never had a suitor. He got hold of me when I was fourteen and after that, after the things he done to me, there's no one would look at me. Nor would I want them to,' she added harshly.

She was standing facing me, her head thrust forward and her eyes glowing with the memory of old fears. I wanted to stop her, to make her go back to the careful silence that she adopted whenever I asked questions that were dangerous. I was frightened of the confidences I had unleashed. I wanted her to stop but I couldn't say it and slowly, her words began to spill out, shocking and startling in their revelation.

The tapping of the water in the sink took on a

nightmarish quality. It ceased to be the homely noise of a kitchen and became instead the thudding background to Mary's disclosures. Nothing in a Quaker village had prepared me for what she was saying. I did not want to listen; I wished I had never listened, but bitterly, Mary's voice droned on, telling me things I did not fully comprehend—terrible, horrible things that could not possibly be true. And yet I knew they were true for no one, least of all the guileless Mary, could possibly have invented them. I tried to put my hands over my ears, but that was no use for I could see her mouth moving, forming words that seemed to be worse than they actually were. She was crying, thick tears streaming silently down her cheeks, and after a while I found I was crying, too. My fear of what she said faded a little and left in its place a deep, sorrowing pity for her.

'Could thee not have gone away?' I asked her.

'Where to? I was twelve when Mrs. Tancred took me from the Union. I was a charity child and when I came here the old man was away on one of his trips. He used to be gone two or three years at a time.' She looked up at me, tears still coursing down her face. 'I thought this place was paradise. There was more money then, and there was three other maids as well as grooms and a cook. She was so kind to me, the first person in the whole world to speak nicely and say "please, Mary" and "thank you, Mary." She was the loveliest lady I ever met.'

Her words were so jumbled and confused that they gushed forth in a welter of distress, and at first I thought she was meaning that the cook had been kind to her. Then I realized that she was speaking of Mrs. Tancred.

'Then he came home and everything changed. And when he went away again it wasn't the same. It was better than when he was here, but it was never the same. She tried to make it up to me, but there wasn't anything she could do, not really.'

'Mrs. Tancred *knew*? And did nothing about it?'

Mary gave me an odd stare, as though trying to make me understand something. The kitchen was suddenly quiet, for the tap had stopped dripping.

'She couldn't do anything.' She paused and added softly to herself, 'She's afraid of him.'

Cold air moved up my back, although the kitchen was warm and it was still daylight outside. I don't think Mary had realized that she spoke of old Richard Tancred as though he were still alive, as though Mrs. Tancred lived in fear of a man who would return again at any moment. Mary went dreamily on, 'He stayed for a year that time. Then Mr. John ran away and that nearly broke Mrs. Tancred's heart.'

'Why did Mr. John go?'

I had asked something that bore onto one of the forbidden secrets of Tancred. Mary suddenly came to herself and turned sharply away to scrub potatoes at the stone sink in the corner.

'They quarrelled,' she said curtly, as though fearing she had said too much.

'What about?'

'I don't remember. And anyway the old man went away again, stayed for four years that time.'

I began to clear the table, ready to prepare the meal. I thought of the strangeness of the house, the silences that ensued when ordinary questions were asked. I thought of Esmee, barring my way to the east wing because she thought her mother was there. 'Mary, how long is it since John Tancred's wife died?'

She had turned right away and her back was toward me, but I had the oddest feeling she was furtively watching me. 'A few years back,' she said impassively. 'She was always a poor, sickly creature. Wasn't none of us surprised when she went. Are you going to fetch me the ribbon now?'

She wanted the subject changed and I liked her enough not to make her uneasy by pressing more

85

questions on her. But I was becoming increasingly unhappy about many things. Things I could not ask about—or if I did they were not answered. Esmee talked a lot of queer nonsense, but it was nonsense that had a sinister background to it, and whenever I tried to get a sensible explanation from the child, she shifted into one of her unbalanced changes of mood.

I had almost given up hope of making any progress with the girl. At least twice a week she led me on an elusive chase over the hills, calling me first from one direction, then another. I would hear her thin, small voice call, 'Miss Wakeford, over here Miss Wakeford,' and when I hurried across to where the voice was coming from, I would hear her laughing from the other side of the hill. Once, when the wind had been blowing a gale, she had led me up to the chalk split again and even though I knew the danger of that place and was on my guard, the wind had nearly caught me and thrown me over the edge.

I had altered the clothes to fit her, and at least she was decently clad. No stockings were forthcoming, however, and eventually I gave her some of mine. As to schooling her, the task was hopeless. I was appalled to find that she had no idea of how to read or write. At the age of twelve, when laborers' children were finished with school and setting out to earn their keep, this perverse daughter of Tancred could not even write her name.

When I had been at the house a week, Mrs. Tancred asked me rather grandly one evening how Esmee's schooling was progressing. I took this to mean that I should try to teach the child something, though with all the other tasks that were put upon me I had little time for educating a backward girl. However, the next day I painstakingly started Esmee on her letters.

It was useless. Day after day we would struggle with crayon and paper until my nerves were taut with frustration. Sometimes she would listlessly copy a few outlines, then she would move her crayon quickly over the paper and draw shapes that were not only unrecognizable but also unpleasant. Once, for a whole morning she sat and looked past me at something that was not there. Other mornings she would ask question after question, so that I was hard put to keep my sanity. And it was through Esmee that I had my second ill encounter with Matthew Johnson.

He had not forgiven me for hitting him across the mouth; every time we met he would remind me of the morning in the kitchen when I had lost my temper. Crossing the yard one day he pinched my arm so hard that it left a bruise. 'I'll get you,' he hissed and turned away very quickly as John Tancred came out of the stable.

I had, by some supreme effort of will, managed to get Esmee clean and tidy and sitting at table every night—although I think it was only because she was taken with the notion of annoying her grandmother and drawing attention to me. One evening, however, after I had seen her wash and prepare for the meal, she disappeared out into the night. Her disappearance came after a long and depressing day, and this last failure on my part produced in me a stubborn determination to sit that child at table, even if it took all night. I flung my cape about my shoulders and unlatched the kitchen door.

It was so dark outside that for a moment I hesitated, tempted to let the child run alone on the bleak hillside if she wished. Then I heard her laugh—the noise coming from the other side of the yard, somewhere by the stables. Gropingly I made my way across the shingled ground and felt for the latch of the stable door. Esmee was making no noise but I felt quite sure she was hiding inside, and although the stable was only dimly lit by one small lamp, I made my way to the stalls at the back to try and find her.

The door slammed shut behind me. Leaning on the wood, grinning and fat, was Math Johnson.

'Now, Miss Prissy,' he said, and he turned and put the bar up on the door. 'Now we'll see if you can stand up to big Math when there's no one else about.' He began to walk slowly toward me, his arms hanging loosely by his side. 'No Mary to come and stop me when you fight back. You're alone now, little Miss Prissy, with your stupid hat and fancy ways.'

I tried to stand my ground against him, but the sight of his great hairy body coming closer was more than I could bear. A small dog-cart was standing on my right and I darted behind it.

He began to laugh. Then he jumped at me from one side of the cart, catching the skirt of my dress in his hand before I was able to dodge away. 'Run all you like. I'll catch you in the end, for you can't get out of here. Not 'til old Math has finished with you.'

He was sweating so much that drops had fallen onto my dress, and in the faint light from the lamp his face shone with wetness. I lifted a small bag of meal, and the next time he hurled himself at me I threw it hard in his face and then ran to the door and tried to lift the latch. I managed to get it undone but before I could swing the door open I heard his furious bellow behind me, and I had to throw myself on the ground to avoid his murderous leap.

The bag of meal had burst. His hair and chest were covered in oats embedded thickly in the dirty red hair. I had not been frightened of him until then—not frightened, that is, in the same way that the queer things in the house frightened me. But when I saw his small eyes glaring wildly at me I began to scream. I tried to stand up and run behind the cart again, but I stepped on the inside of my hem and plunged forward once more into the straw. This time I felt his hand close to my head and, as I managed at last to throw myself headlong behind the cart, he grabbed hold of my cap, wrenching it violently from my head so that the tapes scorched along underneath my chin.

Now I could not even scream. I had no breath to do anything except run, a futile, hopeless running that could only end in one way, with the feel of his hand jerking my ankle and the eyes of an angry bull glaring into mine. He hit me so hard on the face that I bit the inside of my mouth and tasted the warm saltiness of blood on my tongue. I was jerked to the ground and then I felt his heavy body fall across me, so hard that the air was knocked from my lungs. The horrible smell of him, unwashed skin and stable manure, made me retch, but I tried to push him away, scratching at his face and kicking whenever the weight of his body would allow it.

And then, when I was sobbing with a wild, despairing panic, because there was nothing more I could do to fight Math Johnson, I felt a strong wind blowing from the doorway. And I heard an angry voice thunder through the stable.

'Johnson!'

Matthew did not hear. Or I think it more likely, he was so maddened with rage that he could not hear. Footsteps raced across the stone floor and then Matthew Johnson was lifted by his hair and shirt and flung against the side of one of the stalls.

John Tancred, his face furious, the blood boiling up from his neck to flame lividly behind the scarred tissue of his cheek, stood over the fat man blubbering on the floor. 'Get up,' he hissed angrily. Matthew raised his head from the ground; he was moaning and blood was running from a cut in the side of his head.

'I said, get up!'

He reached down, grasped a handful of Matthew's shirt and pulled the big, flabby valet to his feet. Matthew Johnson was a heavy man but John Tancred swung him around like a rabbit. He hit Math twice across the face and if I had been frightened of Matthew's vile temper, I was even more afraid of this man's raging anger.

'Have you forgotten!' he shouted. 'Have you

89

forgotten that the old man is dead and I am master here? Do you still bring his ways to this house?'

He shook the man, like a dog shakes a rat, to break its neck. Then, with a violent kick, he hurled Math out through the door to stumble and crash to his knees on the sharp gravel outside.

I knelt behind the dog-cart and was quietly sick into a wooden trough. Math was whimpering out in the yard and I could hear John Tancred still shouting at him from the doorway.

The inside of my mouth was bleeding and when I thought I could stand without my legs crumpling beneath me I went over to one of the horses' drinking buckets and washed my mouth. My hand was trembling so hard that I spilled most of the liquid; but the second time I managed to ease my face with the cold water. When I turned round, John Tancred was leaning against the wall watching me. His face was white now and the scar even more pronounced against his cheek.

'Why did you come out here?' he asked icily.

'I heard Esmee. Every time she runs away she makes me chase after her over the hills. But this evening I thought I heard her come in here.'

'Esmee is in the kitchen. I have just seen her.' His coldness was so apparent that he made me feel as if I had come out here from choice. I was grateful to him for stopping the fight with Math, but I had taken too much that evening to stand and be accused of lying to him.

'Thy daughter is always where she is not supposed to be,' I said tartly. 'I spend all the time I have trying to catch her in whatever weird haunts she hides. That is, when I am not cleaning, or cooking, or seaming, or caring for thy mother.'

The opaque fury died slowly from his eyes. He rubbed his hand over his face, looking confused and troubled.

'Yes,' he said hesitatingly. 'Yes. Of course. I am sorry for all this.' He waved his hand vaguely about the stable. Then the uncertainty vanished and he said slowly: 'Matthew will not trouble you again.' I did not like the way he said the words. It struck me that he would make a silent, implacable enemy.

The wind made the light in the lamp dance a little. Now that his anger had faded, the distorted side of his face did not stand out so brightly and the dim light was kind to him. I could see how he must have looked as a boy, very gay and smooth-skinned with bright eyes. It was quiet now except for the horses moving restlessly in their boxes and I suddenly became aware that John Tancred was staring at me with the oddest of expressions. I felt faintly alarmed, for a sojourn at Tancred had taught me to beware of strange, obsessional stares.

'Is something wrong?'

He walked toward me, raised his hand very slightly in the air, then let it drop to his side. 'Your hair,' he said slowly. 'I have never seen your hair before.'

His eyes moved to my shoulders. My hair had come right down and I could feel it catching the fastening at the back of my dress. I thought he was going to say something to me. Once again he raised his hand in that curious half-gesture.

The moment was gone. He turned abruptly to the door and held it open. 'Go back to the house,' he snapped, and I did as I was told.

5

At the end of February I was called in to Mrs. Tancred's room to receive my payment for the two months I had been at the house.

The old lady's wheelchair had been pushed to stand beside a small Chippendale table. On the table was a metal cash-box from which she took a sovereign. Then she carefully re-locked the box and handed me the money.

'Your wage for January and February, Miss Wakeford,' she said graciously. 'I shall settle with you every two months. It is easier that way.' She set the cash-box further back on the table and moved her chair away a little.

'I . . . we are very pleased with your work here. You have managed well for such a young girl.'

She smiled politely and impersonally, and then gave a brief nod as though to dismiss me. There was something I wanted to say, however, and I stood firmly in the center of the room, trying to find courage to speak.

'Was there something else, Miss Wakeford?'

'Please, Marm, I should like to have a Saturday off.'

She turned her head slowly and I got a direct, piercing stare from the stark black eyes. 'A Saturday, Miss Wakeford? For what?'

'I should like to go to see the Friends in Brighton. And there are things I need to purchase.' I swallowed nervously, for when Mrs. Tancred decided to be imperious, she could be most daunting. 'In any case, Marm, I believe I am entitled to a day off every two months.'

'Is it really necessary?'

She was plainly loath to let me leave the house, even for such a short time and it crossed my mind to wonder why she was so reluctant. But I am a stubborn creature, as Grandmother has told me on many occasions, and the more she questioned me, the more determined I was to have my day.

'I want to go, Marm.'

She tried to stare me down, her gaunt old face dominant over the high lace collar about her neck. She rattled her fingers angrily on the arm of her chair and frowned at me, but I stood my ground and at last she said fretfully, 'Well, if you are so determined, I suppose you must. We shall expect you back here in good time for supper though.'

'Of course, Marm.'

My hand was actually on the handle of the door ready to go when in a different tone she said:

'Miss Wakeford.'

'Marm?'

I turned around back into the room to face her and saw that the haughty command on her face had gone, that she was looking at me anxiously, with concern and worry.

'Miss Wakeford, you are happy here? I mean you are not thinking of searching for another place?'

'Why no, Marm. I just need to buy things, and to see my friends.'

'You are happy here?' she asked again. 'You find everything agreeable and pleasant, do you not?'

I could hardly tell her that I abhorred Matthew Johnson, that I was frightened of her granddaughter and indeed a little frightened of Mrs. Tancred herself.

'You must tell me if anything bothers you, or if you are in trouble. You will come to me if you are concerned?'

'Ye-es, Marm.'

She leaned forward, clenching her hands tightly over the arms of the chair.

'Is there anything that troubles you, Miss Wakeford? Something that you are not happy about?'

I said 'No,' but she could tell from my face that I was not speaking the truth, and she moved her chair forward so that she could look right up into my eyes.

'What is wrong, Miss Wakeford? Tell me what is wrong.'

'It is nothing, Marm. Only that . . .' I paused, uncertain of what to say.

'Yes?'

'It is the house, Mrs. Tancred. It . . . it does not seem to like me.'

As soon as I had said the words I realized how stupid they sounded. I thought she would laugh or even rebuke me, but oddly enough she seemed relieved, as though she had expected me to say something else.

'It is an old house, Miriam, and a big one. You will soon grow used to it. Perhaps it is because you are lonely. There are no other young people here for you.'

'No, it is not that, Marm.' I had always been lonely and that did not bother me. The circumstances of my birth had prevented me from mixing with girls of my own age and I was used to my own company. She took no notice of me but continued, 'We entertain very little. And there are few callers. But perhaps later, when I am well again, we can see about receiving guests.'

I found it both pathetic and embarrassing the way she spoke to me, as though trying to bribe me to stay at the house, like a child with a piece of cake.

'And soon, perhaps,' she said, her face brightening at some inner thought, 'soon, if my son marries again, there will be parties and visiting and lots of young servants about the house.'

I was so startled that I dropped my sovereign and it rolled across the carpet and underneath a wardrobe of stained mahogany.

'Thy son is thinking of marrying again, Marm?'

She had been staring dreamily into the air, seeing

some private, pleasant thoughts of her own; but when my question penetrated, her expression changed suddenly and she said harshly, 'He has to marry. There have always been Tancreds on the Down. Always. He has no choice. He is a Tancred. He must marry.'

She appeared to give no thought to the wishes of the man in the east wing, living alone with his scarred face and only the unpleasant Math for company. I thought it highly improbable that John Tancred would want to go through all the formalities and customs of courtship and marriage. He was not a man who seemed to care either for his family or the company of other men and women. Neither had Mrs. Tancred appeared to have considered that it might be difficult to find a young woman who would be prepared to take on a vast decaying house and its scarred, taciturn master.

With difficulty, I reached under the wardrobe and retrieved my sovereign. Then I said, 'Perhaps he does not want to wed, Marm.'

Her eyes flashed so wildly that I stepped back a pace, alarmed by the rigid glare on her face.

'He has no choice. No choice,' she said again, and then abruptly she asked: 'Have you seen the Stones, the Stones up on the Down?'

'The Druid's circle? Yes, Marm.'

'They are called the Tancred Stones,' she said fiercely. 'There is a folk story told that when the Romans came, they massacred the old men up by the circle—all the ancient old priests who have left no trace of themselves other than the Stones. The Roman general who had led the killing took the chieftain's daughter for a wife, and in the passage of time she persuaded him to build his villa here, on the side of the hill beneath the slaughtered bodies of her people.'

She paused and I noticed that the lamp on the dresser was making a tired, thudding noise. In a strange, detached way I recalled that I had forgotten to fill the lamp that morning.

'What happened after that we are not sure. There are all sorts of nonsensical old stories told, and much is exaggerated by the ignorance of those who tell the tales. But certainly it is true that when Mandel Tancred received the deed to the land, we had already lived here for many generations.'

She gazed wearily out of the darkened window, then turned back to look at me. 'Our roots are in this house, Miss Wakeford. My son has no choice. He must marry again.'

In an odd communion of weird misunderstanding, we stared bleakly at one another. Then the plopping of the lamp intruded into the old woman's consciousness and she turned impatiently to the dying light.

'Go and fill the lamp.'

I lit a candle, placed it on the dresser and picked up the lamp. I turned, and my eye was held by the sight of the wooden loom. It had changed. I remembered clearly that the last time I had been in the room the tapestry had ended with an acid green; now a violent mauve-like pink, the color of raspberries that have been squashed, had been added on—and not even in a straight line but in a jagged fork that hurt the eye. No one else in the house could possibly have used the loom, yet it was incredible to believe that Mrs. Tancred would weave such designs. I averted my face quickly, before the colors could create an uneasiness in my mind. When I was at the door she called me: 'You can have the first Saturday in the next month.'

'Thank thee, Marm.'

'And Miss Wakeford. It is only an old legend, a folk tale—about the stones, I mean.'

I wished she had not reminded me, for on my way to the kitchen the lamp went out and I had to feel my way along the broken walls remembering the murdered bodies of the old priests lying above me on the hill.

On the first Saturday in March I rose very early, and by seven o'clock I was on my way along the path leading to Loxham. I had visited the village once before with Mary, to buy the provisions for the month, and had learned on that occasion that Reuben Tyler, the vintner's man, came up to the village early every Saturday morning. I felt sure the good man would not mind me riding along on his cart.

I had done all my tasks back at the house—lit the fires, set the breakfast and put the food out for the evening's cooking. As I hurried along the rough track, I felt a sudden lifting of the spirits, a keen anticipation toward a day spent in the great city of Brighton. The morning was a bright one. The wind still threw itself against the hill but as I turned into the landward side of the Down, the strength of the gale dropped and I could walk without hunching myself against the cold. Once around the hill the house could no longer be seen; it was hidden by the slope above me and a great weight was lifted from my heart. The day, begun so brightly, promised to be even better than I hoped. I started to run along the path, anxious in case I should be late and miss the vintner's wagon. Two buck rabbits who were sitting on their haunches rubbing their whiskers looked up, startled as I ran past, and fled into their warrens with feverish haste.

When I reached Loxham I was out of breath and very warm. There was no sign of the cart coming up along the road and I went to the inn and sat outside on a wooden bench. There were plenty of people about, crossing and recrossing the square that formed the center of the village. No one spoke to me, which struck me as being unfriendly. At home if a stranger was seated outside on a bench, there were many of us who would inquire why he was waiting and even suggest that he should enter a house and wait by a stove.

A little girl no more than three or four years old came up to me, and in the forthcoming manner of small children she began to chatter and ask questions. What was my name? Why did I wear a funny hat? Had I a doll? And so on. She was a bright little thing, neat and cheeky, and I wished I had a comfit in my purse to offer her. I took my handkerchief and folded it crosswise, then the corners in, turned back, rolled—and I had made a rabbit. She chuckled and held her hand up to take the white linen toy.

I had hardly put the animal in her hand when a woman came running from out of the shop. She snatched the child up in her arms and threw my handkerchief at me.

'Keep away,' she snarled. 'We don't want your sort coming down here. You leave us alone, you hear?' I was too surprised to speak coherently. I could not think what I had done to merit such rough treatment.

'I have done nothing. I was only . . .'

She interrupted me and held the child well away, as though I was about to harm it. 'I saw what you was doing. We don't want you folk from the house in our village. We let's you buy your food here, but don't think you're welcome, cause you ain't. We're decent folk, living in fear of the Lord and worshipping on Sundays. You keep away.'

She gave me a venomous look and hurried back to the shop, clutching the child in her arms.

I could feel hot color mounting in my face. Everyone was staring at me and one or two were grinning at my discomfiture. For the first time I noticed that the glances I had received whilst sitting outside the inn were not friendly. The women especially were more than merely curious. In their faces was an animated dislike combined with an emotion I could not at first define. I sat quietly on the bench, hoping that Reuben Tyler would come soon, and as I watched the people of Loxham skirting widely around the place where I waited, I realized what was on their faces. It was fear. A cold, loathing kind of fear.

When I had visited the village with Mary we had done no more than drive the dog-cart straight to the shop, purchase the provisions and return directly to Tancred. We had spoken only to the store-keeper, and if anyone had looked oddly at us I had been too preoccupied to notice.

I began to wish that the vintner's wagon would arrive quickly. A group of boys came up and stood on the other side of the square, whispering and watching me. I tried to smile at them but there was a big, uneasy lump in the middle of my throat. They edged nearer to me in a solid, coalescing group. I took no notice, pretending to be interested in the seam of my glove, hoping they would find something else to divert them and go away.

One of them picked up a stone from the ground and tossed it lightly up and down in his hand, looking across at me as though challenging me to some kind of contest. There was a quick scuffling amongst the youths, a flurry of movement and the boy with the stone was pushed forward to the front of the group, urged on by those behind.

The palms of my hands were damp. I looked behind me. The doors of the inn were closed; the shop across the road was on the other side of the boys; and in any case the woman with the child had been joined by two others. They were standing blocking the entrance into the shop, and I had the feeling they would not allow me to push past and take shelter inside. The boy with the stone stepped forward several paces.

At the same time as he swung his arm back in the air, I saw the homely, wonderful sight of the vintner's cart turn into the road. The stone struck against the empty bench, for I was running down the track toward the cart, calling to Reuben Tyler as loudly as I could.

He stopped the wagon, climbed down, and at the sight of his good-natured face I burst into tears.

'Now then, now then,' he said in a puzzled manner.

'What's the matter with ye?'

In a babble of confused relief I poured out my fear of the people of Loxham, my request for a ride into Brighton and the adamant statement that I would not leave his side for a moment until we had left the village. He looked angrily up the path, glaring at the youths who were sheepishly wandering off in different directions. The women had gone into the shop and shut the door firmly behind them. Reuben patted me awkwardly on the shoulder.

'Now don't ye worry, little Missy. I've to unload the cart, but you can sit up top and I shall be in and out of the inn every minute. You call out if there's any trouble and Reuben Tyler will be here to thrash the young devils.'

He lifted me up and we drove right up to the inn door. I watched very carefully as he and the innkeeper came in and out of the cellar doorway, carrying and unloading the big wooden barrels. The women and the boys were still watching me, but the large and ordinary figure of Reuben Tyler seemed to afford a protection of some kind. The empty barrels were finally loaded onto the cart. Reuben Tyler climbed up beside me and flicked the horse into movement. He turned once to look back at the village.

'Miserable folk,' he said crossly. 'Taking out their grudges on a girl.' He patted my hand kindly and asked, 'Ye're all right now?'

I was slightly ashamed of my outburst. In the company of Reuben Tyler's ordinary good sense, the menacing mood of the village seemed unreal—almost as though I had imagined it.

'They're superstitious people,' he said. 'They live up in the hills and keep themselves to themselves. They ain't really cruel, just afraid of anything that's strange.' He looked down at my clothes and went on: 'You dress differently, you see, and that—coupled with the fact you come from Tancred—makes them wary.'

I blew my nose loudly on the crumpled handkerchief that the woman had thrown at me, and we drove in silence for a few minutes. Then he said: 'Ye're a funny little thing. Ye've survived two months up at that house on the Down, yet ye're frightened to tears of the people in the village.'

'They were angry. I think if thee had not come when thee did, they would have hurt me.'

'Oh, aye,' he said, and looked curiously at my black dress and cape and the white cap. 'You'd be a Quaker then, I suppose? Them as believes that everything should be done by words instead of actions?'

'That is what we are taught,' I said defensively. Too many people are ready to scorn us for our lack of fight. We do not, in these enlightened times, get put into prison for our beliefs, but there are many who like to use us as a butt for mockery. And our menfolk, especially, have to suffer much in the way of sneers and ridicule because they will not fight. I was drawing in to myself, preparing for a criticism from the good Mr. Tyler and trying to decide if it would be best to defend myself or just to let him have his say, when he spoke again.

'I suppose,' he said thoughtfully, 'I suppose if a girl is reared like that it would make her nervous of a gang of village boys.'

It seemed I had misjudged him.

'Anyway, ye'll find some o' your folk in Brighton. I've seen 'em about. But even so, young Missy, why should ye fear the people and not the house? I tell ye, I've been that worried since I took ye up there, I've been in two minds about coming to fetch ye down again.'

It had been so long since I had spoken to anyone who was normal, who was not either hiding a secret or terrified almost to insanity, that I began to tell Reuben Tyler of some of the things at Tancred. Not all, for there were things—about the shabbiness and poorness of the house—that I had no right to speak of to an

101

outsider. But I told him of the way no one would speak of old Richard Tancred, or of Esmee's mother, and I asked him about John Tancred's face. He was thoughtful for a while then he said: 'There's not a lot I know, Missy, only what is hearsay. You've seen for yeself the folk at the village ain't fond of strangers. They don't, or won't, say much. Sometimes I overhear things, though.'

The horse trotted briskly along the road. We were going downhill, leaving the smooth countryside of the Downs and coming back to where there were fields and trees.

'O' course, Tancred weren't always such a black place,' he said. 'I remember my father telling me that in the old days there was always parties and balls going on. He, my father, could remember as a lad, the old King driving up to the house from the palace in Brighton.'

In spite of myself I felt faintly awed at the thought of wicked old King George attending a party at Tancred.

'It weren't too bad neither when Mrs. Tancred first came there as a bride. The old man was away a lot, but then the Tancreds was always a merchant family and have forever been over to France or someplace. At one time they had a house over Boulogne way, and another in Holland. The old man, he would be gone three years, maybe four, but still there was parties and suchlike when he came home.'

The horse had slowed his pace a little, lulled by the sound of his master's voice, and Reuben Tyler flicked him gently with the rein.

'He was always after the girls. Didn't matter too much at first, but then it got so as none of the girls from Loxham would go to work up at the house, and they had to take charity children from the Union.

'Then one day Mr. John disappears. No one sees him go, he just disappears and turns up again six years later with a French wife, a little daughter and a scarred face. I was put onto a different run about that time, over to Arundel way. When I come back to the Loxham drive four years ago, both the old man and Mr. John's wife was dead.'

'Did thee ever see Mr. John?' I asked. 'I mean after he came back with his wife?'

Reuben nodded and gave the horse a reminder to keep up his pace. 'Saw him once, poor wretch, with his face all twisted and marked. Such a pity. He was nice looking as a lad, too.'

'Was he?' I said quickly—too quickly, for the kindly man at my side looked curiously at me. We could see Brighton lying ahead of us, hundreds of houses, or so it appeared to me. I think Reuben was tired of answering my questions but there was one thing I wanted to know.

'Mr. Tyler. What did they die of? Richard Tancred, I mean, and Mr. John's wife?'

He shrugged and turned the horse onto a path leading straight down into the town. 'That I don't know,' he said. 'Asked the parson up at Loxham once, but he didn't know either. Seemed they had a preacher come special from Canterbury way to bury both the old man and the girl. Now then, here we are,' he said, pulling up in front of a big, wooden, victualler's house. 'If ye want to ride back with me you must be here at three o'clock.' He gave me another curious glance and said, 'I'd like to persuade ye not to go back. There's much I don't know about Tancred, but I do know it's a bad place for ye to live in. Still, you're a quaint little thing and ye seem to be managing, so there's no point in me persuading ye against ye will.'

He lifted me down and set me on my way. 'Three o'clock now,' he said, and I waved goodbye.

Brighton was huge. Huge, splendid, exciting and wicked. I had never seen such beautiful shops, nor so many people who apparently had money enough to buy from the choice of extravagant things. I needed hair-pins and stockings. Esmee had been wearing mine and she was always ripping them when she chased over the hills. In a town so large, hairpins and stockings should have been the easiest things to purchase, but I was so confused that I was not even sure which of the vast emporiums to enter. I wandered down the streets, looking in the windows and trying to avoid getting in the way of the people who were hurrying past. There was a man playing a fiddle on the pavement. He had a little dog in a red jacket who danced on his hind legs.

Down on the front, by the sea, men were pulling up boats onto the beach, and big nets of slippery fish were lying on the pebbles. I had grown used to the sea. It could be seen clearly, though several feet below, from the front of Tancred. But here on the beach, the waves came right up close, washing frothily round the fishermen's shiny black boots.

I found a draper's store at last and went in to buy my hairpins and stockings. There were bolts of cloth over the counter, and from reels at the back ribbons of all colors hung over a board. I bought a blue piece for Mary to go with the blue dress, and a doll with a red apron for Esmee. I doubted if she would like it. She was not a child who played with dolls or indeed, with any of the things that most children like. But I hoped to please her with my gift.

There was a shop in a side street and from its open door wafted the smell of hot pastry and cooked meat. The smoky aroma curled up into the morning air and searched out an answering rumble in my stomach. In the big, glass windows, in plain view of the passers-by, a chef was making pies: crisp golden pies newly taken from the oven stood on a scrubbed, wooden bench, and the steam from them hovered mistily on the glass.

There was never enough to eat at Tancred. I know it is vulgar to think always of food and mealtimes, but often when I had gone to bed at night, I would lie dreaming of chickens and loaves of bread, hard to ignore the emptiness inside me. There was enough, I suppose, but only just, and as Matthew took his and

John Tancred's share first, before it came to the table, we had to rely on his fair division for there to be enough left over. Usually not much was left.

I stood outside the pie shop, sniffing discreetly at the beautiful odor of well-cooked meat and pastry. Then I went in and bought six pies.

The man wrapped three and put them in a box for me to take back to Mary. The rest he placed in a bag.

Grandmother had taught me that it was vulgar to eat in the street but she, I am sure, had never been as hungry as I was on that cold morning. I found a seat a little way up the road and I sat down and studied the pies before biting into one of them. It was hot and full of rich gravy with the kind of pastry that crumbles in the mouth. When I had finished I stood up and brushed the crumbs from my skirt, took a piece of paper from my purse on which Grandfather had carefully written a name and address, and asked a passer-by to direct me to the house of Ezekial King.

There are many who think that the Friends are a queer, outlandish group. Perhaps they are right. Certainly the fact that we dress and speak in a strange way and hold beliefs that are considered unmanly and contrary to the convictions of the times, has resulted in our drawing inward to ourselves. We are not great in number, and this has brought about a unity of fellowship within our group. No matter what part of the country a Friend comes from, he is assured of welcome and hospitality at any Quaker household he may visit.

I knew that when the young woman, whom I supposed was Ezekial King's daughter, answered the door, her pleasure at seeing me was sincere. But I was astounded at her dress. It was green. A dark green, it is true, but nonetheless it was colored. I thought perhaps I had come to the wrong house. I said tentatively, 'Miss King?' and she nodded, smiled and kissed me on the cheek. Mr. King came out of a room at the back of the house and drew me into the warmth.

'Miriam Wakeford?' he said, holding his hand out to me. 'We have been expecting thee, ever since we received the letter from thy Grandfather.'

He was a thin, big-boned man with gray, crinkly hair and a hawk-like nose that jutted sharply out from the rest of his face. I had not seen him for ten years and had only a hazy recollection of his staying in our farmhouse when he came to preach in the village.

'Thy Grandfather is well? And thy Grandmother and cousins?'

'They are well.'

The young woman took my cape and the box of pies and put them on the hall cabinet. I realized that I was staring rudely at her green dress and I hastily averted my eyes and looked back at Mr. King. He held a door open and let me go through into a back room.

'Deborah and I have been concerned about thee,' he said. 'We expected thee to come before now.'

In an undefinable way he annoyed me and I could not think why. He meant well and was kindness itself as he led me to a chair by the fire and told me to sit down.

'Thee has been at Tancred for over two months and not been once to worship,' he said chidingly.

I suddenly recalled why I felt a dim resentment of him. A picture came to my mind: a scene in Grandmother's kitchen where I knelt on the floor and this sharp-featured man had prayed over me, asking that evil should be cast away and redemption granted to this child, a sinner.

'I have only one day in two months, Mr. King. It is a big house and there is much work and few servants.'

'Time must always be found for the Lord,' he said righteously and folded his hands piously together on his knees. I wanted to give a sharp rejoinder, a comment that some of us had to earn our living and could not walk out of a house whenever we wished. Deborah looked quickly at my face.

'Now, father, do not chide the girl. I told thee the journey was a difficult one and that she would come as soon as she could. She can come to Meeting with us this afternoon.' She turned and asked if I could go with them.

'Well . . . It is difficult, thee sees . . .' I had been going to explain about the ride back on the vintner's wagon but Mr. King gave me no time to answer.

'Come child, has thee no wish to pray with thy people?'

This was grossly unfair. Albeit I was an unfortunate young woman, a child born in sin, yet I had worshipped regularly, and in spite of people like my Grandmother and Mr. King, I took comfort from the security of the Meeting House. I explained a little curtly that I had to be outside the victualler's house at three o'clock.

'Thee shall remain here,' said Ezekial King complacently. 'I have a pony and trap and shall ride thee back to Tancred in good time.'

I felt ashamed. It was a long ride, both there and back in the late afternoon, and it was purely because of his kindness that he offered. I thanked him, rather more humbly than my previous words had been, and felt my guilt grow worse when I was asked to stay after the Meeting and eat with them.

I did not like walking into the Meeting House. If the Fellowship of the Quakers has resulted in a universal welcome, it has also resulted in a universal knowledge. I was well aware that when I sat down, everyone in the hall knew that I was Edward Wakeford's illegitimate granddaughter whose mother was forbidden to come home. I faced it out and after a while experienced the peace that comes from being with one's own people. I was glad I had sought them out.

I was even more surprised in the Meeting House than I had been when Deborah answered the door to me. Several of the younger women were, like Deborah, wearing colored dresses. One even had a robe of light blue. After the Meeting, I tried to broach the subject with her.

'Thy gown,' I said diffidently. 'Does thee . . . I mean some of the dresses are colored and . . .'

'Thee is surprised because we do not wear black, Miriam?'

'Well, yes. In the village we sometimes have a dark blue, for weddings maybe, but never green or brown.' I hoped she did not think I was remarking personally on the color of her dress. She laughed and said kindly:

'The customs are changing, Miriam. It is only in the villages that things remain the same. In London and the cities, hardly anyone wears black.'

'It would be nice to wear a colored dress.' I thought of the silk gown that Mrs. Tancred had offered me, then common sense asserted itself. 'Still, I cannot see Grandmother letting me deck myself in bright colors.'

Deborah hesitated. She looked a little distressed and then said quietly, 'Miriam . . . You must not feel ashamed because of . . . because of what has gone before.' A flush spread up her neck and flooded her face—a flush that was reflected in the heat of my own cheeks.

'It is not us, not the Fellowship, that makes things difficult for thee. We do not care for what happened in the past. It is because thee lives in a village, and village people are slow to forget things like . . .'

'Like my mother?' I asked bluntly.

She nodded and looked uncomfortable. 'Let us go home and eat,' she said quickly and turned and hurried out of the hall.

We walked back to the Kings' house in silence. She was right of course about my village; and even then it was not entirely my neighbors who shunned me. It was Grandmother who had somehow erected a barrier between me and normal folk.

It was good to sit down and eat in a Quaker home with food that was plentiful and well-cooked, in a house that was bright and warm and had no wind screaming its way through locked and forbidden parts. It was good to

108

ask a blessing on the food without a queer, strange-eyed child watching me from across the table.

I said goodbye to Deborah and climbed into Mr. King's trap. I was warm and contented and I reflected how foolish I had been to grow afraid of the old house up on the Down. The pony trotted smartly along the road and Mr. King turned to me.

'Thee will come again, Miriam?'

'In two months time. My next day will be in two months.'

'Then we shall see thee then,' he said decisively and again I felt the warning of resentment at his assumption of authority.

'If thee wishes to stay in my house, my daughter and I are pleased to welcome thee.' He smiled, baring large and slightly protruding teeth. It gave him a wolfish look and with difficulty I stifled a giggle.

'Thee is very kind, Mr. King.' He smiled again and I felt uncomfortable. He was a stern and serious person and his attempts at affability were out of character.

The pony and trap set up into the hills on the Loxham road, and the first tendrils of the wind began to come from the Downs. Gray clouds made the late afternoon appear darker than it was, but I thought and hoped that it would still be light by the time we reached Loxham.

We came to the village and Ezekial King made no attempt to stop the pony. He went smartly up along the road to where the Tancred track branched off.

'I can walk from here,' I said to Mr. King, but he shook his head and flicked the pony's reins.

We drew near to the house. At any moment we would turn and see it hanging over us, gloomy, depressing and black. The old sense of foreboding hovered familiarly over my heart. As we came round the side of the Down and saw the house watching from beneath the brow of the hill, the cold, uneasy feeling that I had grown so accustomed to descended and wrapped itself about my spirit.

I gazed up at the hill and suddenly recognized what frightened me about the Down. It was alive. The great, towering hill, in all its smooth immensity, loomed over the house like a sleeping giant, waiting to reach out with a somber hand at the people who dwelt on the hill.

It was a horrible place to build a house. The old Druid's daughter must have had her revenge a thousand times on the man who had murdered her people, for wherever one stood there was no way to avoid the hill. It was above and below, to the right and the left, and I could even feel its huge presence dragging my feet down into the smoothness.

Mr. King was not impervious to the menace of the Down. He looked uneasily about him, at the wind-scorched grass and the house hovering above him. A small frown gathered between his eyes. 'Here, Miriam? Here is where thee works?'

I nodded and he looked furtively up once more at the gray hill.

'Did thy Grandfather see the house before he agreed for thee to come?' I did not want to talk about the house, not to anyone. 'It is well suited inside,' I said briskly and jumped down quickly from the trap before he had a chance to ask me further questions. He climbed down after me, apprehensively staring at the house. Then to my surprise he kissed me on the cheek.

'We shall pray for thee,' he said severely, looking up at the stone walls. He got back into the trap and drove quickly away, turning his face back once, nervously, over his shoulder.

I stood watching the tiny horse and cart disappear down the hill, dwarfed by the Down to the size of a child's toy. It was some few moments before I sensed I was not alone. I turned and saw John Tancred standing on the grass, holding the rein of a big gray and white horse. He must have moved there silently; I had not heard him come up. He smiled at me—a cruel, uncomfortable smile that twisted his mouth even more. He was wearing a soft, wide-brimmed felt hat that he could easily have pulled down over the scarred side of his face if he had wanted to. It was set well over— deliberately I thought—on the other side of his head, the side that was unharmed.

He removed the hat and gave me a curious small bow. 'Good evening, Miss Wakeford,' he said smoothly. 'I trust you enjoyed your day in Brighton.'

He was mocking me, because he had seen Mr. King kiss me goodbye. I felt my face flame in the gathering dusk.

'I did,' I answered curtly, and went quickly into the house and closed the door behind me.

6

The three of us had just begun our supper that night when the door opened and John Tancred came in, strode across the room and sat down at the fourth place at table.

Dimly, from the other side of the room I heard Mary give a small gasp and drop a spoon back onto a dish. Mrs. Tancred had been in the process of speaking to me, asking about my day in Brighton, and her words trailed off faintly into the distance. I could not tell if she was merely surprised, or if it was alarm that registered on her face. Her eyes widened imperceptibly and I saw the gaunt old throat move once as she swallowed some private concern.

John Tancred unrolled a table napkin and flicked it across his lap. He nodded briefly, both to his mother and to myself, stared once across the table at Esmee— a stare that was completely devoid of any expression whatsoever—and then began to eat.

For once I was not hungry. I had eaten only a short while before with the Kings. But even had I passed the day on the usual sparse diet of Tancred, the presence of that inscrutable man at the table would have successfully destroyed my appetite.

The meal proceeded in utter silence. Mrs. Tancred, with a stony face, set her knife and fork to one side, having hardly touched her food. John Tancred appeared to notice nothing but what was on his plate. He neither looked at nor spoke to any of us. He was seated on my right side, revealing the scarred part of his face in closer detail than I had seen it before. The

112

lamp on the table lit the disfigurement with brutal clarity and the words of Reuben Tyler—the remark that John Tancred had once been a good-looking man— came back to me; and with it came the thought that whatever he had been in the past, John Tancred would never be handsome again.

One could see the remnants of beauty, if beauty is a word that should be ascribed to a man approaching middle-age. Below the scars, the skin of his neck was smooth and olive brown; the hair that curled forward over his forehead was thick, soft and dark. To this day I am not sure of the color of his eyes, neither brown, nor gray, nor green, but something of all three. It was, indeed, the very comeliness of the rest of his face that made the multi-colored whorls and twisted mouth seem even more horrible. The blemish on the skin of an apple is all the more noticeable if the apple is a smooth one and if John Tancred had been a rougher man, with an uneven complexion and features that were irregular, the full disastrous effect of his appearance would have been modified a little. I wondered how and when he had received the wound—before or after marrying his French wife.

I was slowly and shamefully aware that he had turned his head and was watching me.

'Yes, Miss Wakeford?' he asked crisply.

I was deeply mortified and the embarrassment showed in the color that moved up into my face. No one likes to be caught staring, and John Tancred made it quite plain that he was well aware of my curiosity. I looked down at my plate, wishing that the meal was over and that we could all return to our separate ways. Esmee, who had been watching her father with a bright, secret smile, suddenly said into the silence, 'Bonsoir, Papa.'

He did not stiffen or grow restless as Mrs. Tancred did when Esmee spoke in French. He looked up at the child and answered, 'Good evening, Esmee,' in a weary manner. It struck me that this was the first time I had seen John Tancred either with his mother or his daughter. There were rare occasions when he was exercising the horses on the Down and he passed Esmee; but usually he did no more than glance at her with the same non-committal acceptance that I had noted earlier.

She began to sing: the melody that I now thought of as her mother's song. John Tancred finished eating and set his fork down on his plate. The song grew louder. Esmee was waiting furtively for something to happen, deliberately trying to taunt her father into participating in one of those horrible atmospheric silences that were quite usual in this house.

He seemed to take no notice of the song, but then I looked down and saw his hands clasped tightly together on his lap; the knuckles, partially concealed by the linen tablecloth, were white, each finger gripped rigidly against the palms. The air in the room tightened to a barely-controlled thread of sanity. Hysteria hovered crazily over all of us, even I who did not understand the meaning of the song, and Mrs. Tancred was plainly frightened. She watched her son with open concern, yet she made no attempt to stop the soft humming from the child across the table. Again I looked at his hands and now they were shaking. I had the overwhelming conviction that if I did not do something very quickly John Tancred would start to scream.

'Esmee, I have brought thee a present from Brighton.'

The tuneless murmur ceased and her eyes, bright with speculative interest, turned upon me, though not because she was interested in the gift. I knew Esmee Tancred well enough by now to appreciate that she was impervious to the usual inducements of childhood. Her interest lay in why I had chosen to shatter the tension of the room. Her speculation was concerned with what new game of weird provocation she could play as a result of my intervention. I had willingly participated in the scene; therefore, I, too, should be a victim to the various diversions she delighted in.

'A present, Miss Wakeford? Why?'

Any other child would have asked what the gift was, but unfailingly Esmee Tancred had asked a question that started off a whole new round of uncomfortable emotions. This time, however, Mrs. Tancred appeared to be on my side. I think in her own way she was grateful to me for breaking the mood, and now she quickly followed my lead and said in her best drawing room tones: 'How kind of you, Miss Wakeford. Esmee, you must thank Miss Wakeford properly.'

I watched John Tancred's body slacken, and decided it was worth drawing Esmee's attention to myself if doing so resulted in his relief.

'You may leave the table, Esmee,' said Mrs. Tancred abruptly.

At first I thought the child was going to stay and embroil us all in some fresh machinations, but suddenly she tired of her game. She looked at us, no longer with any interest, then her gaze fastened on the window, on the empty night outside. She smiled at something she either liked or recognized—something that flitted batlike and invisible in the darkness—then she darted across the room and slipped past Mary's outstretched hand to disappear into the gloom. I had still not grown accustomed to Esmee seeing things that were not there. My eyes strayed briefly to the window. The night was completely empty.

'Shall we have the curtains drawn, Mrs. Tancred?' I asked.

She looked up dully, then nodded without interest and motioned to Mary to go to the window. There was no further attempt at conversation. John Tancred and Esmee, between them, had successfully destroyed whatever small socialities we indulged in.

In silence we waited until Mary had set small cups

of poor coffee upon the table. Then, as soon as we had finished, I rose thankfully to push Mrs. Tancred from the room. He waited until I was halfway across before he spoke to me.

'Miss Wakeford. I should like to speak to you. Privately. In my rooms.'

Unaccountably, I began to tremble. I was glad I could not see Mrs. Tancred's face.

'You can speak to Miss Wakeford here. What is it that is so private you must talk in your rooms?' She was terrified. Her face was hidden from me but her voice was hoarse with a familiar anxiety. She tried to twist around in the chair, to look at the face of her son, but he was standing well back in the shadows of the room.

'There is no need for you to be concerned. I have a matter of business I wish to discuss with Miss Wakeford. Mary,' he turned coldly away from the table, 'be good enough to take my mother to her room.'

The back of the chair was removed from my nerveless grasp. Unprotestingly I watched Mary push Mrs. Tancred away. As she twisted the chair around the doorway, Mrs. Tancred was able to look back at us. Her eyes were so black they seemed to have receded right back into her head.

'Miss Wakeford,' she said shrilly. 'You will come to my room as well. When my son has finished, you will come to see me. You understand?'

I was caught between them, enmeshed in some weird conflict that I did not understand. I looked from one to the other. John Tancred wore the usual expression of inscrutability that told me nothing. I had been employed by Mrs. Tancred and she was the mistress of this house. Therefore, in some respect, I felt my loyalty was to her. I searched her face for some guide to my behavior.

'Immediately after my son has finished with you, come to me,' she said again.

'Yes, Mrs. Tancred.'

116

Mary moved the chair away, and Mrs. Tancred could no longer be seen. Mary darted one worried glance back before leaving.

'Miss Wakeford,' said John Tancred, 'you will please follow me.'

He went to the door, leaving me to pick up the lamp. I think he would have been quite happy to stride along the passages in the dark, knowing his way surely on each cold, stone floor. Once more I rustled along those endless corridors, silent except for the narrow tunes of wind blowing through the crevases in the walls. Again I traversed the great gallery, brooded over by dead Tancreds. The dim cloud of light from the lamp made only a tiny mark in the impenetrable gloom. Occasionally an old portrait would be lit briefly, just for a second, giving a sudden life to the watching face of a man or woman, and when I passed Richard Tancred's portrait on my right, I carefully averted my face. I could hardly keep up with the man ahead of me. He never once looked behind to see if I was still following or to ask me if I was all right. At the end of the gallery he flung the door open and strode through.

I had thought that we would have to trail along another endless maze of passages, but to my surprise he stopped almost immediately at a small door on his left, just outside the gallery. This time he did hold the door open for me, and I went through into what was, for Tancred, a remarkably cozy and warm room.

A Jacobean table stood against a wall and a big padded chair rested in front of a small fire—the fires at Tancred were never large. Matthew was in the room, removing cutlery and plates from the table, for this was apparently where John Tancred usually took his solitary meals.

Matthew looked first at me, then at John. A sly smile hovered unpleasantly about his mouth. 'I wondered where you was,' he said nastily.

'I ate with my mother.' John Tancred slammed the

117

door shut. It closed with a heavy, vibrating thud, and he walked to the big winged chair and sat so that I could not see the scarred side of his face.

Matthew turned to me once more and grinned evilly. 'I see.'

For the first time John Tancred appeared to notice Matthew's insinuating smile. He sat further back in the dark chair and his voice growled out from its depths. 'Get out.'

Matthew scooped the clean plate and glass onto a tray, moving quickly and obediently. Before he left the room he turned once and gave me such a black, malevolent stare that I knew he had not and would not forgive me for the beating he had received in the stable.

'Sit, Miss Wakeford.'

I sat, gingerly on the edge of a high, hard-backed chair.

'I saw you today, Miss Wakeford.'

'I know, sir.'

He waved his hand impatiently in the air and made a small 'Tut' of dismissal. 'I do not mean on the hill. I mean in Brighton.'

An uncomfortable suspicion began to form at the back of my mind. He leaned forward and looked right into my face. 'You were enjoying the pies, Miss Wakeford?'

There was no one, no one at all I could blame except myself. Grandmother had warned me time and time again that my appalling behavior, my unmannerliness and general disposition, would prove my downfall. The only comfort I could take was that at least she was not here to witness the rightness of her accusations. My face grew so hot I could even feel the tips of my ears burning. A picture came to my mind of how I must have looked earlier that day, sitting with my feet swinging from a bench and a paper-bag of pies on my lap. I hastily thrust the vision away but the hot, uncomfortable feeling it had aroused stayed with me. There was nothing I could say. I was sitting facing John Tancred, and I could feel his eyes raking cruelly over my mortified face.

'You were hungry, Miss Wakeford?'

'Yes, sir.'

Again he leaned forward in the chair and asked: 'Miss Wakeford, are you often hungry in this house?'

I took courage enough to look at his face and saw that after all he was not taunting me. Rather he was bothered, puzzled by some new problem.

'Tell me, Miriam Wakeford. Are you often hungry or cold in my house?'

I did not know how to answer. We sat silently for a moment, then he asked brusquely: 'How much are you paid for working here?'

'Six guineas, sir.'

He wrinkled his forehead in some kind of consideration. 'And is six guineas the usual payment for what you do?'

'I was employed as seamstress, sir. Six guineas is fair for seaming.'

He stood and placed his hand on the mantel over the fire. 'I am embarrassed, Miss Wakeford. It seems we at Tancred have been relying on your charity, and abusing your terms of service. We have been noted for many things, but parsimony to those who serve us has not previously been one of our vices.'

I suppose he did not count Mary, who had worked for no more than her keep since she was twelve.

'We are no longer a wealthy family, Miss Wakeford. No doubt you have observed the condition of the house.' He left the mantel and turned to face me.

'We had a fine trading business once. Our ships moved some of the most profitable cargoes in the world to our own trading stations. There was hardly a country around the globe that did not have a Tancred house somewhere along its coast. Now,' he shrugged

119

despondently, 'now this is all we have left.'

I hardly knew what to say. I did not understand if he was trying to apologize to me for the poorness of my keep or if he was just telling me a story, another of those interminable stories about the Tancreds.

Suddenly he swung violently across the room and flung the door open. 'There is something I want to show you,' he said abruptly. 'Come here.'

I could not have stood another nightmarish journey around the gallery, listening to the macabre exploits of the weird old men and women. I followed him out of the room, and to my relief he passed straight through the gallery. Again I hurried behind him, carrying the lamp until we came to one of the doors leading out to the stable yard.

'In here,' he said when we had crossed over to the stable, and he held the door open for me. I had of course been in the stables before, once with the unpleasant Math and a few more times when I had been seeking Esmee. Vaguely I had appreciated that they were very large. Indeed, in many ways they were better appointed than most of the house. Once or twice it had struck me that there were too many horses considering the penury and smallness of the family.

He opened one of the stalls and beckoned me to join him by the side of a fine black mare. 'Do you know horses, Miss Wakeford?'

'My Grandfather uses workhorses on his farm.'

He dismissed our two splendid old shire beasts with a quick wave of his hand. 'It has taken me eight years to breed this strain, Miss Wakeford. Eight years of selection, disappointment and quite incredible care on my part. At the beginning I lost a good foal, but we managed to recover. Matthew,' he darted a quick, inscrutable look at me, 'Matthew is the best man with horses I have ever known. Between us we have bred a magnificent strain.'

He led me to another stall, a box containing the big

gray and white animal I had seen him with earlier in the evening. 'I purchased St. Jean while I was still in France. I had very little money and what I had I used to buy St. Jean.' He smoothed the horse's flat, oiled neck with a gentle, almost loving hand. 'He is a beautiful beast, is he not, Miss Wakeford?'

'He seems very sleek, sir,' I answered hesitatingly.

'Sleek! He is a superb animal. He has sired eight winners at Newmarket. And now,' he turned back to the black mare. 'Now I have a buyer for Noire. The Tancred breed is beginning to be known amongst the buyers, Miss Wakeford. They are starting to seek out my horses as once they sought our ships.'

He paced up and down the stable, opening stall after stall, pointing out the beauty of each animal, the age, the condition, the hopes and prospects. I was called upon to comment, to admire, and before I could properly speak he was off on some new track. The change in him was fantastic. The morose, moody figure striding darkly about the house had vanished. I forgot that he had an ugly face, because he himself had forgotten. He was a knowledgeable, energetic man, sending out a contagious enthusiasm even to me who knew nothing of horses.

'For Noire, I am getting an excellent price. And here,' he led out a filly nearly full grown, who whinnied softly and bit gently at his hand, 'this is Suzie. She will fetch an even better price. I have a breeder who is already willing to take her.'

The young horse tapped fretfully on the ground. I think perhaps my presence disturbed her for she shied nervously away when I came near. He said her name and backed her carefully into her stall, rubbing the side of her head all the time he was talking to her. He had very good hands, strong and square-fingered.

I wished we could have stayed there, talking without fear or strange misunderstanding, but no one in that house was ever permitted to relax for very long.

From outside the stable door came a sound I had grown to dread, the noise of Esmee, laughing as she ran away up onto the hill. The brisk, almost gay atmosphere of the stable vanished. John Tancred's face closed abruptly and resumed its bleak harshness. For a moment he did not seem to recollect what had brought him to the stables. He stared blankly at me, then turned and savagely thrust a bolt back into one of the boxes.

'You see, Miss Wakeford,' he said tersely. 'We are not entirely penniless.'

'I did not think thee was, sir.'

He turned quickly from the bolt and looked suspiciously toward me. When he had assured himself that I was not speaking grudgingly he continued: 'I am taking Noire to Newmarket on Thursday. When the monies are received, perhaps you will be good enough to tell me what things are needed about the house. Comforts for my mother and so forth.'

'I will do that, sir.'

He was plainly not at ease. I guessed it was so long since he had spoken graciously to anyone that he had almost forgotten the art of being pleasant.

'Later, when Suzie is sold, we must see to the house and maybe take on fresh servants. I am aware, Miss Wakeford, that your duties are onerous.'

'I am able to manage,' I said stiffly, worried in case he had observed that I was not of much use in controlling his daughter. 'Esmee is difficult at times but . . .,' I broke off as I saw how my mention of the child induced a tensing of his features.

'Leave Esmee to herself, Miss Wakeford. There is nothing you can do.'

I felt it was time I spoke to someone about the child. For too long I had tried to pretend that she was merely highly strung—a lonely, imaginative child. But I knew there was something more than this, something bad in Esmee Tancred's mind that refused to answer to the normal disciplines and affections of childhood—something that I seemed unable to control.

'Mr. Tancred,' I said nervously, 'I have tried to teach Esmee her letters. And, too, I have tried to keep her dressed and away from the hill. It is . . .'

Once more he interrupted me. 'Leave her, Miriam Wakeford. Leave her. She is not like other children. Surely you have gathered that by now?'

His face was so terrifyingly empty I was almost too afraid to go on. I should have stopped there, taken him at his word and left him to pursue his agony in private. But a foolhardy rashness made me continue. I clasped my hands tightly together and said: 'A doctor? Perhaps if she were to see a doctor?'

The dark-pitted eyes glowed briefly in the marked face. 'She has seen a doctor, Miss Wakeford. When she was three she was taken to a specialist in Vienna. I have told you, there is nothing you can do.' He stopped for a moment and stared at me. Then the silence was shattered with cruel brutality as he said: 'My daughter is insane, Miss Wakeford.'

There was nothing to say, nothing that would remove the cold pit of shock at the base of my stomach. I knew that Esmee was not like other children. Her wild ways, her strangeness, her cleverness in some things and obtuseness in others had convinced me some time ago that she was not normal. But there is a wealth of difference between admitting that a child is a little 'different,' and hearing a father rasp the word 'insanity' into the air. It was a cruel, irrevocable thing to say, and once said there was no drawing back from the significance of its meaning. Perhaps I should have said something, denied the truth of what he thought about his child—asked him to be kinder, both to himself and to his daughter. But the sudden ugliness of the words left me completely bereft of speech.

'Feed her, clothe her,' he said hoarsely. 'Then leave her alone.'

'But . . .'

His body slumped suddenly against the side of a stall. He brought his hands up to cover his face and I was conscious mostly of a deep relief because I would not have to look at the pain in his eyes—the misery that was there because of my foolish and persistent questions. I closed my eyes, unable to bear the sight of his racked form turned inward to the side of a wooden stall. I could not comfort him. I did not even know if he wished to be comforted and I had said too much already.

'I am sorry,' I muttered chokingly. I turned, stumbled clumsily against the stable door and hurried away.

I was already back in my room, my mind a turmoil after what had just happened, when I recalled that I was supposed to go to Mrs. Tancred's room. Wearily—for I had had too much of conflict that night—I tidied my cap and hurried down to her room, hoping that I was not going to be embroiled in yet another scene of moods and intensity.

'Come in! Come in!' she shouted before I had even finished knocking at the door. I turned the handle and went in.

She was seated before the great loom, her hands raised in the air and wound about with a leprous yellow shade of silk that she was adding to the bright pink already there. She stopped and put the thread down when I came in and pulled her chair around to face me.

'What did he want?' she said sharply. 'What did my son have to say to you that was so private? What secrets and confidences have you been sharing?'

She was wound taut like one of her own threads of silk. I was glad, dreadful though it seems, that she was confined to the wheelchair. If she had been able to walk, my fear of her would have been even greater.

'There were no secrets, Marm. It was only matters of business.'

'What business?' she rapped to me.

124

I wished she would ask me to sit down. That way I could concentrate on seeing that my voice did not shake. 'It was matters of the household, Marm. Details of monies and on what I should spend them.'

'Explain yourself!' She glared suspiciously at me.

'Mr. John . . . Mr. Tancred was saying he intends to sell some of his horses, and when he does he wishes me to purchase some things for the house.'

The frightening glow in her eyes faded a little but still she was not satisfied. 'Is that all? There was nothing else?' My hesitation was prompted more by nerves than consideration of how much more I should tell her. She pounced on the pause with all the suddenness of a silent black cat. 'Come now! What else? You must tell me for I shall know.'

'About . . . about Miss Esmee, Marm.' I swallowed.

'Yes?' The alarm had returned to her face and her black eyes burned their way into my head.

'That Miss Esmee is . . . unwell.'

Again the heat in her face dimmed and this time did not reappear. It was replaced by the look of discomfort she always wore when she spoke of Esmee.

'Ah yes. Well of course, Miss Wakeford, I told you when you came that Esmee was not an easy child to handle. You must take no notice of my son. He has little to do with Esmee. I am quite sure I know more about the child than he does.'

'Yes, Marm.'

She turned her chair slowly back to the loom and I began to leave the room. 'You will stay for a while, Miss Wakeford,' she said over her shoulder, and it was a command, not a request. 'You will read to me, please.'

'But, Marm. It is after eleven.'

'Read!'

I sat down and picked up a book, any book from amongst those lying on the table. It was a study of Talleyrand and no sooner had I commenced reading

125

than she turned once more to the loom. I was aware of the movement of her hands and the weaving of the brilliant yellow threads. I droned on—page after page of dull text about the dead statesman, and found, after a couple of hours had elapsed, that my voice was reduced to a dull, spasmodic grumble, at times ceasing altogether. When I finally stopped reading she took no notice, but continued to pass the shuttle through the long threads.

I was nearly asleep in my chair, but she was sitting tireless and erect over the loom, her body, arms and neck corded and stiff with nervous energy. I watched her white hands through eyes heavy with sleep. They wove a macabre dance of color and design over the silks, seeming at times, to hover disembodied in the air. Her body swayed in time to the shuttle, faster and faster, with incredible speed as though she were possessed by demons who gave her a never-ending strength. The movement hypnotized me into slumber and I suddenly came to when I found myself falling off the chair.

The sound of the shuttle ceased. Mrs. Tancred dropped the silk and let it lie where it had fallen. Her body was slumped forward over the loom, a dried, empty shell completely denuded of energy. I thought she had fallen asleep, but she turned her head and said slowly: 'You may tell Mary to come now.'

She had faded. She was a gray, washed-out specter of the erect woman I had known up to now. Her eyes were dull, lifeless, and even her hair seemed to have lost its color. I stood and made my escape from the room. She murmured something and it sounded like, 'Now, I shall sleep,' but I was so tired I could not really hear.

The next day I tried to approach Mary on the subject of Esmee Tancred but she avoided answering, saying only that the child was greatly improved since I had come. I asked her, too, when Mrs. Tancred had first become confined to her wheelchair and to this she replied vaguely that it was some time ago, she couldn't quite remember when. We were busy repairing the linen of the house, cutting the sheets down the middle and turning the thick part to the center.

'What caused Mrs. Tancred's accident?' I asked. I had been careful until then not to press questions, but I was worried and increasingly perturbed and bothered by the secret ghosts that flitted about the house.

'She had a bad fall,' said Mary evasively.

I am not a curious person. I do not like people asking me questions about my parents, and am therefore reticent about inquiring into the business of others. I resent prying or interfering folk and, for this reason I had carefully refrained from asking questions at Tancred. But there were too many secrets, too many strange, unpleasant things that blew through the house along with the wind. There were many nights when I was afraid to go to sleep and afraid to look out of the window. It was not just Esmee who sent shadows over my heart, it was Mrs. Tancred, and John, and yes, I was forced to admit that the creeping presence of old Richard Tancred had affected me as much as those who had known him in life.

I wrote a carefully guarded letter to Miss Llewellyn. If I said too much about the condition of the house and the strangeness of the family, I knew my Grandfather would be down straight away to take me home. I was not ready yet to admit defeat and be borne back to the village for Grandmother to triumph over. I told Miss Llewellyn what a dear lady Mrs. Tancred was and how bravely she bore all the misfortunes of widowhood and illness. I asked Miss Llewellyn what she knew of the tragedies of Tancred, and I tried to make it sound as though I was no more than idly curious.

An answer came—a thick, voluble letter full of village gossip and details of seaming and dresses she was working upon. Then, on the last page I saw the name Tancred leap at me from the scrawling print, and later that night, in the gloomy privacy of my room, I held the letter up to the light from a candle:

As to your questions about the Tancreds, my dear, there is not a great deal I can tell you. I was with Mrs. Tancred before her marriage, and a gay, high-spirited girl she was. I came with her when she married and I must say I was surprised to hear that there is little or no entertaining at the house these days. Mrs. Tancred was always one for parties and musicales. I recall one time when she changed straight from a ball gown to her riding habit and rode off with the hunt after a night of dancing. Mr. Richard was a very well-set-up man, although I must confess he made me a little nervous. I believe, too, that he was not very skilled in the ways of business. During the time I was at Tancred, he had to sell four of his merchant houses and I believe that after I left, his financial affairs did not improve. Indeed, it may be said in strictest confidence, dear, that he squandered the family wealth in a number of nefarious ways. There were many unpleasant rumors of his behavior, but he was always very correct with me—at least in his rather odd way he was. I stayed with Mrs. Tancred for just a short while after John was born. Then, as you know, I moved to join my dear aunt in the village. But Mrs. Tancred has never forgotten me. Every Christmas and Easter we correspond and she gives me news of her family. Of course I never knew Mr. John's wife, only that she was French and died when the little girl was six. And now, dear, I must tell you about the girl your cousin Stephen is courting . . .

The letter trailed off with messages and precautionary warnings. I set it carefully to one side and began to prepare myself for bed. It seemed as though no one either could, or would, tell me what was wrong at Tancred. There was an elusive unsoundness in the house—an impression, a significance of blackness that I could not define or link with any particular thing or person. It was not Mrs. Tancred's fantastic pride in a dead generation; it was not the insanity—for as such I now admitted—of Esmee Tancred, nor the lonely misery of her father. It was not the lechery of Matthew Johnson, nor the pathos of Mary's dreary life; yet it was something of all these things.

I climbed into bed and gazed upwards to where the candlelight made mysterious runes upon the ceiling.

It was not the wind, nor the east wing, nor the portrait of Richard Tancred, but all these things were part of it. They twisted and whirled round a vortex of unknown horror, an oozing secret that by mutual unspoken agreement was kept carefully covered under a blanket of silence.

The light danced sinuously in the draft. The shapes on the ceiling changed, a skull, a hand, a bird.

Whatever was wrong at Tancred I would have to discover for myself, for certainly no one was going to tell me. Perhaps it was not the people or the past that seeped eerily from the stone walls; perhaps it was the house itself.

The wind blew the candle out.

7

Summer came, but it made no difference to the Down. There were no trees to leaf, no flowers or shrubs to stand brightly in the air. Only the tough, grained grass changed color, turning from faded yellow to a virulent, creeping green, as though feeding on the sourness of the hill.

It seemed to me that the Druid's Stones grew bigger, their monolithic roots fastened into the ground, waiting with dreadful passiveness for the evil to occur. With increasing conviction I knew that a malady of some kind would be enacted, that nothing could be done to avoid the disaster.

The wind did not drop; it only blew less coldy with a tepid, almost stale scent.

I had tried to discover more about the secret of Tancred, but had met with baffling silence from every source I pursued. When I had ridden to Loxham to purchase the month's provisions, I had endeavored to draw the storekeeper into some kind of discussion. It was useless. He had the same bland hostility as the rest of those villagers.

I had been into Brighton twice, once in May, once in July, to spend a day with Ezekial King and his daughter. I no longer waited for Reuben Tyler in the village, however. I did not like the people of Loxham and they cared even less for me. I would walk purposefully through the village street, looking neither to right nor left, until I reached beyond the bend in the road. There I would wait for the vintner's wagon. Once in June, Ezekial and Deborah King had ridden out especially from Brighton to see me. I had taken them in to meet Mrs. Tancred, wondering nervously how such an encounter would develop.

I need not have worried. Mrs. Tancred seemed as anxious as I that a good impression be created. When she chose, she could be extremely gracious, and on this visit from my two friends she exerted all possible charm and affability, even asking if they would like to take some tea with her. We now were so fortunate to possess a set of matching cups, plates and so forth, for John Tancred had been as good as his word. He and Math had ridden off with Noire, the black mare, one morning and when they returned, the master of Tancred had called me once more into his rooms.

'I have received payment for Noire,' he said bluntly. 'Have you decided what things you need to buy?'

'There are clothes for Esmee. And fresh linen for the house. And perhaps, if there is enough, some . . .'

He interrupted me rudely. 'I am not interested in trinkets and hairpins, Miss Wakeford. Tell me how much you need. I have no wish to be bothered with detail.'

I felt plain and silly, as though I were a fussy, over-garrulous creature. He made no attempt to hide the fact that my preoccupation with the details of the house was tedious and boring. I thought his abruptness was uncalled for. I had not been the one to suggest buying things, and there was no need for him to be so contemptuous of me. I told him how much we needed and coldly he counted out the money saying, as he handed it to me, 'I trust you can handle the management of this place without constantly coming to me, Miss Wakeford. I have a great deal to do with the breeding and transactions of the horses. In a household of three adult women I feel my participation should be unnecessary.'

'I did not ask thee for help!' I was so angry I wanted to throw the money back at him, but we needed it. 'If thee remembers, it was thee who . . .'

'That will be all, Miss Wakeford. You may go.'

131

I was seething with fury and hidden hurt. He was more than rude; he was unkind and openly derisive of me. Of our warm, friendly discussion in the stable, when he had told about the breeding of his horses, nothing remained. It might never have happened, and now he was even colder and more brusque toward me than he had ever been. I left him. Whatever misery he carried in his soul, he had no right to make me its object.

Mary and I rode into Brighton on the trap—a day that I remember even now as one of the happiest of my life. Our relationship was one of uneasy friendship: it could be nothing else with the secrets of the house between us. But away from the house we became two people who, until this time, had lacked friends and the companionship of our own sex. With amazement I learned that Mary, who was older and generally more worldly-wise than I, had never been into Brighton. She had come straight from the poorhouse to Tancred, and from then on her outings had consisted solely of trips down to Loxham.

This was only my fourth visit to Brighton, counting my first arrival at the station, and I was still a little in awe of the size and bustle of the town. But in the presence of Mary's dazzling bewilderment, I affected a superior woman-of-the-world air that I was far from feeling. I swept from shop to shop like an experienced devotee of the town, pointing out what I considered places of interest: the Regent's palace (and I carelessly dropped in the piece of information learned from Reuben Tyler—that old King George had traveled up to Tancred); the draper's store; the fishermen on the front and the Quaker Meeting House. In my purse I was carrying an amount of money that made us both nervous in its magnitude and possibilities. John Tancred's unpleasantness when he had handed it to me still rankled; but as the day progressed I firmly pushed his sarcasm to the back of my mind and began to enjoy the scattering of his wealth.

We bought sheets and bedding, clothes for Esmee,

and new drawers and bodices for Mary. I had been going to ask John Tancred if any of the money could be spent on Mary, but as he had not waited for me to finish I bought them anyway. We drove to the hardware store and purchased things for the kitchen and a set of matching china and glass: not so good, of course, as the odd pieces that were left up at the house, but still of fair quality. And because neither of us had ever had the opportunity to buy anything before, we took an unpardonable time in selecting what we were to have, hovering between pink roses, purple and gold Prince Albert, pansies and leaves in colors that no garden had ever seen, and generally driving the poor shopkeeper mad with our dithering.

We bought preserves and fruits for the larder and a big side of bacon that brought a keen sense of anticipation to both of us as we watched it loaded onto the back of the trap. Then, with a flourish, I led Mary to the pie shop and magnanimously handed over a threepence— but out of my own money—in exchange for a bag of pies. It says much for Mary that she accepted my treat with all the spontaneous delight of one who has an innocent spirit. I have observed, since those days, how much easier it is to be a gracious giver than a gracious receiver. It is harder by far to give pleasure in the acceptance of a gift than it is merely to offer a present. I understood nothing of this on that day in Brighton, but I was aware of a tremendous sense of well-being and happiness because I was able to bring delight to Mary's face with the humble gift of threepenny-worth of pies.

We ate them riding home in the trap, each of us taking turns to hold the reins while the other ate. We were being rather silly, I suppose, giggling like children on an escapade, and even when we had left Loxham and were on the track back to the house we were still laughing. Mary brushed the crumbs of pastry from her lap and pointed to the pony's fat rump jogging along in front of us.

'Sometimes I think the horses at Tancred eats better than we does.'

It made us laugh again, and then I realized that it was the first time that Mary had ever said anything even faintly critical of Tancred. As we approached the turn in the track I noticed that the pony, under her guiding hands, had slowed almost to a walk. We came through the Down and suddenly, very quietly she said, 'I don't want to go home.'

The pony stopped. I looked at her. 'Why, Mary?'

For a moment I thought she was going to tell me—to share with me the knowledge that made Tancred the somber place it was, so that I would know why it was forbidden to speak of Richard Tancred and a thousand other things about the house.

She looked up at the house above us, her hand tightened on the rein, then her shoulders slumped forward defensively and she jerked the pony forward.

'Come on,' she said. 'We'll have to get the dinner soon.'

In August Ezekial King rode up to see me, but to my surprise, he was alone. I asked him to come in and sit in the house, but he shook his head.

'I will speak to thee out here, Miriam. It will not take a moment.'

I waited, curious to know what had fetched him all this way on his own.

'I have been making inquiries, Miriam, and I have found a place for thee in Brighton, a very commendable position with a banker's family.'

I was puzzled. He spoke as though I had asked him to seek out something for me. 'But I have a position, Mr. King. Here, at Tancred.'

He pursed his lips together and allowed a small frown to settle over the bridge of his jutting nose. 'I have not been at all at peace about thee staying here, Miriam. I do not think the place is at all suitable for a

134

girl of thy background. I have been most careful in selecting this new position. Thee will care for the six children of the house and Mrs. O'Brien, the housekeeper, is an extremely capable and competent woman.'

I felt a small knot of anger gathering in my chest. It was not entirely his managerial ways that annoyed me but his reference to my background. I knew full well what he meant. With my inherited bad blood I should work at a place where I could be constantly watched and supervised.

'I thank thee for thy kindness,' I said stiffly, 'but I am well suited here. I am learning the craft of running a large house and I prefer this kind of work to nursemaiding.'

The frown of displeasure between his eyes grew more pronounced. 'This is an ungodly house,' he said icily.

'Then I feel it is my duty to stay here and work the Lord's will.'

It is to my credit that I managed to conceal how furious I was. Mr. King was furious too, but his was not so well hidden, for his face went white. 'I have already settled the matter with the banker's family,' he said. 'I think, Miriam, this is a time when thee must be guided by those who are concerned for thy welfare.'

'I am very sorry, Mr. King. Thee has no doubt gone to a lot of trouble on my behalf. But this place was arranged for me by my Grandfather, and I shall remain here until I think it is time to leave.'

It was a neat if rather dishonest answer. Grandfather had arranged for me to come here only at my insistence and on the good recommendation of Miss Llewellyn.

Mr. King's mouth tightened to a narrow line. He could hardly press his point without being discourteous to Grandfather. He did not give up without a struggle, however. 'When I write to thy Grandfather, he will see I have done what is best.'

'I am sorry, Mr. King. I wish to stay here.'

'Thou art a disobedient and ungrateful young woman!'

I was truly astonished. His peremptory assumption of authority I could, to a certain extent, understand; but the degree of familiarity with which he addressed me was completely uncalled for.

'Good day, Mr. King.'

He climbed back into his trap. His nose was even bigger and bonier against the rigid whiteness of his face. 'I shall write to thy Grandfather, Miriam.'

'Good day, Mr. King.'

If he had not gone then, I think I should have been rude to him. He rode stiffly away down the hill leaving me boiling with indignant rage as I walked back into the house. I was even too angry to worry about what would be the outcome of his letter to Grandfather, although later I began to feel anxious about it. I did not want Grandfather turning up at Tancred, seeing what a dreadful place it was, with hardly any servants and a family that never went to worship.

That night I sat down and wrote to Grandfather myself. I told him exactly what had happened with Mr. King. I also told him that perhaps the house of Tancred was not quite as splendid as we had been led to expect from Miss Llewellyn's glowing accounts. However, I pointed out, I was certainly needed at the house. There was a crippled mistress and an undisciplined child. I felt it was not right to run away just because Mr. King wished it. The letter left much unsaid and I supposed it was not entirely honest. I could do nothing then except wait to see what would happen.

Only later that night it occurred to me to wonder why I was so loath to leave the house.

The following morning I really began to worry about Ezekial King's visit. All night I had been haunted by thoughts not only of Grandfather, but Grandmother too, descending on me at Tancred and carting me off home, or back to the position at Brighton to be watched over by the gloating self-righteousness of Ezekial King.

I dropped a pan of porridge on the kitchen floor, nearly the last of the month's supply. Finally, when I went to find Esmee to teach her her letters, I found she had torn the centers out of three of my books and tipped the ink over what remained of them. I don't know why I still bothered to try to teach the child. John Tancred had removed such responsibility from me, but a stubborn perverseness made me continue to sit with her for a few hours each day, trying to instill at least some kind of learning in her. I was upset by what she had done to my books. To those who love reading and learning, books and living things, almost as precious as pets are to other folk. She had completely ruined the pages, and it was impossible to restore them in any way at all.

I walked out of the house and began to climb the hill—not that I had any great love for that bare landscape, but there was nowhere else to walk and I needed to get away from the house for a while. When I came to the Stones I turned westward and strolled unhappily over the rolling Down, climbing up and down over the tussocks of grass and carefully avoiding the strange little rings of different colored moss that appeared almost overnight on the hill.

I could see John Tancred exercising the gray and white horse a little way beneath me, trotting him straight across the slope of the hill. He looked up once and when he saw me he hesitated, then pulled the beast round and began to gallop up to where I stood.

'Miss Wakeford,' he said hesitatingly and bent his head slightly toward me.

'Good morning, sir.' I nodded morosely back and went on my way over the hill. I saw no reason to stand waiting, merely to be snubbed by him.

He did not ride off, however, but slowed his horse to

137

a walk beside me; and as I marched, somewhat aggressively I am forced to admit, he paced the animal carefully to suit my stride. 'I observe you had a visitor yesterday,' he said.

I could never understand this man. Sometimes he could be friendly, almost pathetically unsure of himself and then, when I was expecting his goodwill, he would turn on me with deliberate rudeness. I had endured enough that day of the changing moods of Tancred and I wanted no more. Rather tersely I said, 'Yes,' and strode on.

'Miss Wakeford, I have observed that gentleman here before. Are you thinking of getting married?'

I was so astonished I stopped walking and turned to face him. The ridiculousness of his question made me forget the bother of Ezekial King's visit. I thought that John Tancred must be using me to sharpen his unpleasant sense of humor, but when I looked at his face I could see nothing but genuine curiosity.

'Marriage! With Mr. King?'

Suddenly the thought of hook-nosed Ezekial King proposing marriage began to make me chuckle. John Tancred, of course, could not know of my background, but the idea of serious, worthy-minded Mr. King proposing marriage to an illegitimate, disobedient young woman such as myself was so absurd that my grins turned to laughter.

I think laughter is an infectious thing in the same way that tears and unhappiness are. For as I stood on the hillside thinking of Mr. King and laughing so loudly that not even the wind could drown it, I looked up and saw that John Tancred, too, was smiling.

The day suddenly took on an unreal quality. It was a gray, heavy morning full of distance and cloud, and I had the strangest feeling that I had been swept into a looking-glass world where ordinary thoughts and emotions no longer existed.

He smiled at me again, and for a second I forgot who

he was. 'Would you care to come for a ride, Miss Wakeford?'

He could only mean on the gray and white horse. There was no other beast about. I thought he meant that he would climb down and let me ride in his place, but instead he held his hand down to me and pointed to the stirrup. 'Put your foot in the stirrup, Miss Wakeford.'

I threw caution and good behavior to the wind. I was tired of behaving seriously, spending all my life working and remembering that I must always be circumspect because of my bad blood. I did not even think whether or not I should climb up beside him. I took hold of his hand, put my foot in the strap, and he pulled me up to sit in front of him.

It was all unreal, so it did not matter that I had no right riding on a horse with a man I hardly knew. It was a silly dream—with him behind, one arm around each side of me holding the reins—and soon I would wake up and find him growling or ignoring me, and Esmee would be singing away over the hills and Mrs. Tancred guarding her unpleasant secrets with glittering queerness. But until I woke up, I would enjoy my dream.

He spurred the horse to a gallop and then we were away, racing over the Down, leaving the house and the Druid's circle far, far behind us. The hills went on in a never-ending series of smooth undulations. The horse did not pause once; he kept the same speed ascending the slopes as when he raced downward. The wind flapped my skirts, but away from Tancred it was not such a brutal, cruel thing and merely lent excitement to the speed of the horse.

We came at last to a point high up over all the other hills, from where we could see both the ocean and the valleys stretching inland behind us. The horse was reined in for a second and John Tancred said: 'Take off your cap. It is in my way.'

139

I untied the bands and held it in my lap, then we were off again, racing down toward the sea to where the white bands of foam split the gray fantasy of water and sky, the wind blowing my hairpins away and streaming my hair out into the air around me.

The slopes grew lower until eventually they dipped right onto the beach itself. A narrow, grassy verge intermingled with the beginning of the shingle beach. St. Jean—for I had remembered the horse's name—trotted straight toward the firm band of ground. He was obviously used to coming here and now he walked leisurely along, pulling his head up every so often to smell the air from the sea. John Tancred took his hands from the reins. The horse knew the path better than he did, and when at last the grassy shingle led to a small ridge over the sea, he went forward and stood still on the promontory looking out across the water.

And then, as though I had half expected it, I felt John Tancred's hands upon my hair.

Such a wealth of feeling surged up into me that I could not speak. I had never felt like this before, not even when Joseph Whittaker had asked to walk me home from Meeting. I was frightened to move in case the dream was broken and I woke to find myself back in the huge, drab bedroom at Tancred.

I wanted to say something, but words would take the fantasy out of the air and make everything mundane so that I was Miriam Wakeford who had no right to be sitting on the master's horse. Each time his fingers touched my skin a drowning cataract of warmth flooded outward from somewhere inside me. Not from the heart, as one would believe from reading modern novels, but from the throat and stomach, suffusing me with heat so that at that moment I would have done anything for John Tancred.

His hands were strong—maybe squarer and thicker than was commonly supposed elegant—for he was, in any case, a heavily built man. But he was so gentle it was as though a boy were touching me. I felt him lift the hair from the back of my neck, weighing it carefully in his hand before letting it fall again. Then he smoothed it back from my face, tucking it neatly behind my ears away and out of the wind.

Now I could admit to myself that this was why I stayed at Tancred; because like myself, John Tancred was lonely and ugly. But more than this, because he was a man and I loved him.

The movement of his hands stopped and I took courage to turn my head and look at him. I was so close to his face that I could see every tiny mark and vein of his scar, every piece of seared tissue and puckered skin, and strangely enough it did not repel me in any way. In his face was so much misery that, after a brief glance, I looked no more but closed my eyes.

Then, still in my dream, without self-will or any voli-, tion on my part, I put my hands up to his neck and kissed his face.

The horse moved, whinnied fretfully and pawed irritably at the ground; and with its sudden movement I realized that it was not a dream and the enormity of what I had done flamed across my face.

I tried to put my hair back but the wind had taken all the pins. The more I fumbled, the more wild and unruly it became until at last I bundled it back into my cap and tied the tapes fiercely beneath my chin. I think I was crying; certainly I remember that I wanted to do no more than hurry home and lock myself in my room away from my shame and abandonment. Ezekial King was right; Grandmother was right. There was bad blood in me inherited from my father and, to a lesser degree, from my mother. I had climbed up beside the master of Tancred. I had removed my cap and let my hair blow out into the wind. And then I had kissed him. The dream was shattered.

I dared not look at the man behind me. When I had finished tying my cap he bent forward and picked up

141

the reins, brushing my cheek briefly with his as he did so. In silence he turned St. Jean back the way we had come. This time we did not gallop but went at a sharp trot back to the hills and the sloping Down of Tancred.

I would rather he had left me at the top of the hill by the Druid's Stones, but I could not bring myself to ask and so we rode straight back to the stable, directly opposite the kitchen door. He got down first, then reached his hands up to my waist to lift me down and hold me, very briefly against him for a second. I wanted to look up at his face to see if he were amused or contemptuous or even disinterested. I could not. I broke quickly away from his grasp and ran toward the kitchen.

Mary was standing in the doorway watching me, a puzzled frown marking her eyes. As I pushed past her she followed me quickly.

'Where've you been? Mistress has been asking for you and I looked everywhere. We've company.'

'Company?'

I looked up quickly. Mary was excited, her face flushed and I noticed she was wearing a clean apron. 'Aye. They arrived about an hour ago. She's been asking for you ever since. Called me over to her quiet like and whispered that you was to go at once. Where've you been?'

'I . . . I was looking for Esmee, up on the hill.'

I dared not try to tidy my cap. As soon as I untied the tapes my hair would come down again. A horrid notion struck me.

'Mary. The visitors, it is not Mr. King is it?'

'Course it ain't,' she said wonderingly. 'Why should it be? It's friends o' Mrs. Tancred's, friends from before she was married. Hurry now, she's waiting.'

I smoothed my dress as best I could, clenched my hands tightly to regain control, then knocked on Mrs. Tancred's door and went in.

There were three other women in the room, one a

plump, florid matron who was perhaps a little younger than Mrs. Tancred, but not nearly so striking in appearance. She was wearing a maroon traveling dress, and in spite of being very well corseted it was really too tight for her.

Mrs. Tancred was relieved to see me. 'Ah, Miss Wakeford. We were wondering where you had got to.'

'I was looking for Esmee, Marm, I . . .'

'Yes, of course.' She turned smiling to the plump woman by her side and said blandly, 'Miss Wakeford takes her duties as governess very seriously. When she is not teaching Esmee, she insists on spending every moment of leisure with the child.'

If I was startled at my promotion to the official rank of governess, I managed not to show it, appreciating that Mrs. Tancred was playing some social game of her own. The plump woman beamed at me and nodded approvingly at such keen devotion to duty.

Mrs. Tancred stared hard and asked carefully: 'And where is Esmee now, Miss Wakeford? Settled for her afternoon rest?' She made sure I did not answer by turning to her companion and saying quickly, 'Esmee is a delicate child you know, Grace; we have to ensure that she leads a quiet, well-rested life.'

Grace clucked sympathetically and Mrs. Tancred again gave me that hard stare. She need not have worried. I had gathered very quickly that she did not want Esmee coming into the room, singing her weird little song and looking at things that did not exist.

'Miss Wakeford, this is a friend I have known since girlhood, Grace Thorburn. And here,' she waved one of the other women forward, 'is her daughter, Mildred, widowed alas, like her dear mother.'

The plump Grace touched her eyes briefly with a wisp of linen in formal acknowledgement to the late Mr. Thorburn.

'Miss Wakeford,' she said, extending a large white hand very briefly toward me. 'We have had such a journey. I cannot tell you. If only we had *appreciated* how far it was, I can *assure* you we would have left our visit until later.'

She was sitting down, but from the way she spoke, in a quick, breathless fashion, one gained the impression she had been running or hurrying up a flight of steep stairs. The maroon dress was really most unflattering. She had a puffy, bad-complexioned face, and her tight gown and breathless voice gave one the uncomfortable feeling she was about to come undone at any moment.

Mrs. Tancred turned once more to me. 'Grace and dear Mildred have ridden over all the way from Chichester, Miss Wakeford, just to renew an old acquaintanceship.'

Mrs. Thorburn bent forward as gracefully as her corsets would permit. 'Oh surely not just an acquaintanceship, dear. Why we were always such *close* friends. I remember when Richard was courting you, we used to tell each other absolutely *everything!*'

I found it hard to picture Mrs. Tancred as a girl, giggling and sharing confidences. I found it even harder to understand why she was bearing with this silly, over-voluble woman now. Mrs. Tancred was many things, but she was not a woman who enjoyed gossip or noisy company and I could not reconcile her apparent eagerness to please this noisy creature with her former desire for solitude.

I realized suddenly that I had made no contribution whatsoever to the conversation. 'Is it far to Chichester?' I asked politely.

'An absolute *age*, my dear. I thought we would never arrive. We are moving to Brighton very soon, you see, and once our plans were definite I said to Mildred, we just *must* call on dear Emma and tell her that from now on we shall be *neighbors*.'

I looked anxiously at Mrs. Tancred. She knew, as well as I, that we at Tancred were in no position to indulge in social interchanges. If her friends thought that she would be able to launch them in Brighton society, they were about to be dismally shocked. To my surprise she was in no way perturbed, rather there was a hidden excitement about her—a feverish anticipation of delights to come.

'I have told Grace that we shall have to give a party—nothing ostentatious but perhaps some friends and a little dancing—to welcome her to Tancred.'

I tried desperately to hide my startled discomfiture. I respected her keenness enough to appreciate that she knew quite well what she was saying, but the thought of a ball at Tancred . . .

'Emma, my dear! How delightful, and how kind. Now that poor Mildred is out of mourning we shall really look forward to coming.'

I turned to look at Mildred. She was a smoother, slightly slimmer replica of her mother; probably in her early thirties, unfortunate in her complexion and, truth to tell, not very comely, although she had quite a pleasant manner. Mrs. Thorburn reached up and took her daughter's hand sentimentally in hers.

'Poor Mildred. The boys are at school, you know and she has only her old mother for company. I fear I am not very gay for her.' She beamed pathetically up at her daughter who answered with a cursory smile.

'Has thee many sons?' I asked. The two ladies exchanged sly smiles and after a moment I realized it was my speech that amused them.

'Two boys, Miss Wakeford.'

Mrs. Tancred leaned forward and interrupted quickly. 'And you must find it a thankless task, Mildred, bringing up sons without a husband to help you.'

Suddenly everything clicked into place: Mrs Tancred's forced affability, her promise of parties and so forth, her eagerness to display me as a worthy and devoted governess and her frantic desire to keep Esmee out of the way.

'My own dear son has been very lonely since his wife

died. Only those who have suffered such bereavement can understand the sorrow of others in the same position.'

The two elderly ladies exchanged a look of silent agreement. There was a brief, mutual acknowledgement of the marital situation of their respective children, a foray, a bargaining and an unspoken signing of contracts.

I wanted to draw Mrs. Tancred back to earth, back to the bleak, rotting world of Tancred: to a house already falling into decay and a grandchild about whom the less said the better. Above all I wanted to remind her that her son was a recluse—an ugly, scarred man who preferred to live alone.

'Miss Wakeford, perhaps you would care to see to the bringing in of the tea.'

I turned to go and Mrs Thorburn said, 'Miss Timkins could help you.'

The third occupant of the room I recognized at a glance as one of those poorer relations who act out their lives as unpaid companions. Doomed never to marry, they are further impeded by the fallacy that women of breeding should not earn a living for themselves. They live a life of secondhand emotion, fetching, carrying and generally obliging without any kind of payment. Miss Timkins was so pale and colorless, so generally nebulous in her bearing, that the moment after I looked away from her, I had difficulty in recalling what she looked like.

'Miss Wakeford can manage, thank you, Grace,' said Mrs. Tancred quickly. She did not want Miss Timkins going into the kitchen and seeing the deplorable condition of the rooms and passages or, even worse, perhaps colliding with Esmee or Math Johnson.

I was just going out of the door when she suddenly spun the wheels of her chair and glided swiftly towards me. I never ceased to be amazed at the way she could move herself when she wanted. She put her chair between me and the other women in the room. Then she hastily thrust a small bronze key at me.

'The china in the cabinet,' she hissed and turned at once to smile at Grace and Mildred Thorburn.

I hadn't a notion of what she was saying but I knew this was not the time to ask. I trotted dutifully back to the kitchen and asked Mary the significance of the key. She was impressed.

' 'Tis the last of the old lady's good things,' she said. '*He* took nearly everything and sold it, and what wasn't sold soon got broke. But she hid a few things. Here, in the old pantry.'

Next to the kitchen was a big, old stone room, once used for the hanging of game and meat but now just a shabby repository for old furniture and discarded rubbish. Mary unlocked the door of a small lacquered cabinet and very gently removed a tea service of Chinese porcelain.

'We haven't had these out since Mr. John's wife first came home,' she said nervously. I was as tremulous as she. The cups were so exquisite I hardly wanted the responsibility of bearing them back into Mrs. Tancred's room; but when I set the tray beside her she took no notice of the delicate cups, and one would have supposed that we drank from them every day. Calmly, with no apparent effort, she poured out the tea and handed the cups to me so that I could pass them round the room. When I had served the negligible Miss Timkins, I too was handed a cup and I gathered I was supposed to join the tea party. I went and sat with Miss Timkins, knowing my place instinctively. In other circumstances I felt quite sure I would not be invited to participate in such socialities, but on this occasion I was a very useful piece of background. I was a comparatively normal person in a household of abnormalities. I could converse politely and be presented as Esmee's governess. Mrs. Tancred needed me that day.

The tea over, the ladies began to say their departures. There had been no reference to the non-appearance of John Tancred. She must have surmounted that hurdle while I . . . while I was riding over the hills with him.

The recurring thought of how I had passed my day brought a flood of color to my face. Resolutely I thrust the memory away, trying to dismiss it all as the dream it had seemed.

The ladies kissed goodbye, and even Miss Timkins was given a perfunctory brushing of the cheek. With protestations of regret and promises of an early reunion, they were led to the door where Mary, waiting with a graciousness recalled from her earlier days, took them and shepherded them away, whisking them quickly, I imagine, through the shabby passages. I heard Mrs. Tancred sigh, but it was not an expression of tiredness.

'At last,' she murmured gloatingly to herself. 'At last.'

I felt it was time I reminded her of the way things were at Tancred. I had helped her to play her game, for whatever purpose, but the charade could not go on indefinitely.

'Thy friends, Mrs. Tancred,' I said carefully, 'will they be visiting often?'

She turned her head sharply and snapped at me, 'I shall see to it that they do, Miss Wakeford.'

I measured my words very carefully. It was a difficult thing to say. 'Thee . . . thee mentioned a party, Mrs. Tancred . . .'

She did not allow me to finish. 'I promised them a party, Miss Wakeford. And there will be a party! Do you think I have so few friends that I cannot find guests enough to make up a ball?'

'No, Mrs. Tancred. But,' again I sought for the right words. 'But does thee think we are equipped to entertain, Marm?'

To my surprise she looked neither offended nor strange. Instead she said irritably, 'Of course we are not equipped to give a party, Miss Wakeford. Do you think I am not aware of the condition of my own house? We are hardly equipped to live at all. I am not a completely foolish old woman living in the past, you know.'

As this was exactly what I had been thinking, I felt my face growing a little hot. 'Not at all, Marm. I . . .'

'We need money for a party. Servants, food, musicians. Very well then. We shall find the money.'

She moved her chair and glared at me. I did not know what to say. With every passing second the sheer ridiculousness of the whole thing became more apparent to me: the panelling splitting from the walls, the lack of lamps, the improbability of persuading anyone to visit this house; above all the insanity of supposing that John Tancred would dress in a suit of black and receive guests.

'Well, Miss Wakeford?'

She had been watching me, plunging into my thoughts with her scaled black eyes.

'It is . . . Well where could we hold a ball, Marm?'

'In the gallery,' she snapped. 'Where else would we hold a ball?'

'But there are no lamps.'

'Lamps will be purchased.'

'And the walls, Marm. The panelling is gone in places and the wind comes through.'

'If there is enough to eat and drink, with plenty of dancing and gossiping, they will not notice the walls.'

She was looking at me as though she hated me, and yet I knew full well that she did not hate me. I was not sufficiently important to arouse any lasting emotion in her.

'Have you any other complaints, Miss Wakeford?' she asked icily. There were many things I could have said but one look at her indomitable face convinced me of the uselessness of further argument. However I tried just once more.

'Well, Marm, thee sees . . .'

'Yes?'

'It is me, Marm, I do not think I know how to manage the events of a big entertainment. The cooking and the ordering and such like.'

Again she shot me a look of impatient dislike. 'I repeat, Miss Wakeford, I am not yet completely devoid of usefulness or intelligence. I am well able to conduct the running of an event. You will do as I say, spend as I direct and follow my instructions exactly. We shall set the date for September. That will give us a month to prepare, but the weather will still be warm enough to avoid the necessity for heating.'

To this very day I do not know if she was mad or terribly sane. Her will was such that no one could stand before her. Call it courage, or pride or merely the iron spirit of a crazy old woman. Certainly at this time I could say no more to her. I was confused. Such was her tremendous gift for evoking a dream about her, that I found myself almost believing in the coming to pass of the entertainment.

'Go to the fireplace, Miss Wakeford. If you look carefully you will see a small depression to the left of the mantel. Press it and bring me the case inside the cupboard.'

It was a small hidden cavity, so carefully built that, although I had helped clean the room many times, I had never guessed at the existence of the secret cupboard. A flat jewel case rested inside and I carried it over to Mrs. Tancred.

She took it from me and paused for a second, holding the dark leather case carefully on her lap. She wiped the top of the box slowly, almost tenderly with her fantastically long fingers. Then, very gently with a ceremonial precision of movement, she opened the case and looked at the contents.

'The last,' she said softly—so softly that I could hardly hear. 'These are the last.'

They were pearls, row upon row of deep, glossy, round pearls, milky in color because they had not been worn for a long time. But their richness was apparent, even to me.

Dreamily she stared at them, stroked them and let them twine loosely in and out of her fingers.

'The last,' she whispered again. 'He took everything else, everything that was mine as well as ours. But the pearls were my parents' marriage gift and I told him I had lost them.'

She held them up against the light so that the bloom on their convex surfaces shimmered against the background of her face.

'I knew the day would come when I would need them—when I would have to have something for myself. You see how beautiful they are?'

She was not speaking to me, but to herself. She had forgotten I was there, for otherwise she would never have said what she did about Richard Tancred. Suddenly she thrust the pearls into my hand.

'Take them. Tomorrow you will get Matthew to drive you into Brighton. I will give you a letter to take to Mr. Dreugh of Dreugh and Warner. You will sell the pearls. They are a good firm and will give you a fair price. Then, when you have the money, you will come home and we will decide how it can best be apportioned.'

The whole affair had gone too quickly for me. My head was spinning with the realization of the value of the pearls and her references to Richard Tancred. Vaguely I could see just which way events were moving, but she had left me far behind.

'Surely thee should save the pearls for later when thee might have serious need of them.'

She threw my suggestion into the air derisively. 'What need should I have? The need is now, here at Tancred. We are a dying house, Miss Wakeford. You know this; and if we die so will the house.' Her hands gripped tightly at the empty case. 'We have a chance,

Miss Wakeford—a chance to save ourselves.'

I was lost, devoid of strength to fight the madness flowing from her out into the room, pulling me into her macabre dreams.

'I must go now.' My head ached. The pearls were hot and heavy in my hands. I was at the door before she spoke to me again.

'Miss Wakeford.'

'Marm?'

She looked across the room towards the tapestry loom—a look compounded of triumph and dislike. 'Send Mary to take down the loom. I do not want it here.'

She said no more, and after waiting for a second, I hurried away and returned to my room.

There was shouting that night—shouting and angry voices came from her room. I could not hear what words were said, but it was John who rebelled against her, and she who screamed and wept back at him. The voices echoed back from the dark walls and I pulled the pillow up hard about my ears. I looked back to the morning and wondered who it was that had ridden on a gray and white horse with the man whose voice now filled the night. I was right. It had been a dream, a dream that now, in the terror of the darkness, could not even make me feel ashamed. There was no shame in this house, no love, no remembered caresses as my hair was stroked back from my face.

There was nothing in this house except fear.

8

I rode to Brighton the next morning. The pearls were wrapped in a piece of felt and fastened tightly with a safety pin to the inside of my purse. I was no longer in any condition to protest or reason against the sequence of events. I was conscious only of a small knot of pain, high up in the back of my neck and an increasing effort to fight the rising nausea in the pit of my stomach. There was a hopeless inevitability about what was going to happen. I was not strong enough to set myself against it.

Matthew rode beside me. I had no will even to refuse his presence and in any case, I knew that he would never touch me again, at least, not while I had to return to Tancred and live amongst the people there. He did not speak to me, not all the way into Brighton, nor on the way back when I had a promissory note from Messrs. Dreugh and Warner in my purse. But when we passed round into the Down, he turned and spoke quickly to me, in a voice thick with spite.

'I haven't forgotten. Don't think I've forgotten!'

I looked at him dully, not particularly shocked or dismayed by his unforgotten hate. So much was gathering speed towards a cataclysmic disaster, that his addition to my general malaise could make no further impression upon me.

Mrs. Tancred had pushed her wheelchair to the top of the steps and was waiting for me with bright excitement. I handed the promissory note to her and apparently she was satisfied. She nodded slightly and moved her lower lip into a semblance of a smile.

'Good,' she said huskily. 'Now, Miss Wakeford. You will come to my room bringing pen and paper. Then you will write down all I tell you, each item as I say it, until there is no doubt in your mind what you are to do.'

I nodded and went dumbly to my room to fetch the things she had said. Then I went and sat beside her, to receive the first of the many instructions which would be spread over that month.

Although the sheer incongruity of the entire scheme was never entirely lost upon me, the power of the old woman who directed me in the coming weeks was such that there were long periods when the plans laid down no longer seemed bizarre, when I came to believe that Tancred would glitter splendidly with beautiful men and women and that John Tancred, resplendent in evening clothes, would appear charmingly amongst his guests and take the first steps towards acquiring a new wife.

I was forced to admire the old woman's magnificent generalship. Although mostly she gave the impression of one lost in the past, living amongst old dreams and nightmares, she had a core of practical common sense that she could, when she so chose, exert to the full. I sat with her and prepared the invitations; there were seventy in all and each one was written in hand either by her or by myself. I spent a day in Brighton delivering some of them, and four days more driving around the country calling upon old houses and leaving the crested envelopes with a variety of maids and manservants.

I lost count of the time that, accompanied by either Mary or Matthew, I drove down into Brighton. Servants were hired for three days from a new and rather fashionable business house that specialized in assisting with entertainments. From the same place I arranged to hire glasses, plates, napkins and in fact almost everything that was needed. Another day I waited at Brighton station for the arrival of the lamps ordered specially from London. We had to make two trips on that occasion, for there were eighty lamps and the carriage would not take them all. A man came up to Tancred to rivet them along the walls of the gallery, onto the places where once the original silver lamps had hung. The new ones were only gilt but they were made by a firm of craftsmen, and each one was slenderly designed with the outer globe of glass traced delicately in a design of ferns and tendrils.

I hired an orchestra of four musicians, and a piano was moved down from one of the attics. It took the tuner six days to make it fit to play upon. I ordered wines and sherrys to be sent up to the house and the only piece of sanity I saw in the month was when Reuben Tyler drove his cart right up to Tancred to deliver the order.

Each trip I made, each portion of money that I spent, was reported back to Mrs. Tancred in minute detail. She sat in her somber red and gilt room, listening, directing, making last minute readjustments, checking constantly to see if I had obeyed her instructions. She had an indefatigable memory and could recall not only each piece of furniture that remained in the house, but in what room it now resided. She had me draw a plan of the great gallery, then she told me what tables, screens, couches and so forth were to be moved down from the various old rooms and where, exactly, they were to be placed in the gallery. I grew to dread the mornings with her, each one a tiring examination of why this or that had not yet been accomplished.

On Wednesdays, Mrs. Thorburn, her daughter Mildred and the wavering Miss Timkins, would ride out to take tea with us. The play of the Chinese porcelain was repeated on each occasion, with Mrs. Tancred adopting social irrelevancies along with the fine china cups. The talk was all of the party, of what the ladies would wear, and of whom was going to come. Sometimes I wanted to stand up and scream that it was all foolishness, and that they had no idea what terrible madness they were bringing down upon themselves. There was no point in protesting, however, the days moved forward with inexorable relentlessness.

On the third Wednesday visit, Mrs. Tancred told me that I should escort the ladies to their conveyance. The formalities of farewell were said, leathery old cheeks brushing briefly against plump ones, and I led the ladies to the door.

'Miss Wakeford,' said Mrs. Tancred from her chair at the far side of the room. 'When you have seen Grace and dear Mildred safely on their way, I should like to see you again.'

I felt an increasing wave of the lethargy that was with me more and more these days. Too much of Mrs. Tancred tore at my control and I had hoped to have done with her leech-like presence that day. I listened with half an ear to the irrelevancies of Mrs. Thorburn, panting along the passage behind me.

'. . . *such* an event . . . no idea how quietly we live . . . *so* delightful for dear Mildred . . . company of people her own age . . .'

We came to the door and as I swung it open to allow the ladies through, Mrs. Thorburn's meanderings came to a fading halt. I heard a tiny gasp from Miss Timkins who was just in front of me and when, at last, I followed the ladies through the door, I saw the reason for the uneasy quietness of the party.

John Tancred was leaning lazily against the door of their carriage. He had placed himself deliberately so that his face was exposed at the worst possible angle, so that one's first view was only of his disfigurement.

Miss Timkins gave another shadowy little cry and I noticed Mrs. Thorburn turn to glare at her. John Tancred slowly unwound himself from the carriage door.

'Ladies,' he said smoothly and bowed slowly from the waist. Then he permitted himself to smile—a smile

156

so different from the one I had received on the Down the day we had ridden together, that I shuddered. It was a cold, one-sided smile that lifted the good side of his face and left the scar unaltered. It was done on purpose. I had seen him smile. I had seen him laugh. When he chose, he could overcome the cruelty of his face.

Mrs. Thorburn sailed down the steps, hand extended. 'My dear John,' she said throatily. 'It is quite years since I have seen you. Indeed you were only a boy and now, here you are, full grown and . . .'

She paused, not quite certain what to add. She had permitted her useless extravagances to run her into an awkward phrase. But I had to admire her just the same, for she gave no sign that John Tancred was different. She plucked her daughter forward by the arm.

'I expect you recall Mildred. You used to play together so prettily when you were small.'

Mildred did not have her mother's composure. Her slightly blotchy complexion had flamed to an unflattering plum color and she was looking very carefully away from his face.

'Dear Mildred,' purred John Tancred. 'You have hardly changed at all.' Whatever she might say in answer to that could only accentuate the fact that John Tancred had changed, and she wisely chose to remain silent. He took her hand and smiled again, forcing that horrible distorted smile right into her face so that she could not help but look at him. Mrs. Thorburn again flung herself majestically into the unpleasant calm that followed.

'Now, dear. We have to hurry away. But we are looking forward to a really long talk when we come to the entertainment next week.'

Then, to my astonishment, she stretched up, and standing on her toes, gave him a brief peck on the cheek. It was an address permitted by an older woman who had known him since childhood, but nevertheless

157

my admiration for her grew. Until now I had considered her only as a silly, overgarrulous woman, not understanding anything more serious than gossip and sentimental nonsense. I was wrong. She had the same veiled sense of purpose as had Mrs. Tancred, sharing with that indomitable old woman waiting for me upstairs, an ability to accept anything or anyone who would participate in her plans.

She pushed the fluttering Miss Timkins unceremoniously up into the carriage. It was as well the pathetic companion had not been introduced, for her nervous twitterings would have dwindled to petrified terror had she been obliged to stare much longer at the horror of John Tancred's face. The two other ladies climbed up and the coach set off down the hill, two plump hands waving out of the window. John Tancred watched them, a small gleam of appreciation showing in the darkness of his eyes. Then he turned to me.

'I suppose you are participating in this charade?' he asked coolly.

'I am employed to do as I am told.'

If it were possible for me to have felt even more miserable, I would have done so. I was enmeshed in a tangle of hopeless emotions and fears from which it was impossible to escape. I did not think, in spite of that strange day on the Down, that he cared for me. I did not think he was a man who could care for anyone. He was beyond such tenuous emotions as affection or tenderness. But I remembered what had happened on the promontory overlooking the sea. There was a boy beneath the smiling cynicism of the surly man, and even though he was incapable of love, I wanted nothing more than to see that he lived his life in the way he chose. He looked down at me quietly, inscrutably.

'Miriam . . .' He spoke softly, then reached down and touched my hand shyly with his fingers. Stupid, inexplicable tears suddenly welled up in my eyes and

158

he lifted his hand and touched one of them.

'Poor little Miss Wakeford,' he said softly. 'You should never have come here. And now you are trapped, are you not? Trapped in all the intensities of the Tancreds.'

I swallowed hard, then nodded, not trusting myself to speak.

His mood passed quickly as they always did.

'You had better go to my mother now.' He slumped tiredly against the door leaving me to do nothing else but go.

I had hardly opened the door of Mrs. Tancred's room when she snapped at me: 'Such a time you take, Miss Wakeford. I have been waiting for you a good fifteen minutes.' She pushed herself to the table and asked, 'Now then, was John at the door? Was my son there to see them go?'

'Yes, Marm.' I had not realized that John's presence had been part of the plan. Her face took on an added warmth.

'Good, good.' A doubt crossed her eyes and she added, 'Was he polite? He did not behave abruptly, Miss Wakeford?'

'He was polite, Marm.' I could not tell her that his very politeness had been an affront, a studied insult to the wishes of his mother. Something must have showed in my voice for she looked sharply at me, then she paused and said, almost apologetically, 'You think I am a crazy old woman, Miss Wakeford.'

'No, Marm.'

'You think I am mad to force my son into a marriage with Grace Thorburn's daughter.'

'It is not ...' I began, but she interrupted me forcefully.

'You have seen my son, Miss Wakeford, and you have seen the house.' She paused drily and added, 'We are not going to find many candidates who will care for a surly husband and a rotting home.'

She had never spoken like this before. Always she had maintained the illusion that Tancred was a place of splendor.

'Perhaps you are surprised that Grace Thorburn even entertains the proposition of encouraging her daughter to marry my son?'

I did not answer and she went on bluntly. 'Let us face it, Miss Wakeford, my son is no great catch; and the house in its present form, leaves a lot to be desired. But wait a while, let them see how the house can look and how, when there are lights and music, it is a place of magnificence.' She bent forward to me. 'Can you not see what a great house this is; what glory and splendor is here, just waiting for us to return in our strength and give ourselves back to the house?'

The familiar cold air moved over my body.

'When they see Tancred, with dancing and people moving about, they will understand. They will understand and she, Mildred, will want to come here as mistress of Tancred.'

'But thy son, perhaps he will not want to marry Mrs. Thorburn's daughter.'

'He will do as he is told,' she said angrily. 'Mildred is not such an ideal bride as we would like. She is not comely to look at, she has two children and she is over thirty. Moreover her late husband died of alcoholism. But it is these very things that make her suitable as a wife for my son. She knows full well that she will find it difficult to get a husband elsewhere. She, like my son, will have to take what she can get.'

She had not really answered my question and I asked again, 'But why should thy son obey thy wishes? He is a full-grown man and it seems, Marm, that he lives his life according to his own tastes.'

The old head, erect like that of a giant lizard, swiveled slowly and faced me. 'He knows his duty to the house,' she hissed. 'He will do as he is told.'

I began to appreciate, for the first time, that the

fanatical spirit of Mrs. Tancred could possibly make
everything happen just as she wished. The idea of two
misfitted people, similar only in their general ineli-
gibility and unattractiveness, being forced into a
union purely to ensure the line of Tancred, was repel-
lent to me. But it had an insane reasonableness about it
—an obviousness that could only have been born in the
mind of Mrs. Tancred. And with the same steadfast-
ness that she had waited for her hopes to materialize,
she would wait and plan ruthlessly for them to come to
fruition.

'And what of Esmee, Marm?'

Her eyes flickered slightly, then returned to deliberate obscurity.

'It was Esmee I wished to speak about. You must
ensure, Miss Wakeford, that Esmee is in bed well
before our small party commences next week. And
after, when Mrs. Thorburn and her daughter come out
to visit, which they will do more and more frequently,
you must see that Esmee remains absent.'

'And after ?'

She waited carefully before speaking. 'After my son
is married, Esmee can either be sent away, or moved to
the east wing where you will have complete control of
her.'

I felt sick. Even my own grandmother, who had no
great love for me, would not consider locking me away
as an embarrassment to other people. I reminded
myself that none of this could come to pass, that John
Tancred would never bring himself to marry. But
unbidden, my mind leapt forward to a life where I was
locked eerily in the east wing with Esmee Tancred,
growing old in the care of a strange child, watching a
man I cared for living in weird anonymity with his
unsuitable wife.

I had no ridiculous dreams for myself such as young
girls sometimes indulge themselves in. At the time of
Joseph Whittaker I had resigned myself to a life with

few friends and certainly no husband. I could not marry outside the Fellowship and no one inside would have me. But even so, I did not like the idea of passing my life at Tancred watching that unhappy, lonely man whom I loved, living in an enforced misery.

'And now, Miss Wakeford, let us go, once more, over the list of furniture to be carried down to the gallery.'

I picked up my pen and settled for another hour to bear with Mrs. Tancred's orders.

Two days before the party, the extra servants arrived at the house and events began to move rapidly. The floor in the gallery was waxed, the portraits dusted, the tables and chairs set in intimate groupings around the edge of the hall. Small retiring rooms to the left and right of the gallery were fitted out as best they could be. Five extra girls in the kitchen began to cook and Mary retreated into a non-committal silence from whence I could not draw her.

The musicians arrived at four on the afternoon of the entertainment and at five I began to look for Esmee with a growing sense of panic. She was not on the Down, nor by the Stones. Mary had not seen her, nor Math, nor John Tancred. The guests were bidden to arrive at nine o'clock, and at seven I was still searching, not knowing quite what to do if she could not be found. At last I returned briefly to my room and discovered her there, sitting on my bed, cross-legged and watching the door.

'You've been looking for me, haven't you Miss Wakeford?'

I was so relieved I didn't even have the temper to be angry. I hurried over and pulled her from my bed. She had soil from the hill over her shoes and it had come off on my pillow.

'It is time thee was in bed, Esmee.'

She rocked back delightedly, laughing softly to herself.

'You've been looking for me. *Grand-mère* is so frightened I'll come out and speak to you all. Do you know *Grand-mère* is afraid of me, Miss Wakeford?'

'Nonsense,' I said, taking her into her room and beginning to unbutton her dress. 'Now get thee undressed and I will see thee washes properly before thee goes to bed.'

I watched her prepare for the night, heard her say the simple prayer that exorcised her own particular ghosts and then pulled the covers back for her to get into bed.

'I shall stay with thee,' I said. I did not trust Esmee and I had no intention of leaving her until she was truly asleep. I took up a book and began to read. In the distance I could hear the movement of wheels on gravel as coaches began to arrive. The gallery was too far away for me to hear anything properly, but occasionally a dim chord of music would float along the silent passages, reminding me that the dancing would begin at any moment. There was the odd sound of china or pans being dropped in the kitchen and sometimes a voice as one of the hired servants hurried along between gallery and kitchen.

I stayed with Esmee until it was midnight. When I was sure she was asleep—her thin body was relaxed, her breathing slow and very soft—I closed the door of her room carefully and went into mine.

I had letters to write, books to read. I sat dutifully trying to fill my time with inconsequential thoughts and actions. At one o'clock I ceased pretending to myself that I was not interested in the happenings of the great gallery. I opened my bedroom door and moved quietly along the passages, following the sound of the music. There was a narrow balcony that ran along the upper wall of the gallery. A door from one of the upper passages opened straight onto it and I opened this and stepped onto the narrow ledge, moving quickly back against the wall in case anyone should look up and see me.

The scene in the hall below me was like a grotesque vision born in the mind of someone who hated men.

I remember once, in the village, when I had been delivering a dress to the doctor's wife, I had been asked to wait in the drawing room until it was convenient for me to be seen. There had been a picture on the wall. It was only a black and white drawing, but it had an arresting quality that drew my attention more than any colored paintings I had seen. It was a gathering of men and women in a London street and there was not a single good or beautiful thing in that drawing. All the faces were greedy or lecherous and all the bodies fat or evil—sometimes both. The doctor's wife had come in while I was staring at the picture and she had asked me if I admired the works of Mr. Hogarth. When I replied that I had never seen his drawing before, she fetched a book from the library and said I could borrow it if I wished. The pictures were all like the one on her drawing-room wall. The people were not always evil or greedy; sometimes they were stupid or diseased or poor, but the faces were always harsh, never kind or innocent.

Looking down at the guests in the long gallery, I thought it was one of those drawings come to life.

Of the eighty or so people gathered there, not more than ten were under the age of fifty. Most were considerably older than that. Indeed there was one old woman who was so decayingly ravaged that she must have been at least approaching ninety. She wore a wig of bright auburn piled high over a puckered mask of skin on which a face had been painted. The costumes—for I cannot call them dresses—had been pulled out of old trunks and were high-waisted in a fashion that had not been worn since the beginning of the century. It was a ghastly carnival of old women wearing girl's clothes.

The men in the room were few—old men die more quickly than old women—but those that were there showed the same moribund decay as their partners. Their clothes were not so easily dated, but the black coats hung like shrouds over withered shoulders and bandy legs. Yellow faces cackled nastily over glasses of punch and sherry. Crooked, wizened fingers were stuck playfully at scraggy throats encircled with cameos and bands of black ribbon. A few bent, distorted couples danced with capering madness to the incongruous music coming from the end of the hall.

I need not have worried about the condition of the house. The gallery and the guests were well matched. The broken walls, the outlandish collection of furniture, all of it old and most of it shabby, provided a fitting background for the caricature of humanity that paraded itself beneath mo.

Mrs. Thorburn, Mildred and Miss Timkins stood out amongst the guests only because they were not diseased or awaiting the presence of death; but some of the travesty of the other guests had rubbed off onto them.

At the center of the hall, presiding like some terrible queen at a witches sabbath, sat Mrs. Tancred. I suppose she was the most beautiful woman there, beautiful in a dreadful way. She wore a white dress, high-necked, long-sleeved and only a woman as bizarre as Mrs. Tancred would have dared to have worn such a gown and, having done so, not looked ridiculous. Her hands were stretched passively over a black and silver shawl that draped much of the wheelchair, and the combination of black, silver and white, together with her glittering erectness made me feel that at any moment, she would stand from her chair and glide across the floor.

It was a warm night, but the wind fluttered idly through the cracks in the walls, making old shoulders pucker slightly and table napkins stir in the breeze. The lamps, strikingly new against the poverty of the walls, lit the rows of portraits and gave them new colors and an animated life of their own. Indeed there seemed little difference between the portraits and the guests and I would not have been surprised to see one of the old men bow before a portrait and suggest they dance together.

With growing concern I searched amongst the figures on the floor, admitting to myself that I had come for only one reason: to see how John Tancred stood out in this company. He was not there. It was foolish of me to think I would not have seen him the moment I entered, for amongst the assembled guests he would have been instantly obvious.

Then Mrs. Tancred turned and beckoned in my direction and for one hot second I thought she had seen me. A figure moved out from beneath the balcony and I realized that John Tancred had been standing right below me.

He was magnificent. I had tried to imagine how he would look and now, seeing him, dark and big in a black suit and tucked white shirt, I felt a pounding in my throat—a pounding I had not felt since the first time I met Joseph Whittaker. He was taller and slimmer than he normally appeared and the white shirt set off the olive skin of his face. He was so fine it hurt me to look at him, and it was not merely because he was the youngest man in the room. I watched him for a long time and then I realized that I could no longer see his scar, although it was there. I had come to accept his face as it was so that now, when I looked at him, I saw only a smooth-skinned, dark-eyed man without blemish or disfigurement.

He walked slowly to where his mother sat and I noticed how the old men and women stared furtively at him and then quickly away. I had almost found it in my heart to pity Mrs. Tancred—to waste compassion on her for the macabre carnival she had assembled about her—but when I saw the way he walked through the curious eyes of his guests, my pity was all for him.

She drew him forward, making him stand by Mildred, trying to set some kind of gay conversation round the small group. He had the same unpleasant smile on his face that he had worn on the day when he had waited by their coach.

The horror of the whole room struck me afresh: the aging men and women called back from their graves to witness the ill-mating of an ugly man with an unattractive woman; and the entire formality presided over by a fanatical old woman in a white satin dress.

I turned away, sick of the music and people, wishing I had not come. As I reached my hand to the door I felt the first tendril of evil premonition steal into the gallery. The air became taut with apprehension and the old woman in the red wig laughed too loudly and too nervously at something that was not funny.

The music was still playing, but the musicians had unwittingly paid homage to the darkness of Tancred. Melodies that should have sounded gay were slow and heavy, making funeral pavanes of waltzes and polkas. The air was cold—colder than it should have been for September—and in the gap between two murmurs of music, I heard again the whine of the Tancred wind.

The old woman in the green dress was the first to notice something amiss. She had been on the point of lifting a glass to her lips, but her hand was arrested in mid-air. Her mouth, already shaped to sip the liquid in the glass, remained foolishly puckered as she stared up the length of the long gallery. Another ancient crone saw almost at the same time. She stopped in the middle of a conversation and, without looking at her companions, directed their attention to the other end of the room. The music faded weirdly away, the last chord of a violin echoing thinly through the air, and in the oppressive silence that followed, I could hear a sound so tiny, so minute, that at first it seemed no more than the humming of a small insect. I turned my head and looked to the end of the gallery.

Esmee Tancred, barefoot, with her black hair un-

braided down her back, stood waiting by the massive
iron door.

Carefully, moving on her toes, she weaved her way
delicately in and out of the guests. Her arms were
arched out in some kind of pattern by her side, and in
a curious, half-human rhythm she danced slowly up
along the gallery until she came to Richard Tancred's
portrait. The faint murmur of sound grew to a soft
singing and she stopped in front of the picture and let
her arms relax softly at her side. The whole room
waited, sensing something uncanny about the small,
bird-like figure of Esmee Tancred.

I stood paralyzed, holding my breath as though any
movement on my part would precipitate some violence
from the child staring at her grandfather's portrait. I
dared one look at Mrs. Tancred, then tore my eyes
away from her wax features and moving throat.

At some point, I cannot remember exactly when,
someone rustled a skirt, or perhaps the wind did it, but
the movement of hissing silk and the singing in front of
the portrait were the only sounds in the room.

Esmee began to laugh. Softly at first, without moving
her head, then the noise grew a little louder, a little
shriller and she hugged her thin arms to her sides and
rocked smoothly back, to and fro. When the first note
of a scream crept into her laughter, I was suddenly
able to move. I wrenched open the door of the balcony
and hurled myself headlong down the stairs and into
the gallery. By the time I got to Richard Tancred's portrait she was screaming—a wild, unbalanced noise
composed of fear and insane delight that threw her
head violently back with each fresh burst of sound.

I tried to hold her arm but she broke away from me,
running up the length of the gallery, the old men and
women drawing back from her as she passed. I called
but she laughed again and ran in and out of the tables
to avoid me. It was the running dream, the dream that
everyone has at sometime during their life: either

running towards something that moves away, or fleeing from an unpleasant thing behind. For me it was a garish combination of both, for although I was chasing Esmee, there was also something in the gallery that seemed to pursue me.

Every so often she would allow me to draw close enough to reach out my hand, then she would dart quickly away, laughing, singing, watching me with her bright malevolent eyes. I heard John Tancred shout, but she took no notice except that her actions revealed an added glee. He shouted again, and the next time she swung away from me he stepped abruptly forward and grasped her firmly under one arm.

The old men and women watched us silently as we hurried along the gallery. John Tancred, the child now passive under his arm, strode angrily towards the door and I followed close behind with the growing realization that the whole affair had been my fault. I should not have left Esmee, not even to go to my room. Surely by now I knew that her perverseness would delight in the scene she had just provoked.

The walk down the gallery was the longest of my life. The room was no longer so silent, whispers blew softly about the portraits. Old eyes watched the three of us and old memories drew forgotten pieces of scandal from the corners of Tancred.

I looked neither to right nor left. I kept my eyes fixed firmly on the dark coat covering John Tancred's shoulders and told myself that the walk must soon come to an end.

We reached the door, and once on the other side, he made no attempt to stop, but raced along the passages and up the stairs until we came to Esmee's room. He kicked the door violently with his foot, strode through and dropped Esmee on the bed. Then he turned to me with a face so furious that I backed against the door.

'You fool! You crazy fool,' he shouted. 'What on earth possessed you to leave her?'

'She was asleep. I thought . . .'

'Surely by now you have learned never to believe anything Esmee does or says! Can you not even be trusted to look after a twelve year old child?'

The first points of anger edged slowly into my mind. He was hardly fair. At one time he told me to leave her to her own devices, at another he accused me of neglecting her.

'I am sorry,' I said. 'I should not have left her, but I had no reason to think she would behave as she did.'

He swung savagely across the room and kicked over a small wicker stool that stood in his way.

'You think too much! You come here believing that kind words and soft deeds will put the world to rights. And all the time you cannot even control my daughter.'

The thread of calm in my mind snapped suddenly, worn to shreds by the strains of the evening, and I knew the glorious freedom of losing my temper. 'No I cannot!' I shouted back at him. 'I cannot control Esmee because no one has tried to control her until now. She has been left to run without discipline or manners for twelve years, and now thee—all of thee here in this house—expect me to put the matter to rights in a few months.' I stopped to draw breath, shaking at my own temerity, but still angry enough to go on.

'And then thee has the impertinence to blame me for thine own shortcomings.'

I thought he was going to hit me. He raced back across the width of the room and stood right over me, where I gazed up at him from the welcome support of the door.

'And what should I have done? Tell me that, you who believe your God has all the answers. Go on, Miss Wakeford. Tell me what I should have done!'

A small nerve was trembling at the side of his brow but by now I didn't care anymore. I had gone too far to stop.

'Thee could have taught her to honor her father and

her grandmother, to have respect for things and people about her.' My legs were shaking, but I am not sure whether it was from anger or fright; I could hear myself shouting defiantly into the room.

'Does thee know, John Tancred, when I came here she could not even say her prayers?'

'And you set great store by prayers, do you not, Miss Wakeford?'

'They are better than nothing!'

He grasped hold of my wrist and bent my hand back against the wood of the door. 'You believe in prayers and all the nonsense of "Thou shalt not kill" and "Honor thy father and mother," don't you?'

'Yes!' I screamed back at him:

He pinned me back against the door and suddenly thrust his scarred, distorted face right up close to me. The livid skin was no more than half an inch away.

'And would you honor a father who did this to you, Miss Wakeford?' he shouted. 'Tell me! Tell me if you would love and cherish a man who did this to his own son?' He put his hand up to his face and pulled the disfigured cheek right around into the light.

'Look at me. Look and see what my father did to me, and then tell me again that I should teach Esmee the Commandments!'

I closed my eyes, wanting to bring my hands up to cover my face, but I was held too rigidly to allow such a movement. He shook me roughly by the shoulder and there was such vitriolic hate in his voice that I was afraid to open my eyes.

'Why do you close your eyes, Miss Wakeford? Can you not bear to see what a beloved father did to his son—his eighteen year old son— Miss Wakeford? Eighteen, the same age as you are now. Look, Miss Wakeford. Look at me. I order you to open your eyes!'

I opened them, but his face was blurred and watery.

'Are you listening?' he asked hoarsely. I nodded and he went on. 'You must listen, Miss Wakeford, for I

171

doubt you have heard anything like this before. You see when I was eighteen I was old enough to hate him, old enough to see what he did to my mother, and to Mary, and to everyone else who came to this house. Are you listening, Miss Wakeford?'

'I can hear thee,' I sobbed.

'Good. I want you to hear. When I told him what a brutal, evil man he was he picked up a lamp and threw it at me. You understand, don't you? The lamp was alight and it was my father who threw it.'

'I understand,' the words came out of a choking throat.

'I am glad you understand, Miriam Wakeford, for now you will not tell me what I should teach my daughter.'

He let go of my shoulder suddenly and stepped back, and I was able to turn my face against the door and weep. The misery that welled up in me was not only for him, but for me and for my mother, for Grandfather, for Esmee, and for the old woman in the white satin dress. I cried until I had no tears left in me; and when my heart was empty, I felt a strange soothing peace enter the room and settle around the silence. Nothing happened except the patient clicking of Esmee's small clock on the dresser. I turned at last and saw his face. He was staring at me, shocked and disbelieving. The rage had gone from his eyes and he had the bewildered look of a man who has been caught in something he does not understand.

'Miriam?' he said slowly.

I tried to straighten my collar and tuck the bands of my cap away. He frowned and raised his hand diffidently to touch mine.

'I did not mean . . .'

'It does not matter,' I said quickly. I could stand no more raw emotion that night.

'I had no right to say . . . to say what I did. I know you do what you can for Esmee. It was not your fault. What

172

happened tonight was not your fault.'

There was shame in his voice and I could not bear to hear it. I loved him so much that it hurt me to see his confusion and distress.

'Thee must not worry. I was lacking in my duty, and indeed, I know it is my fault that the party is ruined.'

He shrugged disparagingly and made a small noise of disgust. 'I have no care at all what happens to that foolish collection of men and women downstairs.'

'Then why . . .?'

'Have you any idea, Miss Wakeford, how my mother has relived her girlhood with this party? They are useless people and they deserve whatever upset they have suffered tonight. But I wish my mother had not seen it.'

I could hardly believe that he did not know why the party had been assembled, the real reason for the reception of guests. He must have read my thoughts for he smiled bitterly and added, 'I am not sure quite how far I would be prepared to go, merely to satisfy the ambitions of that unhappy woman. At least I thought I could do no less than participate in some of her more harmless wishes.'

'And Mrs. Thorburn, and Mildred?'

The smile faded quickly. His mouth looked pinched. 'I have a little dignity left, Miss Wakeford, and I am not unaware of the ludicrous nature of what was planned for me.'

I made no answer. I heard a tiny laugh from the bed and realized with appalling clarity that Esmee had been watching and listening to the entire scene.

'Thee had better go now,' I said quickly to John Tancred. 'I suppose thy mother will want to see me.'

He opened the door, then looked back and shook his head. 'She knows there is nothing to be done now. I think perhaps she knew all along that there was nothing to be done.'

He left me and I had to turn and face that gloating child sitting on the bed. The evening had been one of unsurpassed delight for her. Whatever John Tancred said, I knew that Esmee was not insane in the ordinary meaning of the word. She was too clever, too weirdly old for those poor folk to whom that word usually applies. She lived in some horrible reach where she found pleasure in tormenting others. When she chose to, she could pretend an act of normality, but it was always to further some uncanny scheme of hers. I think I was more afraid of Esmee than of any of the others in that house.

'Were you upset, Miss Wakeford?' she said sweetly.

'Get into bed, Esmee.'

She smiled nastily at me. 'You were afraid, weren't you? Down there in the gallery, you were all afraid of what I would do next.'

I wished she would not always stare at me. It reminded me of a stoat waiting at the entrance to the run of a small, soft animal.

'Grand-mère was frightened too. She was worried in case I said something about Grandfather.' She laughed quietly to herself, hugging her throat with thin, tight hands. I had been folding her cover back and I stopped and looked at her.

'But Esmee, I thought thee was afraid of thy grandfather?'

She shook her head. 'Oh no, Miss Wakeford, not any more. Not since you taught me the words. Now there is no one I am afraid of.' She began to sing her unpleasant French melody, then suddenly she stopped.

'He is dead. Grandfather is quite dead. I saw them bury him up on the Loxham hill.'

Something struck suddenly at my bemused mind, something that would reveal itself to me soon.

'Thee has ruined the party, Esmee, so it does not matter what thee does now. Stay in bed or not, as thee wishes.' I pulled the covers up.

Her eyes gleamed at me, then she lost interest and thumped her head down into the pillow. When I left she was singing again.

In the gallery, events had come to a hasty conclusion. The women were fetching their cloaks and old men waited by the doors for the coaches to be brought around from the back. Mrs. Tancred was nowhere to be seen, she had left them all to make their departures as they chose. Fragments of whispers and laughs floated across the hall ... 'Like the old man ...' 'We remember when ...' 'The money has all gone ...' 'Him too, he is strange like the rest ...' 'So ugly, coming to a party when he looks so horrible ...'

Mrs. Thorburn, Mildred and Miss Timkins, already caped, sat stiffly on small Malacca chairs waiting for their carriage. Miss Timkins had been crying and had an even more watery look about her. One of the hired servants hurried over and spoke to Mrs. Thorburn, apparently telling her that the conveyance had come, for they stood quickly and walked towards the door, passing me on the way.

Mrs. Thorburn hesitated when she saw me, then came over. 'I am sorry for you, Miss Wakeford. I realize now what an unpleasant task you have, living in this house with ...' she paused, then added, 'with this family.'

Mildred, in a lavender dress and gray cape, tried to pull her mother away, but Mrs. Thorburn was set on speaking her piece.

'I was prepared to overlook much, Miss Wakeford. The dilapidation of the house, the general disfavor of the family, even that poor, afflicted man. But there are some things we cannot take and I advise you to get away from here before you end up like the rest of them.'

Mildred tugged again at her mother's sleeve. 'Come away, Mother, please. Let us leave now, at once.'

She grimaced a weak smile of distant dislike at me and at last persuaded Mrs. Thorburn to leave. They hurried down the steps, into the early morning light and away down the grassy track.

Slowly, a few at a time, each decrepit little group dispersed: quavering voices and pinched cheeks huddled up in the coldness of dead festivities. The last beady old gentleman giggled back into the gallery, then hurried down the steps, leaving me and the hired servants to clear everything away. The men and girls who had come two days previously to help prepare, now looked at me with open insolence. They had received their payment and they had no loyalty to a family that was so obviously impoverished. The general malaise of the evening had not been lost upon them, and with the superiority of all servants who discover their masters are no better than they themselves, their derision of the whole affair was open and aggressive. As soon as they had packed all the cutlery and glass, all the hired equipment, they hurried away down the hill in the big cart that had brought them.

I waited by the door until they had completely disappeared, then I turned back into the gallery to see that Mary had just come in at the other end.

'She's gone to her room,' she said nervously. 'She says everything is to be put back exactly as it was, all the tables and chairs taken away as though nothing had happened.'

I stared uncomprehendingly at her for a moment until the meaning of the words penetrated. 'But the servants,' I protested. 'They have all gone.'

Mary nodded miserably. 'I told her they was going but it makes no difference. It's all got to be the same as it was.'

'Will Math help us?'

'He's gone. So has Mr. John. I saw them saddle and ride up over the Down.'

The selfish uselessness of men struck me, even at that emotion-charged time. Mary and I looked bleakly into each other's faces, waiting for the other to say the tiring words. In the end it was I who shrugged and bent to pick up a canebacked chair.

'Then I suppose we shall have to do it ourselves.'

None of the furniture was really heavy, but most of it came from rooms at the top of the house. Mary was stronger than I and could sometimes carry two chairs at a time. I tried to balance a small, side table on top of a chair, but the journey, up three flights of stairs and along an interminable length of passage, took so long I decided it was quicker to carry one piece at a time. There was a couch which we foolishly left until the end. It took both of us to lift it and by this time we were so tired that we could easily have sat on the stairs and gone to sleep.

We came back to the gallery after the last trip and stared wearily at the empty room.

'What about the lamps?'

I looked up at the gilt lamps. Now that the gallery was empty and denuded of furniture, they appeared even newer and more out of place against the walls.

'There is nothing we can do. Leave them.'

We moved slowly up the gallery, reaching up to each shining globe and shutting the wicks until only a faint, smoky scent of oil was left in the air. Mary had a streak of dirt across her face, and under my left arm I could feel a tear in my dress that had been the result of getting the couch up the stairs.

We shut the door on the gallery and slumped tiredly back along the passages. When we reached the kitchen Mary leaned against the door and said wearily, 'I'm going to bed.'

'Mary, did . . . did she say anything about me?'

She looked back at me, expressionless. 'No.'

'Not that she wanted to see me?' I asked apprehensively.

'She said no one is to go near her. She is in her room and no one is to go in.'

Miserably I turned to go.

'Goodnight, Mary.'

She nodded heavily, and still uncertain, I asked, 'Are

thee sure? She said nothing about the blame of the evening being upon me?'

Mary put her hand up to her face and smudged the dirty streak further across her cheek. 'No,' she said apathetically. 'And what does it matter now anyway?'

She shut the door and I went back to my room. I was tired, very tired but I did not go to bed. I changed my dress and put my cape around my shoulders. Then I went softly out into the passage and hurried towards the door. The house was quiet and empty and its very emptiness held a note of warning. The macabre night was not yet finished and the walls vibrated with grim anticipation. I left the house and hurried down the hill to the Loxham path.

I could not sleep, not yet. There was something I had to do; for the words of Esmee Tancred had opened a small, revealing crack in the mask of silence that shrouded the house.

9

Sometimes we stand so close to something—some particular thing or person—that although we constantly see and observe it, the apparentness of the object is lost upon us.

Every time I went down to the village, I had noticed the small church and surrounding graveyard; but not until Esmee Tancred had spoken of her grandfather's burial, had the significance of the burial ground dawned upon me.

The Loxham church was a comparatively new one, well built with a neat and tidy graveyard. I suppose that instinctively, I had known that the Tancreds would not lie in such a comfortably normal place. But above the village, on the first of the inland hills, was the old church—a ruin of greenish stone around which were scattered the remnants of old headstones and older tombs. And it was here, naturally enough, that the Tancreds had chosen to hide after death.

I crossed the village street and took the faintly discernible track up the side of the opposite hill. The first few hundred yards were well worn but then it petered out and I had to stumble over the rutted ground as best I could. It was early morning; the gray light hung ahead on the hill, and for the moment, the wind had dropped.

Landmarks set upon hills are always misleading in their distance. From Loxham, the ruined chapel seemed only a short way up the hill; but now that I was climbing towards it, it seemed constantly to recede before me and it was a good hour before I at last reached the first tumble of stones. A broken, but

179

clearly defined wall surrounded the burial ground. In some places it had disappeared completely while in others it remained perhaps four or five feet high; and in the center of the mourning stones stood the bones of the church: small, very small, without roof or doorways.

I sat on the wall for a few moments. I was so hot from the climb that I even welcomed the return of the wind as it started to blow in with the turn of the morning seas. The lack of sleep and the frightening episodes of the night made my eyes feel hollow and gritty. I was not even allowing myself to think about what I might find. From the very air about me I knew that I would soon understand the shadow I had been living with for the past months. I stood and walked towards the first group of headstones.

Some of them were so old they were nearly buried, leaving only a small bump of stone standing above the mound. The name Tancred appeared again and again; indeed they seemed to monopolize the hill. There was a family called Perrepont who must have lived hereabouts at one time, but they died out some fifty years before. There were no later tombs for them.

I wandered slowly from stone to stone, feeling myself caught up inextricably in the moody past of the family I now worked for. 'Elizabeth Tancred, aged three, died of a wet fever, February, 1812'; a little further on she was joined by a brother and two sisters, Simon, aged six, Mary and Catherine, one aged four, the other six months, all died of a wet fever in February, 1812; and I wondered what sad epidemic had robbed an unhappy Tancred mother of four of her children. One gravestone was so old that the wording was covered in green mold. I knew it could not possibly be the grave of Richard Tancred, but nevertheless, I picked up a stone and scraped the slimy moss away. Only the letters T. . . . R. . . . were visible and the arm of the R. was broken. The graves were mostly of children and women,

Tancred men more often being killed at wars or at sea. All the mounds were untended, but on the Downs this was not quite so disastrous as it would have been in valley graves. The short hill grass was shared only by moss and there were no nettles and weeds to smother the graves.

I came around the side of the ruin, wondering just where Richard Tancred could be buried and a little way above me, saw a headstone that was still white enough to be recent. With thudding expectancy I read the inscription:

Richard, husband and father,
Master of Tancred. Departed
this life, 8th October, 1892.

It told me nothing—nothing except that Richard Tancred had died six years ago. There was no message of remembrance, no details of his passing; only the brief acknowledgement that he had lived and died. I began to search again, for there should be another grave that was not too old—the grave of Esmee's mother—although if Richard Tancred's passing was marked so tersely on his tomb, I did not expect any further revelations from the grave of his daughter-in-law.

I wandered from grave to grave, carefully reading every one. At the end of an hour I returned to my starting point and methodically examined each grave again, determined to be sure I had missed none of them. Esmee's mother was not there.

The morning was well-advanced and it was a dull, gray day with a pall of dampness in the wind. I looked across to the Tancred Down, to where the big chalk crack cut the hill in a bone-white scar. On the other side of that ugly cliff lay the house, implacable and withdrawn, hiding a secret that I knew I must unravel.

John's wife, Esmee's mother: the body of that sad, unspoken creature must lie somewhere, but it was not here in this mausoleum of Tancred history. Uneasily I wondered if she were really dead or if, like the terrible wife in Miss Brontë's *Jane Eyre*, she was locked away in one of the forbidden rooms of the east wing. It was a foolish thought and I shook myself briskly, climbed through a break in the intermittent wall and prepared to walk home.

On the other side of the wall, standing in lonely silence on the unconsecrated hillside, was the grave of Esmee's mother.

Rachel Tancred, Died 8th October, 1892.

That was all. It was even briefer than Richard Tancred's memorium but it told me more, much more than that other grave, respectably surrounded by its fellow dead. She had died on the same day as the evil man whose presence hung about the walls of Tancred. I had been vaguely and obscurely told that they had both died 'some years back' but no one could possibly forget a double death of such magnitude. And whatever had caused Rachel's demise, it had not been because she was a poor, sickly creature. She lay outside the precincts of the church, forgotten, and, by the teachings of the established church, unblessed.

I hurried down the hill, tripping on stones and tussocks as the steepness of the ground flung me forward too quickly. A shepherd passed me with his dog and the huge shaggy beast sniffed warningly at my skirt. The shepherd called to the dog, 'Heel, boy, heel,' and they both looked curiously at me as I went on my way. There were people in the Loxham street and from their glances I guessed that news of the strange happenings of the previous night were beginning to seep down into the village. The hired servants would have been only too pleased to add their store of rumors to those already in existence. There were one or two sniggers from the children, but most were afraid I think, and hurried away, anxious that I should not speak to them.

Now I was truly tired. I had walked seven miles and still had the long climb back to the house. I remembered that I had not eaten since the previous night and it would be well into the afternoon before I got back to Tancred. When I came through the Down, the sea was flecked with foam, its somber green preparing to blow up into a high water; thankfully I turned my back on it and climbed up to the house.

Everything was silent, calm with the insanity of a deserted house. At three o'clock in the afternoon, no place should be so quiet—so devoid of living creatures. Mrs. Tancred's door was implacably closed to me; I dared not even try to go in. Esmee had vanished and there was no movement from either the stables or John Tancred's rooms. I went into the kitchen. Mary must have risen at some time, for a tray of dirty cups rested on the table. But now, she too, had hidden herself in some private part of the house. I cleaned the cups, then sat at the table and ate a slice of bread, thinking hard all the time about the mystery of the graves on the Loxham hill.

The silence of the house was oppressive. I banged the big kettle and put extra fuel noisily on the stove, but the sounds vanished, sucked away into the heavy air. Finally I unlatched the door and looked up to the hill. There was still one thing I had to do. Whatever mystery lay buried with Richard and Rachel Tancred, the answer would be in the east wing; and now, while it was still daylight, was the time to see what evil secret was locked in that derelict quarter.

I walked the length of the building, my steps growing slower as I neared the crumbling stone of the forbidden wing. The door at the far end was still loose, banging open and shut in the wind and creaking faintly on broken hinges. I waited for a long time by the door, wondering if it were a sensible thing to do. I was almost tempted to go back—to leave whatever black secret lived inside—and continue my life at Tancred with the mystery unsolved. But Richard Tancred and Esmee's mother had died on the same day, and John Tancred had a face that was brutally marked by his father. Mrs. Tancred lived in the past, Esmee lived in fantasy. I wanted to know what drove everyone here to madness before I too, was sucked into the labyrinth.

The passage was a narrow one. It turned after a few yards and led, as far as I could see, into a larger corridor joining the rest of the hallways running through the house. Off to the left was a steep, narrow flight of steps; an oak door barred the way at the top. There was no rail up by the side of the steps and I rested my hand against the cold wall until I came to the door. It was not locked and it led, in turn, to another small passage and yet another door. I had a sudden uneasy notion, born of hysterical fear, that there was no room in the east wing, only stairs and doors leading to stairs. I came to the second door, hesitated, then pushed it open.

There was nothing there. Only a huge dark room filled with misshapen furniture and lit by a small window high up on the wall. I am not sure quite what I had expected to find, but the simplicity of an empty bedroom both relieved and dismayed me. There was a small painting on the wall—only a tiny one—of a young woman, pale-skinned and dark-eyed; I crossed the room to stand beneath it. A brass plaque had been riveted to the base of the frame and although it was corroded, the word 'Rachel' was clearly visible. The face told me nothing. It was merely the portrait of a pretty woman painted by an artist who brought no more than flattery to his work.

Dust hung in the air. It lay thickly on wardrobes, dressers and chairs. A heavy fourposter bed was coated with gray particles that covered velvet and linen alike. A cape lay flung across a chair and that too was coated with grime.

I was foolish to think there was nothing there, for as I

looked about the room I became eerily aware that the presence of Rachel Tancred lingered aromatically about me.

A pair of slippers stood by the side of the bed. A hairbrush upturned on a dresser as though hastily put down. A mirror tilted forward so that a face could be more easily seen.

I was afraid to move—afraid that sudden noise or action might drive her away—for she was there. I had seen her grave on the hill, but she was there with me in the room. I moved softly to the dresser. Three hairpins lay in careless disorder, a crumpled handkerchief to one side. The finger of a lilac glove hung carelessly out of an unshut drawer. The mirror was dirty, coated in six years of decaying grime, but I could dimly see the outline of my face.

Something moved behind me. A hand reached up in the mirror and touched my neck. I could not even scream. The muscles of my throat had contracted into dry silence. I wanted to turn around, but again I could not. I prayed, or at least I think I did. Mostly I was aware of the blood draining away from my body in a flood of fear.

'You've been wanting to come here for a long time, haven't you, Miss Prissy?'

The hand on my neck turned from a ghostly member into the living, fat palm of Matthew Johnson; with the realization that the intruder was a human one, I began to tremble.

'I've seen you snooping about the place in your black frock, asking questions and trying to find out.'

I twisted to face him. His eyes were mean, red with the remembered beating he had received at the hands of John Tancred. When I struggled and tried to pull away from his hand he let go at once.

'Don't worry, little crow. I don't want you, nor never did. You'll have no excuse to run saying Math Johnson attacked you this time.'

185

He spoke softly, carefully controlled as though anxious not to draw attention to his presence in the building.

'Why has thee followed me here?' I was still shaking, but now that the sudden unknown horror had been transformed into the ordinary menace of Matthew Johnson, I was prepared to stand my ground. He leaned back against a wardrobe and grinned at me.

'Well now, I might ask why "thee" came here in the first place.' He spoke jeeringly, rubbing his hand up and down the side of his leather breeches.

'I came because . . .' I did not know how to finish.

'Oh aye, I know full well why you came. Don't think I've not noticed you prying and pushing about the place, pumping Mary with your questions and writing letters to find out about us. Yes, Miss Prissy,' he said as I gasped angrily at his mention of my letters. 'You don't think old Math carries your letters up to the house without finding out what's going on in that stupid little head of yours.'

'Thee had no right to read my letters,' I burst out furiously.

He put his hand in his pocket and grinned again. 'No? And you had no right to poke your fingers into business that don't concern you.'

I crossed the room to go toward the door. Quickly he took his hands from his pockets and barred my way.

'Let me pass.'

'Oh no, little black crow. You came here to find out didn't you? And Math is going to help you. Math is going to tell you what you want to know.'

He took a step towards me and I backed into the room. His big hands hung loosely by his side.

'What is thee going to do?' I asked nervously. He laughed, the big, booming laugh that I hated so much.

'I'm not going to *do* anything. I'm just going to have a little talk with you, to satisfy that curiosity of yours. You want to know, don't you?'

Suddenly I didn't. The room had its secrets and I didn't want to hear them. I had a quick premonition that if I became a participant in the malady of Tancred, everything in my life would change.

'I want to leave.'

He backed me farther into the room, not touching me but merely making me move by the menace of his fat body. 'Perhaps you do, perhaps you do,' he said huskily. 'But not yet, not until Math has had a little talk, for you've had such a busy day, haven't you? Wandering about the graveyard looking at the tombstones, trying to find Rachel Tancred's grave when it wasn't there at all.'

'Oh, but it was,' I answered quickly, without thinking, and at the triumphant gleam in his eye I wished I had not spoken.

'So, you found it did you? Lying out on the hill right away from the others. And you know why, don't you Miss Prissy? You know why the church won't have Rachel Tancred in its graveyard.'

He was still making me move backwards into the room and my heel bumped against the dresser. I could move no further away from him or from his evil face smiling down into mine.

'Come now, tell old Math you understand.'

There was a painful throbbing just above my eyes. It hurt to look at his face and I turned my head to one side.

'Look at me now, straight at me.' He turned my face towards him carefully and went on, 'That's right. Now, you just tell me why Rachel Tancred is buried alone on a hill, instead of nice and cozy with the rest of the family.'

The throbbing turned into a pain stretching right around the inside of my head. 'I want to leave!' I said again and this time my voice sounded higher than it should have. He began to grow angry; beads of sweat stood out on his forehead and chin, the small eyes tightened.

'Not yet, Missy, not yet. Not till you've answered my question. Answer me now, answer! Why is she buried alone on the hill?'

'Because she killed herself!' I shrieked. I no longer had control over my voice. I did not care what I did or said any more. I only wanted to leave the room and to get away from the gloating face of Matthew Johnson. He relaxed slightly when I answered him and his voice dropped to a thick whisper.

'That's right,' he purred. 'A suicide. Right here in this room, at night, when it was dark. Perhaps I'll keep you here till it's dark, Miss Wakeford. Then I'll tell you exactly what happened.'

By now it was dark in the room anyway. I looked up at the small window and saw the wind moving the faded curtains. Clouds of thick dust eddied slowly out into the room and the thin whine of the breeze hovered in forgotten corners. I shuddered.

'You don't like the wind, do you?'

I didn't answer.

'She didn't like it either,' he said softly. 'She hated it, but it got her in the end.' His hand closed tightly over my wrist and he breathed heavily into my face.

'Right up there. See, up in the beam. The wind got her, all right. Look, Miss Wakeford. Look up at the beam and you can see her.'

The pain in my head broke violently into a myriad of light and noise. I closed my eyes tightly, trying not to see the raftered ceiling of the room, trying not to hear the words crawling from Math Johnson's mouth. He was entranced by the vision of his own description.

'To and fro, to and fro,' he said hoarsely, staring into the distance at nothing. 'And the old man standing at the top of the stairs, laughing. Laughing so hard I thought he would burst.'

A vivid recollection flashed instantly through my mind. Esmee, the first day I had come to Tancred, standing outside watching the unhinged door swinging

188

in the wind, using the same horrible words. 'To and fro, to and fro.' Rachel Tancred was a forbidden subject in this house, her songs were sung only to annoy, her language disliked and ignored.

Through the heavy, cloying silence of the room I was aware of Math's labored breathing. He had released my hand and he stood, captured by his private vision, staring up at the beam. Inexorably and unwillingly, my eyes moved to the same spot, to the thick, dark rafter in the center of the room. Another sudden gust of wind shook the air into a swirl of dust around the beam. It hung for a moment, then moved, swayed and dispersed. Ice tightened the pit of my stomach and crawled up the skin on my back.

On the other side of the room a small dark shape darted swiftly from behind a wardrobe. A noise like a scurrying thing made us both turn from our vigil of the beam.

Esmee, like a small black insect, slid across the room to the door. She was no longer a child, not even a strange, perverse child of Tancred. She was a ghost, a macabre reminder of her mother. At the door she paused and looked back. 'I saw them,' she said simply. 'I saw what happened. And after.'

She began to laugh again, the way she had laughed in the gallery. Then she slammed the door upon us and I heard her running down the stairs laughing louder, more wildly. Matthew Johnson's face was white.

'Catch her!' he hissed. 'Catch her quick before she does something crazy.'

The spell of the room vanished. Esmee's shoes running down the stairs brought me terrifyingly back to the danger of the present. She had watched and listened while Matthew Johnson had talked me into a ghastly trance and now she was away, running wildly out of the house, away from the dream he had evoked.

Together we ran across the room. The door was jammed and he pushed me roughly out of the way and wrenched it open. 'You first,' he shouted. 'You catch her. She'll listen to you.'

My skirt caught in my shoe and I finished the descent of the stairs in a stumbling run. I could see her outside, darting up the hill and every so often she would stop and look back.

'Esmee, Esmee!'

I began the climb, running as fast as I could against the rise of the hill. Somewhere behind me I could sense Matthew Johnson lumbering grossly over the grass but he could not run as quickly as I.

'Wait. Esmee, wait for me!'

My chest hurt but I dared not stop for I sensed this was no ordinary chase, no teasing whim of Esmee's merely to annoy and provoke me. I pressed my hand to the side of my ribs and tried to force my body into a faster speed. The distance between us was growing and she was nearly at the top of the Down. I heard another voice behind me; someone shouted, and dimly I recognized John Tancred calling, but what or to whom I could not tell.

Now she was at the top of the hill and she stopped. For one blessed second I thought she was going to let me catch her and persuade her back to the house. She watched me panting up the steep rise, then she called again, thinly down the hill. 'I saw. I saw what happened,' and she was off once more, running faster and faster, straight into the Stones.

'Esmee. Please come back. Please, Esmee!'

Deep sobs dragged at my throat, burning my chest with hot pain. Now I did not even have the strength to hold my hand against my side. I just stumbled forward, calling to her whenever I could tear the breath from my lungs.

'Esmee!'

She was through the Stones and I knew where she was running. I had known when we were still at the bottom of the hill. The chalk crack lay ahead, high

190

against the sky and four hundred feet above the valley floor. My running turned into a driving panic. Hysteria and choking fear pushed me forward. 'Oh Lord, let me stop her! Please Lord, let me stop her!'

She was standing there on the edge of the cliff watching me stumble towards her, watching me pray with sobbing urgency. She waited until I came up to her, close, within arms reach, then she smiled smoothly and held out her arm. 'Here, Miss Wakeford,' she said sweetly.

I raised my hand slowly to hers, watching her all the time, trying, by the sheer strength of my will to keep her quiet on the edge of the chalk. My hand was six inches away from hers, then three. Lightly my fingers brushed against hers and swiftly I grasped the palm of her hand in mine.

I still dream about what happened next. I wake at night with sweat across my hands and fear pulling at my throat. I have tried to tell myself she did not mean to do it, she was not aware of what was happening, but I know in my heart that when Esmee Tancred jerked suddenly at my hand and then jumped sickeningly into the screaming air, she meant me to die with her.

It seemed to happen slowly. At one moment I was holding her hand, at the next I was lurching over the edge of the crumbling chalk, groping desperately with my left hand for something to stop the crazy suction down into the rocks. My fingers curled frantically over a jutting peak of chalk, gripped, held, and then felt the chalk disintegrate into nothing. At some point Esmee's hand came apart from mine. I think I must have pulled so hard she could no longer keep me in her insane grip. My leg hit something hard, slid slightly but stayed. I clung holding to nothing, digging my fingers into crumbling soil and I watched the body of Esmee Tancred, twisting slowly, arms outstretched like a seagull, down, gracefully down, to the bottom of the valley. The gliding, black shadow turned into a silent speck that did not move.

'Help me, Lord. Help me.'

It was half a ledge, half a boulder and already it was beginning to break around the edge. I tried to move, to find something stronger to hold onto, but with every movement the chalk rattl'ed away down the hill and I slid a little further. Carefully I twisted my head and looked up toward the sky. Matthew Johnson, his mouth bloodless in a white face, gazed down from the edge of the cliff. 'Don't move,' he said hoarsely.

I dared not even speak in case the muscles of my face started the soil in another crumbling fall. I stared back into his eyes, begging him to help me, pleading for him to save me somehow from joining the body of Esmee Tancred on the floor of the valley.

John Tancred fell forward against the lip of the cliff so suddenly that grass and chalk fell down onto my face and I screamed to him to keep still. He was six feet above me, but I could see his mouth shaking violently in a rigid face.

'Can you move?'

I shook my head dumbly, terrified to speak again. Math, his eyes glazed, turned to John Tancred. 'I'll get help. I'll get a rope.'

'There isn't time. It's crumbling too quickly. Look.'

They disappeared from the edge of the cliff, went away and I was alone with nothing above me and great distances of sucking space beneath me.

'Oh Lord. Help me!' I knew I must not cry. Tears might make the ledge disappear even more quickly. 'Keep still, keep still.'

John Tancred looked over the edge again. He had taken his coat off and foolishly I noticed that his shirt sleeve was torn. 'Miss Wakeford,' he whispered. 'I am passing my coat down. We have tied the two together and you must try to grasp hold of the sleeve. Do you understand?'

I nodded.

'Good. Try not to move too much. When you are holding tightly onto the sleeve I shall try to pull you up.'

192

I moved my mouth to warn him. The words would not come.

'What is it? Speak, but don't move.'

'The edge,' I croaked. 'The chalk edge. It will crumble when you pull me up.'

'Math is lying behind me. It cannot crumble that far back. Now, carefully Miss Wakeford. Try to catch the sleeve.'

His black coat slid gently over the edge. My teeth hurt where I held them closed against each other. I willed the coat to come down, watched it and made it fall softly next to where I lay. My arm crept along the face of the cliff and at last I was able to grip that blessed, wonderful cloth in both hands.

'Hold on. I am going to pull.'

As soon as I moved, the whole ledge of chalk began to fall away. Every time I put my foot against the face of the cliff to ease the pull in my aching arms, the whole hill seemed to collapse beneath me. He was only a few feet above me and it was hours before his face grew closer—hours of hanging tightly onto the black, woolen sleeve, my face turned upwards, watching his eyes, asking him to manage it somehow.

The distance grew imperceptibly less. Every part of his face was engraven in my mind. The scar, lividly white now, became clearer as we drew closer to one another. He turned his head back once and spoke to Math. There was a sudden tug on the coat, then he reached his arm down and gripped me under the shoulder.

'One last pull. Just one.'

I made my final effort and threw my body upwards, against nothing, using only the coat to brace myself. At the same time he pulled hard on my shoulder and then I felt the lip of the crack grating across the front of my body and I was lying face down on the grass at the top of the Down.

10

I could not stop shaking that night. Even when I slept—
and it was only the exhaustion of a bruised, tired body
that enabled me to sleep at all—I was conscious that
my limbs were trembling in some kind of nervous fever.
The violent shuddering had started almost as soon as
they had hauled me over the edge of the crack.

At first I had been unable to move. I lay, pressing my
body down into the good grass, feeling the solid comfort of flat land beneath me and holding tightly with
fixed hands to the sleeve of John Tancred's coat.

'Are you all right, Miss Wakeford?'

If I spoke I would start to scream and I was not sure
that I would be able to stop. I had done without sleep
for two days—two days of misshapen horror in which
everything seemed to overlap in a confusion of a ball, a
graveyard and a scarred face. The final madness of
Rachel and Esmee Tancred no longer had power to
shock me. It merely added to the gray mist of fantasy in
which I was living.

'Miss Wakeford! Answer me. Are you hurt?'

It was then that the shivering started. It was
involuntary and I was powerless to control it. I stared
back at John Tancred's white face, then managed to
pull myself to my feet and walk stiffly away down the
hill. He came up, to help me I suppose, but I held him
away with one cramped, quivering hand. Hysteria was
surging so wildly in me that I knew the slightest soften-
ing in my spirit would send me over the edge of sanity. I
paced my way deliberately down the hill, making a task
of it, concentrating on where I should place each foot:

now on this blade of grass, but miss that small stone, flatten the tussock with my left shoe, find another of the same size to tread on with the right. Where I stepped was of the utmost importance to me. If I stopped thinking about that I would have to think about other things . . .

Matthew ran past me down the hill. He was calling for Mary to come out of the house and I watched the two tiny figures as though they were on another planet. She began to follow him quickly up the hill, and when she got near, she too tried to put her arm about me and help me walk. I held her away in the same manner I had held John Tancred away. There was something I had to tell her, something about Esmee, about fetching her body back from the floor of the valley. I tried to open my mouth, to stretch the mask of skin over my lips into information. A croak came forth, a sound so guttural and distorted that I said no more.

Carefully she followed me back to my room, fetched me hot water and turned back my bed. She watched while I washed the dirt and blood from my body and took the torn clothes away as I dropped them on the floor.

It was dark now and at last I climbed up into the bed, dreading the ghosts that would emerge during the night. Mary took the lamp away leaving me to be sucked into a sleep of nightmare shapes and fantasies. But when I awoke, the reality of the day was worse, far worse than the dreams of the night had been.

The body of Esmee Tancred was carried home. For the last time, I washed and dressed the tense, childlike body; even in death, I could not like her. I have helped to prepare the dead before. In the village we do not like outsiders to touch our people and this last service to the departed has served to bring us closer to death—to destroy the terror that is so commonly associated with the termination of life. I had always noticed that once

195

the fatigues and strains had left a body, faces would become calm and peaceful, showing that they were already detached from the torments that still beset the rest of us.

With Esmee Tancred, there was no such repose. In death she had the same eerie secrecy that had driven her in life. Her face was not relaxed; she still watched me with the fox-like cunning I had grown to fear. I tried to pray for her. She had no mother and her family was constrained and distant from her, so that there was only I who could sit with her mortal remains. It was no use. Try though I did to mourn her, I was increasingly beset with the blasphemous notion that she would rise suddenly from her bed and say, 'Yes, Miss Wakeford?'

The time came when I could no longer stay in the room with her and I left Mary to renew the lamps. I think she understood. Certainly she never asked me about that terrible afternoon on the Down, although it was obvious she knew something of what had passed. Together we whispered about the house, planning carefully what we were to say to the parson who was riding out from Canterbury. We had no wish to see the child lie unblessed like her mother. Sometimes, when we were speaking softly to one another, I imagined that the furtive murmurs were thrown back to us from the cold, darkened corners of the house, echoed in a soft voice with a French accent.

We told Math Johnson and John Tancred what story had been decided upon, that the wind had caused an accident during a childish game. I left Mary to say what she wished to Mrs. Tancred. Her door was forbidden to me, and to everyone but Mary. I had not seen her since the night of the ball; no messages had been passed to me nor had her wheelchair been seen in the corridors. I lived in dread of the day she sent for me.

On the fourth day they came from Brighton—two black carriages pulled by plumed mares—and we watched while John and Matthew carried the small coffin into the first carriage and then came back to join us in the second.

In conspiratorial silence we jolted down into the village: two men and two women, staring at one another and joined together by more, much more, than mutual mourning. At Loxham we waited for the preacher to arrive, sitting guardedly in our coach while the people of the village stood well back in a sinister, frightened mob. Their curiosity reached out in greedy waves towards us; the faces were cruel and hateful. If they could have harmed us they would have done so. But we four, garbed in black, implacable and white-faced, formed an impenetrable barrier of secrecy. When the preacher came and we moved off, each of us could feel our guard tighten and wall up about us.

Then for the first time I realized that now I was on the other side of Tancred—the side that was dark and hidden, the part that must be shut away from the eyes of ordinary men. It had happened without my knowing. I was still not aware of all the old mysteries of the house; but now there were new secrets, things that I had been part of and I, like Mary and Math and John Tancred, was hiding away from the good light, carrying forbidden things in my heart.

The carriages drove as far as they could up the side of the hill. Then we had to climb down and John and Matthew carried the coffin over the narrow, rutted track while Mary and I stumbled behind. The preacher, a harmless enough man, had been crushed into frightened silence by the menace of the burial. There were no weeping mourners for him to comfort, and mercifully, he refrained from the usual platitudes. I prayed that he would not speak of an innocent child being called to heaven. To him, Esmee Tancred was a twelve year old girl. To us, she was an evil wraith.

The climb was long, but Math and John Tancred took the hill in steady, even strides. At last we came to the ruined graveyard and the minister looked nervously about him at the crumbling walls and the old tombs.

'Here?' he asked uneasily. 'You will bury the child here?' John Tancred turned his scarred face impassively towards the man.

'All the Tancreds lie here.' He led the way behind the tiny chapel, to where a new grave had been opened beside that of Richard Tancred.

The words were said, the coffin lowered and the first soil thrown into the ground. I wanted to cry for the child, to feel some pity, but try though I did, there was no mourning in my heart, no regret for the cessation of this particular life. The five of us stood around the grave, the wind blowing the black dresses of Mary and myself flat against our bodies. The damp air moved thickly about the gravestone of Richard Tancred; Esmee's grave looked small and thin beside that of her grandfather. *'Everyone is afraid of Grandfather, even God is afraid of Grandfather.'*

I looked across to the man who had sired this unhappy daughter of Tancred and from his face, tried to define what thoughts were moving behind his brow. He had stood on this hill six years ago listening to the same words spoken over his father. And then he had stepped outside the graveyard and watched his wife being laid in the ground without benefit of church and clergy. His face told me nothing.

The preacher finished but we made no move. If he wanted to go he could not. He was held in our silence, in the cloud of oppression that hovered over the grave. He gaped his mouth at each of us in turn, helpless and confused, not knowing what to do next.

'Perhaps,' he faltered, 'perhaps the father would care to say a few words? A little remembrance . . .' His voice faded into nothing as John Tancred slowly turned his head and stared at him.

'Finish your task, Parson,' he said thickly.

The man tried to protest at the peremptory rebuke, but under four pairs of bleakly empty eyes his words died away. We turned slowly and walked back across the burial ground waiting a moment while John Tancred stopped and spoke to the sexton waiting by the gate. He pressed a coin into the man's hand, and when I looked back, Esmee's grave was being filled in.

At Loxham the preacher left us, thankfully and unashamedly relieved. He shuddered once as he stepped out of the coach and then he hurried away in the direction of the Loxham parson's house. Whatever he learned there he could do nothing now. The child was buried.

Back up into the sea wind blowing against the hill, back to the empty house where the old woman in the wheelchair waited behind locked doors. The plumed horses, the drivers in the dark clothes, drove away and left us.

I went to my room, washed, and put on my best frock of black dimity, clean starched apron, collar and cuffs. I brushed my hair and tied it carefully with a ribbon, then fastened a clean cap over my hair and took a fresh handkerchief out of the dresser drawer. I sat quietly for a while in the small, upright chair by the table. I opened my Bible and read the Twenty-Third Psalm. And then I left my room and walked along the passage and through the gallery until I came to John Tancred's room.

When I knocked he did not answer. I knocked once more, and, knowing I had made my peace with the Lord, I opened the door and went in. He was sitting in the big wing chair, gazing emptily towards the window where the last light of the day filtered thinly into the room. His hands were resting, one on each arm of the chair, and he sat so coldly and so straight that he reminded me of a carving I had once seen on a crusader's tomb.

'Miss Wakeford.'

There was no query in his voice, merely a fatalistic acceptance, as though he had been expecting me. I nodded carefully towards him, then sat in the chair directly opposite his and folded my hands in my lap.

'I suppose,' he said tiredly, 'you have come to tell me you are leaving.'

'No.'

I think he was surprised. When he spoke again his voice was sharp, querying. 'You have not?'

'No.'

'You understand, Miss Wakeford, that I would not dream of trying to persuade you against your will. You . . . you should never have been employed in the first place. If you remember, I told you not to remain here, the first time I saw you, on the hill.'

'I remember, sir. But still I have no wish to leave.'

He began to move restlessly in the chair. I sensed a fretfulness in him, because the conversation was not going the way he had planned. 'Miss Wakeford,' he said irritably, and then his irritation gave way to a fumbling sincerity, an attempt to speak fairly to me.

'I must try to explain,' he said slowly, 'try to convince you that it would be wrong for you to stay here. This house is a bad place, Miriam Wakeford. It is corrupt and old and already you have been caught into things you do not understand. You should never have come here, but perhaps it ís not too late.' He paused and then said thoughtfully, 'You have strength. You can leave here, and in a little while, you will find that Tancred has not touched you.'

'I do not wish to go.'

It was a very quiet room. We sat in what was almost peace for a moment, then he frowned and asked, 'Then why have you come here?'

Now that the time had come, I was surprised to find I was not in any way nervous. I was no longer an outsider at Tancred. I had joined in the dark brotherhood that held the family together and I felt no fear, no diffidence in what I had to say. 'Does thee know why Esmee ran over the edge of the chalk?'

He raised one hand to cover his face and nodded wearily.

'Does thee know I found thy wife's grave on the hillside? And that Matthew Johnson told me how she died?'

Again he nodded. I was not nervous, but for some foolish reason my heart was thumping heavily and I clasped my fingers tightly together.

'Thee knows too, that Esmee heard us talking?'

He slumped right back into the shadow of the chair, and as the last of the daylight receded from the room, it became impossible to see his face. 'I know all this, Miss Wakeford. Matthew told me all this.'

'But thee does not know, and Matthew Johnson does not know, that I did not fall over the edge trying to save Esmee. She—thy daughter—pulled me with her when she jumped.'

His hand fell slowly from his face and I watched his body lean forward in the chair. I could just make out his eyes, staring at me in shocked disbelief, refusing to accept this final burden of knowledge.

'It is not true!'

'It is true.'

There was a time when I would have lied to save him pain and kept the secret of Esmee's last insanity from him, but now, if I was to help, I must tell the truth, and I must know the truth.

'I have come so far,' I said gently. 'And now I must know the rest. I must know about thy father, and why thy wife took her own life. Thee was unfair to me— each one of thee—letting me come here to work, expecting me to put things right, but never telling me what it was I had to fight against. Now thee must tell me, John Tancred, for the silence of this house has caused another tragedy. And if thee wants my help, if such tragedy is not to happen again, I must know what it is I battle with.'

Now it was quite dark and I could not see his face at

all. We sat still, neither of us moving or speaking. Perhaps he thought I would grow tired of his silence and go away, but I was determined to have the truth. I think we must have sat for ten or even twenty minutes, facing each other in the darkness. After a while I stood up.

'Where is the lamp?'

'By the window.'

His voice grated roughly in the dusty air and I felt my way over to the lamp and groped for the matches. I had just replaced the bowl over the flickering light when I heard him say, 'How much do you know?'

'That thy father was an evil man, that he laughed when thy ... when Esmee's mother took her own life; that Mary and Esmee and thy mother too, were all afraid of him.'

'Do you know just how evil a man he was, Miriam Wakeford?'

I could hardly recognize his voice; it was completely devoid of hope or warmth. 'We were all afraid of him, not just Mary or my mother, but all of us. Even as a child I remember how terrified we were when he came home, and thank God, he did not come home very often.'

'Did he beat thee?' I asked, thinking of my own particular fear so far as violence was concerned. He shrugged his shoulders.

'He could be brutal when he chose, but this was not the secret of his terror over us. He had a gift, an evil delight in discovering our own particular fears and anxieties and using them against us. You have seen enough of my mother, Miss Wakeford, to realize that her vanity is the glory of this house; her greatest pride, that of being a Tancred. But I have seen my mother groveling at his feet like an animal, reduced by his private cruelties to a woman without strength.'

He was slumped in the chair, his heavy body crushed by weary recollections. 'There were times when he would make her invite people to the house, all her old friends and those of society who could be persuaded to visit. And in the middle of the festivities he would arrive feigning drunkenness, with a coachload of Brighton strumpets. I have watched him rip the jewels from my mother's gown and throw them to a street woman, in full view of a room of guests. What he did to her in private, I can only guess at.'

He faced me suddenly and asked, 'Did you know what he did to Mary?'

I nodded.

'Did you know that it wasn't only Mary—that every woman who came into this house turned into a terrified creature devoid of dignity or human bearing? To him they were merely devises for his own especial torments.'

He stared up at the darkened window and said irrelevantly, 'I had a dog once and he killed it—killed it because he knew I loved the animal. He locked it in a room on the top floor and let it starve to death and everytime I tried to go in he thrashed me back down three flights of stairs.'

I began to feel sick. The humiliation of Mrs. Tancred did not seem half so bad to me as the tormenting of a poor dog. I watched him staring morosely back into the past, reliving some small scene that I could not see.

'I cannot tell you everything, Miss Wakeford, even you who think you can abide with the truth. Sometimes the truth is so horrible it is best to leave it covered in lies, or secrets, or any kind of deceit so long as it is hidden.'

My heart began to thump again. I was determined to know the story of Richard Tancred's death, but I was afraid of what I might have to hear.

'There were things so bad, so abominable that you would not understand my words. For all your honesty, for all your strength, you would not understand.'

'Why did he hurt thy face?' I asked carefully. 'Why did he throw the lamp?'

He smiled, the ugly, twisted smile that he had given to Mildred and Mrs. Thorburn. 'Ah yes, my face. That intrigues you, does it not, Miss Wakeford? I have noticed your keen observation of my face.' I made to deny the fact but he continued speaking.

'He threw the lamp partly because he was angry at my defiance. He had stolen a cameo of my mother's and I tried to get it back.'

He paused, then speaking softly, almost to himself, he said, 'But that is not the truth, not the whole truth. He was worried and jealous because he saw I had become a man. When he looked into my face he could see his future. He could see he would grow old like other men—become bent and decayed and one day die. He did not like to see anything about him that was not crippled, or distorted, or bad. To see me ugly made him, once again, the king of Tancred.'

'Thee is not ugly!' I burst out. 'Thee thinks that everyone is frightened of thy face but it is not true. I am not afraid of thy face. I do not even see the scar.' I bent forward in my chair and stared into his eyes, trying to make him believe what I was saying.

He gazed back without seeing me and his voice moved softly forward. 'That was when I ran away; I left this house and the terrible man who was its master. I went to France. We once had a trading house there, until he sold it, but the people in that town remembered the Tancreds and they were good to me. Monsieur Duvoix, he who had bought the trading station, lent me money enough to start breeding the Tancred horses. We had no claim on him for he had paid a good price for the house. But he was a kind man.'

Suddenly he got up from his chair and strode across the room to the window. He stood with his back towards me, looking out into the darkness. 'Rachel was his niece, the daughter of his dead sister. Her father was dead too and Duvoix had cared for her since she was a child. She was sixteen then and the daintiest, kindest little person I had ever known.'

He turned and looked at me across the distance of the room. 'Can you imagine, Miss Wakeford, the shyness and torment of a young man who knows that women cannot bear to look at him; who, at an age when he should be making his first overtures to a woman, has to spend all his time keeping one side of his face hidden? I used to watch them, walking towards me until they saw my face, then carefully averting their eyes, pretending they had not seen me.

'She was the same the first time. When she saw me she made a small shocked noise and ran out of the room. But the next day she came down and said she was sorry, and that if I did not mind her staring at me, she would very soon grow accustomed to my looks.'

I felt I knew Rachel Tancred. I could almost see her coming down the stairs, feeling sorry for the strange, unhappy young man with the scarred face. I could imagine how she would be, shy and very pretty, the girl who had left three hairpins and a lavender glove on her dressing-table before she died.

'That first time, the first two months I stayed with them, it was difficult. She was a timid creature, easily frightened, and sometimes, when I was angry or bitter, I would speak harshly to her and make her cry. But the next time when I came home to the Duvoix house it was better. I had made a little money and I bought her a present. It was only a musical box but she loved it and she played it so often, that in the end, she taught herself the words that went with the tune and she would sing it with the melody.'

I did not need to be told what tune it was. I had heard that melody too many times, drifting over the hills and through the dark corridors of the house.

'She did not like going out very much. She preferred to stay with me and with her uncle and I had no complaint. By this time I had learned how to live with my face and I found that in spite of it, my business flourished.

But I still did not like visiting with people. Society is cruel, Miss Wakeford, and women are even more so. Rachel and I were content to remain at home.

'I waited until she was nineteen and then I asked Monsieur Duvoix if we could marry. I was making a fair living, and too, I knew that one day Richard Tancred would die, and the house would be mine. Perhaps I was no great catch, but Rachel had set her heart on marrying me, and without too much protest, he gave way. She came with me when I traveled, and between journeys we would return to the Duvoix house. We were there when Esmee was born, and once the child was old enough, we took her with us whenever we had to visit in another country.

'I suppose it was a strange marriage. She was so timid and afraid and I so reserved about my face that we made no effort to mix with other people. Truly, I suppose we were not altogether happy. We were too intense, too sensitive to our separate hurts to relax completely. And both of us had to be constantly on our guard, in case the one should hurt the other.'

I watched him leaning against the table by the window, speaking into the past, and I felt my heart swell with pity for the two unhappy, young people wandering alone around Europe.

'The time came when I wanted to see Tancred again. It is an unhappy place and I had known nothing but misery here. Nevertheless it was my home. We knew by this time that there was something wrong with Esmee and things had begun to be bad between us. Sometimes we would deliberately hurt each other— say cruel things we did not mean and that we instantly regretted. I had the foolish idea that if we returned to Tancred, things might be better. I wrote to my mother; I wanted to make sure the old man was away before I went home. And when I had her answer, she was so pathetically anxious to see me again that we booked a passage on the next boat and went home.'

He paused and then said bitterly to himself, 'If only we had stayed where we were. We were not happy, but life was bearable, and at least we were not completely alone.

'At first it was not too bad. The house was always better when he was away, like a sick person recovering from a long illness. He had been away for quite a while and Mary and my mother were even able to laugh sometimes. I told them that we would go the moment he returned and they accepted this. I had made my own break and I could not risk my wife and child to the creeping disease of the old man.'

Again he paused, then softly, in a tone of muted horror said, 'But we left too late. He came home suddenly, in October, and once he had seen Rachel it was too late.'

I did not understand what he was trying to say. Thoughts groped darkly in my brain but still I did not understand.

'He got to her first and he told her that evening. Then he told my mother, then me. But by the time I got there it was too late.'

He was whispering into the room and I felt the old familiar fear crawl up my neck. They were all there in the room with us, Rachel and the old man, and Esmee.

'What did he tell her?' I asked, and I found that, like him, I was whispering. Either he did not hear, or he did not understand. He looked directly at me but I could tell he was not seeing me or the furniture of the room about us. He was standing in the east wing looking up at the body of his wife.

'He was laughing, standing at the top of the stairs laughing, and when Matthew and my mother came in he was still laughing. My mother shouted at him, screamed at him to stop, but he only laughed harder. I never saw her so wild, so crazy. All the years she had hated him suddenly burst from her when she saw him laughing because my wife was dead. I saw her lift the candlestick. It was an iron one painted silver. I remember that especially, and I heard her curse him as she struck, hard across his head. He swayed for just a moment and she hit him again, screaming and shrieking at him; that time he fell, crashed against the wall and then rolled down the stairs. And he was laughing even while he fell.'

He waited, then added, 'But when he reached the bottom he was silent.'

'What did he tell her?' I whispered again. 'What did he tell thy wife to make her want to die?'

'I wanted to stop her from striking out with the iron candlestick. She did not seem to notice that he had fallen and she went on screaming at him, exorcising the years of hate, of vileness and humiliation. Then her face went rigid and her eyes suddenly blanked. I caught her before she fell.'

'What did he tell her?'

'They said it was a kind of heart attack, but I knew it was hate that took the power from her legs. For a time she could not move her left arm, but that came back in the end.'

I could not stop him talking. The flow of words poured incessantly from his mouth as though, now that he had started speaking, he could not stop. He paced wildly up and down the room, describing the scene in the east wing in such detail that I felt I had watched every horrifying episode myself. I could see the body of Rachel Tancred and the figure of the old man laughing at the top of the stairs. I could see John, staring with sick horror at his wife, and the old woman abandoning herself to the glorious release of years of consuming hatred. And I could see something that they had not seen—the small figure of Esmee, crouching behind a wardrobe, watching her mother and listening to the noise her grandfather made as he stood at the top of the stairs. But there was still one thing I did not know.

'John Tancred. What did he tell thy wife?'

He was not listening. He strode angrily up and down the room and at last I stood directly in his path and when he came close I reached up and put my hands on his shoulders. 'Tell me, John Tancred. Why did she kill herself?'

The anger died away from his face. He stared at me bewildered, then the bewilderment was replaced by despair. 'Why?' he said dully. 'Why? Because he told her he had known her mother years before and that, in fact, her mother had never been married. He told her how like her mother she was—how he recognized her at once, even before he knew her uncle was Duvoix. He told her exactly who her father was.'

'And who was her father?' I asked, but in my heart I knew already.

'Why, it was him of course,' he answered softly. 'It was him, Richard Tancred. And now see if the strength you have—the good, wholesome strength that comes from prayer and reading of the Bible—is able to stand against knowledge like that.'

I closed my eyes and thought of many things to stop the sickening nausea in my stomach. I thought of flowers and the making of a good dress; I thought of going to Meeting on a spring Sunday; I thought of Grandfather. And through the pictures in my mind I could see the agonized face of John Tancred watching me, pleading wildly for me to understand. When I opened my eyes the face was there, just as I had seen it. I felt ill, but the greater pain was for him and for the re-opening of a gangrenous wound that would never entirely heal. He was watching me so closely—so carefully to see what emotion registered on my face—that I could not afford to let even a tiny part of what I felt show in my eyes.

'Is that all?' I asked. 'Or is there more?'

'That is all.'

The lamp sputtered softly on the table by the window and I could hear the beating of my own heart, loud and regular like a hollow clock. I had accepted what he had told me. I recognized it to be the truth, and in the face of John Tancred's tormented scrutiny, I bore the news with calm. But I knew that it would take many hours of my own private pain before I could accept this final nightmare of the house.

'Do the others know?' I asked quietly. 'Mary, and Matthew Johnson, do they know?'

He nodded. 'They know.'

With the lifeless tread of an old man he returned to the wing chair and sat down. 'Miriam Wakeford . . . strange little Miriam with the kind heart and the will of iron. I know you well enough to be sure that whatever you have learned, whatever you think about this house, it will remain locked behind that small, gentle face of yours. The gray eyes will observe and learn but no one will ever be sure which way your mind is turning.'

I was thankful that my face had shown nothing of my thoughts, thankful of the training that had taught me to be on my guard against a hasty emotion.

'And now,' he said dully. 'Now I am sure you will want to leave us, and perhaps you are right.' He looked away from me, out again into the darkness. When he spoke once more his voice was so soft I could hardly hear him. 'I had no right to keep you here. I should have sent you away. I tried to tell you to go and then . . . then I found I needed you here. Did you know I watched for you, Miriam Wakeford?'

'No.'

'It was your black dress, or perhaps the white cap. And you were always so busy and so clean. Not just to look at,' he said quickly. 'But your eyes and whatever you did was so clean. I would watch you walk up the Down and all the shadows fell back, afraid to touch you.'

'Not always,' I answered abruptly. 'Not always did they fall back. Sometimes they came out to meet me.'

'I used to wonder what would have happened if you had come here in the old days,' he said dreamily. '. . .

Before I ran away. I think you would have stood against the old man.'

'No. I could not have fought Richard Tancred. Only God could do that.'

We waited, and then, for the very first time since I had been at Tancred, something restful filtered into the house. We did not speak, but there was no strain, no tension between us, only a deep soothing peace.

'You have beautiful hair, Miriam Wakeford,' he said suddenly and then continued hurriedly, 'Do you want to leave?'

'No.'

'You will stay?'

'I will stay.'

The peace in the room grew. There would be days when he would not speak to me, days when I was afraid again, or tired or dispirited; there would be days when the house pressed heavily on both of us. There was no future for me at Tancred, only a life of underpaid usefulness. But I did not mind. If I could just be where he was, and see him riding over the Down, I would be content. And if my presence in the house afforded him a kind of comfort, I would ask no more.

Tancred was a house of bad surprises; nothing ever lasted, or at least nothing good. For a little while, sitting in the soft-lit room together, we were lulled into peace, anticipating a future, perhaps not quite so harsh, not quite so sick. The dream was brief.

We heard the noise at the same time—the noise of a wheelchair grating against wood. We both stood and turned to face the door, but before either of us could move, it swung open and Mrs. Tancred, glittering, crazy with rage, slid forward into the room.

'There will be no staying in this house,' she spat. 'No walking on the Down in a black dress and white cap. Get out!'

I felt no fear of her, only a terrible weariness—a realization that life would never be gentle at Tancred.

'You have ruined my hopes for Tancred. You have murdered my grandchild and now you try to corrupt my son with your slimy ways! You are bad, evil. You have brought nothing but disaster to this house. Get out!'

She was mad with her own anger. Fury had driven her alone through the length of the gallery, pushing the heavy chair by its wheels, whipped by a frenzy of hatred that had given strength to old arms.

John Tancred frowned and stepped towards her. 'Go back to your room. You do not know what you are saying. Miss Wakeford stays here, with us.'

'No,' she screamed at him. 'No! I am the mistress of Tancred and I say she goes.'

She spun the wheels of her chair like a madwoman and suddenly she was right in front of me, staring up with such vitriolic hate that I fell back a step. 'You!' she hissed. 'You with your Bible and your holy ways. Until you came we were safe, safe with our secrets. Then you came, prying and asking questions, trying to teach Esmee how to pray. You have brought trouble with you and now you have murdered my grandchild.'

'No! That is not true. I tried to stop her.'

'Murderess!'

John Tancred took hold of the back of the chair and began to push her back towards the door. The full fury of her wrath turned instantly on him. 'Leave me!' she screamed. 'Leave me or I will kill you, like I killed him.'

Fear returned to me—to my legs and to my throat—fluttering nervously at the violence of the old woman.

John Tancred, his face a mask of puckered skin and dark eyes, strode bleakly toward the door pushing the old woman who was now shrieking at both of us. Near the door was a small walnut bureau with a cigar box resting on the top. With a last mighty surge of strength she snatched it from the bureau, twisted her gaunt old body in the chair and threw it at me with all the force she could muster.

'Get out! Get out!'

The cigar box clattered harmlessly to the floor on one side of me. John Tancred looked down on his mother with anger in his face. And beneath the anger I could see pity—a deep weeping pity for the woman, once so proud and beautiful. She had lived too long with fear and humiliation. And even now, now that Richard Tancred was dead, he had left her his final gift of a body that could not function properly.

'Get out! Get out!' she screeched again.

I pushed past the wheelchair, past the outstretched arm of John Tancred and I left the room. As I hurried through the long gallery I heard him cry out after me. I heard him call my name and the echo followed me down the passages in a wild ribbon of sound. I closed my ears.

I could bear no more of Tancred.

11

I threw my small possessions into the hand grip, left the house and ran directly out of the door and away down the hill. I gave no thought to the manner of my leaving, did not consider whether it was wise to leave so precipitately. My overwhelming desire was to leave the place —to get away from Tancred and the Down—and as I fled down the hill I made a point of not looking back, in case I should see over my shoulder some last, horrible phenomena of the house.

I turned at last onto the Loxham path, my carpetbag in one hand and my cape held tightly together in the other. I was still running and periodically I had to stop and draw breath; but as soon as I was able, I hurried on once more to the village, anxious—frantically eager—to put as great a distance as possible between me and Tancred.

Since that time I have often wondered why it was that the hysterical raging of an old woman should have succeeded where everything else had failed. I had borne all kinds of abuse and all kinds of insanities at that terrible house; even the appalling confidences of John Tancred had not driven me away. But the hate-ridden face of the old woman haunted me all the way down the hill, precipitated me over the rough ground and through the village street. Even now I am not sure what final terror sent me hurrying through the night. I only know that some tiny fragment of instinct warned me that if I did not leave Tancred immediately, I would turn into a facsimile of Esmee or the old woman.

It was late and I did not even think to stop in the village and ask for help. I suppose I knew I would receive short comfort from that sour community. I started down the Brighton road, half running, half walking, thinking of everything that had happened, everything I had learned. It was a long walk. At one point, I remember, I was surprised to find I was crying. Another time, about five miles outside Brighton, I realized I was talking to myself, repeating words in a dreary rhythm that kept time with my pace. When I reached the first houses I found that I had lost my cap and that my best dress had a band of thick mud around the hem.

I knew I should go to the house of Ezekial King. A girl of our Fellowship alone at night in a strange town, should naturally seek shelter in a house of her own people; but I was reluctant to ask him for help. I had not seen him again since the time he had tried to remove me from Tancred. The events of the past month had served to drive his threats of complaint to my Grandfather away to the back of my mind. I knew Deborah would be kind and indeed Mr. King would be the first to help me. But after he had helped me he would want to know exactly why I had rushed headlong from Tancred. He would question and pray over me, point out how my headstrong ways had nearly carried me into disaster. And then, the following morning, he would march me along to the banker's house where he could keep a watchful eye on me and see that I did as I was told.

Suddenly I could not bear it: the very thought of his scoldings and santimonious questions made me start to cry again. I turned away from the direction of the Kings' house, and when I was once more in control of myself, I asked a passing woman to direct me to the house of Reuben Tyler of Wat's Lane. Ten minutes later, dirty and capless, I knocked on the door of that good man's house.

If he and his wife were surprised to see me, disheveled and late at night, they were kind enough not to comment upon it. Mrs. Tyler was already in her nightshift but she set to and made me sit at a table laden with

215

food. My throat hurt so much I could hardly eat and Reuben Tyler looked at me carefully as I tried to swallow a small piece of bread.

'Have you left the house then?'

I nodded. 'She . . . she shouted . . .' Foolishly I began to cry again. 'It was not me, not my fault . . .'

I saw him exchange a brief glance with his wife. He put his arm across my shoulders. 'Now then, now then. Don't get yeself upset after all this time. It doesn't matter what she said. Come now, drink the tea. It's nice and hot and will make you feel a whole lot better.'

I gulped at the scalding liquid and he was right. I felt the heat move down inside me and then spread out in a nice, warm glow.

'They buried the child today, didn't they? I heard someone say the carriages was riding up to Tancred.'

Again I nodded and took another sip of the hot tea.

'Then you'll be wanting to get home, back to your own folk?'

He was a man of poor education, yet he had such kindness, such tactful consideration for my unhappy condition, that I remember him as one of the finest gentlemen I have ever known. He must have been curious, wondering what had happened to send me running through the night. Yet he asked no questions, merely assuming that as Esmee was dead I would naturally be going home.

'I'll go as soon as there's a train. I have money for my fare and . . .'

He interrupted me and put his big, rough hand back on my shoulder. 'You'll stay here tonight, little Missy. Tomorrow we'll see about putting you on the train.'

I tried to thank them—to apologize for the awkwardness I had caused them—but they hushed me and Mrs. Tyler made me up a bed in front of the kitchen fire. It was a tiny house and I could hear the occasional sound of a child crying. There was a cat asleep in the corner and everything was warm and small and ordinary.

I could never go back to Tancred.

I came home to the village and made my explanations as best I could. I told Grandfather part of the truth—but only part—for no one would believe the sequence of horrifying events at Tancred. I told him about Esmee and about her unchildlike ways, but I said nothing of her birth. I told him of the accident that was no accident and when I described how she had tried to pull me over the cliff I thought I detected some kind of concern in his eyes. I told him there was little money and the work was hard, but I did not speak of the ghosts that rode along with the wind and I did not speak of Mrs. Tancred's final fury. When I finished he stared hard at me and then nodded thoughtfully.

'Thee is thinner, Miriam,' he said. 'I think thee did well to come home.'

I received no rebuke, not even from Grandmother. I think he must have spoken to her and told her not to chide me. When I went in to see her she paused from her beating of a cake long enough to receive my dutiful kiss on the cheek.

'So thee is back again,' she snapped, but said no more; there were no scoldings or admonitions and so I guessed Grandfather had told her to mind her peace.

I took up my old place with Miss Llewellyn, and in answer to her questions about Tancred, I told her what I thought she would want to hear—of a family living quietly on reduced means. Everyone accepted the fact of Esmee's death as sufficient reason for my leaving, and of the rest, I said nothing.

I sewed, I worked in the dairy, I went to Meeting on Sunday. Indeed life was just as though I had never been away. There was no cold wind in the village, no eerie shadows chasing me through a dimly-lit house. The people were simple, good, and with loving hearts; yet after a few weeks had elapsed, I was aware that I had not left Tancred completely behind me.

217

I dreamed at night—I think I shall always dream about those terrible months at Tancred—and when I woke in the morning I would start from my bed, wondering if some new horror had beset the unhappy family on the Down. I tried to push the memories away, to fit myself once more into the routine and pattern of the village. I visited Prudence and Joseph Whittaker, and wondered how I could ever have thought that callow young man was handsome. I watched my cousin Stephen marry the girl of his choice, and felt nothing but a restless unease at what should have been a pleasing occasion in our family. Once, I thought I saw Mary in the village and I ran all the way across the fields to catch her, only to find it was Elizabeth Jenkins grown a little stouter.

And whatever I did, wherever I walked, or worked, or sat, the face of John Tancred would crowd into my brain, sometimes smiling, sometimes angry, but always there, intruding on my daily life and cutting me off from the things about me.

And then in March, the letter came: a fat letter with the envelope addressed in a badly-written, mis-spelt hand. When I opened it the fatness proved to be one of my white caps. The letter was from Mary.

Miss,

I was sorry you went. Last month we had trouble again. Mrs. Tancred, she took another bad turn and this time there was no saving her. Now there is just the three of us and Mr. John is sick. The horse jumped on his leg and he is bad, real bad. Me and Math, we does what we can but he asks for you. This is a sad house and I wish you was still here. You was kind to me and I still wear the blue dress. You left your cap.

Yours very truly,
MARY

I slept badly that night. I heard again the wind riding

through black corridors and a child's voice singing an old French melody in damp corners of the house. And when I slept I dreamed of the night when Esmee's mother had died and I saw it all again: the laughing man, the raging old woman with the iron candlestick, and the broken body of a girl who could not stand what the old man had told her. How could I go back there—back to the cold empty rooms and the horrors of the east wing and the long gallery? Mary's letter was a cry for help, but I had no comfort to offer. I was a village girl, used to simple things and God-fearing people. I had no business in a house like Tancred. But even while I tried to persuade myself to keep away, to stay in the village where I was safe, I knew full well that I must go back. I had stayed too long at Tancred to remain untouched, and now it had the power to stretch across two counties and fetch me back.

I returned to Tancred. I made my peace with Grandfather; I told him I must go back and he accepted my decision without question. I think he knew even then that he had lost me. I had seen too much during the last months to ever stand in awe of Grandfather or Grandmother again. I had watched people whose lives were twisted and black and I had lived with an old woman who really was a terrifying creature. Neither Grandmother's temper, nor Grandfather's sternness any longer had the power to restrain me.

I begged a last ride in the vintner's wagon, and with steps that grew faster as I neared the house, I climbed the last few miles up to the top of the Down. The house had not changed. It was still cold and dark and dirty. It was still broken and lonely, sitting up there on the hill with not even a tree to soften its starkness.

He was lying in his room, thinner, older, and with his leg strapped to an ugly block of wood. The room was dirty; the bed was rumpled and untidy and he was staring out of the window, searching hopelessly for something in the gray sky. Then I closed the door and said, 'John? John Tancred?'

His face on the pillow slowly moved toward me—that tragic, ugly, beautiful face that I loved so much.

He called my name and the cry was an echo of that other cry I had heard when I ran from the house. He watched me when I crossed to the bed and then his big hands pulled down on my neck and I felt his scarred cheek against my own.

I promised him much that day, and I have tried to keep my promise. I told him I would never leave him, and I never have, although at first it was not easy. For two months I nursed him and while I sat by his bed watching his fever, cleansing the wound in his leg and trying to ease his pain, I was conscious all the time of the house about me—the bad, shadowy house of Tancred.

When at last he could stand again, the preacher came up from Loxham to marry us, and I knew that I must remain at the house. Whatever its evil past—however bleak and cold—it was the home of John Tancred whom I loved; and for that reserved, taciturn man to live anywhere else would be impossible. Mrs. Tancred had told me—and indeed I had known it was true even before that day in her huge, dark room—that they were irrevocably bound with the house. Their roots were in the soil. I hated the house; I was afraid of it, but there was no other place for John, the master of Tancred.

The first few months were bad—cold and terrifying and borne only because he was with me. Mary and I tried once more to restore the place to some semblance of order: to clean and warm and patch; but I was conscious all the time of fear—of old memories and nightmares that pressed out at me whenever I walked the dark corridors. I could not go into the east wing. I could not go into Esmee's room for fear I should hear a small, high tune playing about the corners. Indeed I found it difficult to enter Mrs. Tancred's old room, although logically, that would have been the most comfortable and pleasant room in which to live.

And then October came, the night I had anticipated with fear, the night when it had all happened—the laughing and the old woman venting her years of hate on the man who had lived so evilly. I sat in my old room, shaking with terror and waiting for the silent ghosts to steal softly through the wind-swept passages. I kept my Bible with me, although I did not open it and that night I contributed my own especial nightmares to the house. And then, when the first light of dawn filtered through the shabby curtains, I became aware of what needed to be done, and I knew that now I had the strength to complete the task.

I blew out the lamp, and in the half light from the narrow windows, I made my way along the length of the house until I came to the gallery. The portrait was still there with those terrible eyes watching, staring out from the canvas, following the figures of those who passed through the house. It was not enough to kill him, as Mrs. Tancred had done. It was not enough to bury him, to remain silent when his name was spoken and forget what he had done.

I lifted the portrait of Richard Tancred from the wall and I dragged it though the gallery and out onto the hill. It was heavy, and the weight pulling at my arms made me hot. But for the first time I was not afraid; at last I reached the cliff overhanging the sea and I felt a joyous spurt of strength. One final push and I heard the portrait crashing and tearing down the side of the cliff, breaking into fragments of canvas and wood that plunged into the sea and then floated away with the flotsam of the morning tide.

Someone should have done it six years before.

We cleaned out the east wing that morning, Mary and I. We scrubbed and tore down old hangings, polished and moved the furniture into the attics. And when we had

221

finished there we started on Esmee's room. That winter—the first winter—there was not much money to spare, but I saw that all the rooms that were used had fires that burned night and day and made the house a little warmer and a little brighter. When the spring came we planted the first row of pines in a long line across the front of the house, pines bought specially from Denmark to stand against the wind from the North Sea. I prayed that year that the trees would live. The significance of those small, slender saplings took on an importance out of all proportion to the other things we were trying to put right in the house. And when the next spring came I was able to hold my son up in my arms and show him the young, green needles of the year's new growth.

Matthew left us after two years. He was a weak, bad man but I bore with him because he knew how to handle the horses. When he said he would go, I was glad. We have three men in the stables now and two lads come up from Loxham every day to learn the art of rearing blood stock.

Mary stayed with us, and is with us still. At one time I hoped that perhaps she would marry and be happy in a home of her own making, but the scars of Richard Tancred were cut too harshly in her. In her heart, I think she was afraid of all men, and at last, I saw that her happiness was bound up with me and with my children. She is stouter now, she has lost the sad unkempt look that she used to have.

And of the silent, forceful man who is my husband, who will never be as other men. I do not understand him, and why should I—I who have not suffered the things that he has suffered? It is enough that when I am gone for the day, visiting with friends—for we have many now—he is waiting at the foot of the Down for my return, and I see the unhappy shadows lift from his face. He puts his strong hands on my shoulders and holds me hard as though he were afraid I would not come back.

He has never mentioned the portrait of his father that disappeared from the gallery. But another picture hangs there now: a picture of me with my son upon my lap.

THE END

A SELECTED LIST OF NOVELS AVAILABLE
FROM CORGI BOOKS

THE PRICES SHOWN BELOW WERE CORRECT AT THE TIME OF GOING TO PRESS. HOWEVER TRANSWORLD PUBLISHERS RESERVE THE RIGHT TO SHOW NEW RETAIL PRICES ON COVERS WHICH MAY DIFFER FROM THOSE PREVIOUSLY ADVERTISED IN THE TEXT OR ELSEWHERE.

☐ 12638 1	SPINNERS WHARF	*Iris Gower*	£2.95
☐ 12637 3	PROUD MARY	*Iris Gower*	£2.50
☐ 12387 0	COPPER KINGDOM	*Iris Gower*	£2.50
☐ 12565 2	LAST YEAR'S NIGHTINGALE	*Claire Lorrimer*	£3.50
☐ 10584 8	MAVREEN	*Claire Lorrimer*	£2.95
☐ 11207 0	TAMARISK	*Claire Lorrimer*	£2.95
☐ 11726 9	CHANTAL	*Claire Lorrimer*	£2.95
☐ 12182 7	THE WILDERLING	*Claire Lorrimer*	£3.50
☐ 11959 8	THE CHATELAINE	*Claire Lorrimer*	£3.50
☐ 10375 6	CSARDAS	*Diane Pearson*	£3.95
☐ 10271 7	THE MARIGOLD FIELD	*Diane Pearson*	£2.50
☐ 09140 5	SARAH WHITMAN	*Diane Pearson*	£2.50
☐ 12641 1	THE SUMMER OF THE BARSHINSKEYS	*Diane Pearson*	£2.95
☐ 12803 1	RUTH APPLEBY	*Elvi Rhodes*	£2.95
☐ 12367 6	OPAL	*Elvi Rhodes*	£1.95
☐ 12607 1	DOCTOR ROSE	*Elvi Rhodes*	£1.95
☐ 11596 7	FEET IN CHAINS	*Kate Roberts*	£1.95
☐ 11685 8	THE LIVING SLEEP	*Kate Roberts*	£2.50
☐ 12579 2	THE DAFFODILS OF NEWENT	*Susan Sallis*	£1.95
☐ 12375 7	A SCATTERING OF DAISIES	*Susan Sallis*	£2.50
☐ 12880 5	BLUEBELL WINDOWS	*Susan Sallis*	£2.50

All these books are available at your book shop or newsagent, or can be ordered direct from the publisher. Just tick the titles you want and fill in the form below.

ORDER FORM

TRANSWORLD READER'S SERVICE, 61–63 Uxbridge Road, Ealing, London, W5 5SA.

Please send cheque or postal order, not cash. All cheques and postal orders must be in £ sterling and made payable to Transworld Publishers Ltd.

Please allow cost of book(s) plus the following for postage and packing:

U.K./Republic of Ireland Customers:
Orders in excess of £5: no charge
Orders under £5: add 50p

Overseas Customers:
All orders: add £1.50

NAME (Block Letters) ....

ADDRESS ....

....